Psychic Surveys: Book Five

Descension

ALSO BY SHANI STRUTHERS

Psychic Surveys: Book Five

Descension

You. Don't. Know.

SHANI STRUTHERS

Authors Reach
www.authorsreach.co.uk

ISBN: 978-1-9999137-9-3

For Mum (who inspired the character of Theo) – flying free at last. Have fun until we meet again. Love you.

Acknowledgements

The subject of the fifth Psychic Surveys book has been a tough one – mental health is not, in my opinion, something to utilise for the sake of ghoulish thrills. With that in mind, I've attempted to write a balanced account, showing the utmost respect for anyone who's ever suffered in such a way. I hope I've succeeded. Thanks to all those who've helped shape this book, giving their opinions, insight and knowledge – these include Milly Haire, Louisa Taylor, Lesley Hughes, Sarah Savery and Robin Driscoll. Thanks also to Rob Struthers and Vee McGivney for their tireless editing and Gina Dickerson for another sublime cover and formatting. As with all my books, it's based on truth, with lots of fact woven in between the fiction. The building I refer to exists and is one I've visited several times – however the name of the asylum and the estate that has grown up around it has been changed. As for the individuals that inspired me with their often tragic stories, thanks for shining a light on a subject that needs no embellishment. Whether dead or alive, I hope you've found peace.

Prologue

HER body rigid, her breath caught in her throat, she watched as he retreated. He was a dark figure, darker than the night that bore down on them, and far more threatening. Not once did he turn back, he didn't even falter. Arrogant! That's what he was. So sure of himself, of his plans, his wants, his needs and his desires. How dare he come here and threaten what was already such a fragile situation? One more crack, that's all it would take, and all she held together would break apart.

Refusing to stare any longer, to give him that satisfaction, she closed the door. There was no slam, although certainly there was anger behind the gesture. Turning, she slumped against it. All was quiet in the house. Some might even say peaceful. Able to breathe now, she had to fight to keep it steady. She inhaled for a count of four and exhaled for a count of four, but still tremors coursed through her.

Where should she go? What should she do? She felt at a loss, unable to cope.

You have to cope. You have no choice!

Not true. There were always choices.

Straightening, she headed up the narrow stairs, thirteen of them. On the landing, she stopped. Her damned breathing, her thumping heart, she had to get them under control. On the right was her bedroom. Everything she needed was in there. Avoiding the floorboards that would protest under her weight, she glided on silent feet. In her room, she closed yet another door on the world. It wasn't just that her breathing was laboured; her eyes stung too with tears begging to be released. But now was not the time for crying. Time was running out.

Across the room was an antique bureau. Going to it, she opened the writing desk to reveal several storage drawers and pigeonholes. On the desk itself were notes she'd written, everyday lists and quite benign. In other bundles were papers she had often referred to: precious papers. That wasn't solely her opinion; many in the arcane world considered them precious too. In a locked drawer, a secret drawer that only she had the key to, was yet more reading matter, that which she'd been avoiding.

Her breathing still ragged, she turned on a desk lamp. She'd need at least a glimmer of light if she was going to delve into such darkness. The key wasn't hidden; it was in amongst the jumble. Sheets rustled as she searched. Finding it at last, she inserted it into the lock and liberated what had lain hidden for so long.

Using both hands to smooth the handwritten notes, she started to read, noting the triangles and the pentagrams that accompanied the words. Symbols of power some might call them, those who believed, though many scoffed. Reading on, she became only too aware that this was very real. As real as the threat that faced her.

Her legs no longer able to support her, she sank onto the chair and, desperate for a touch more light, adjusted the lamp slightly. The words jumped before her eyes: dangerous words – *loaded* words – with belief at their core;

something she and the man who'd come calling shared. One hand reaching upwards, she rubbed at her chest as her heart continued to beat frantically. Some words appeared hastily scribbled; others were more precise, as though hewn from stone. How did it make the scribe feel to write them; to *know*; to sit by a desk such as this one, her hand and mind focused? How was it possible to come this close to the wire and remain sane? Yet the scribe had been the most down-to-earth person she'd ever known.

It wasn't difficult, that was the biggest revelation. None of it was difficult.

It was all so easy.

Which made it all the more frightening.

A sigh escaping her, she closed her eyes – needing that break, that relief.

Could she do it? Was she capable?

She opened her eyes. Yes, she was capable. Love made her so. Ironically.

Although the light seemed to recede, she continued to read, having to squint, to stop in places to decipher the handwriting when it became garbled. An astute pupil, she read and she learnt – she devoured the lesson.

Everyone has choices.

And she had made hers.

Chapter One

THE pub cellar stank. Not overly fond of beer anyway, the stench was enough to put Ruby off for life. Combine it with cleaning fluids and it was just so... *sour*. Beside her, her friend and colleague, Theo, held her gossamer scarf over her nose for protection, whereas Ness and Corinna, the remaining half of the Psychic Surveys quartet, simply wore pained but stoic expressions. As for Jed, a ghost dog that had attached itself to her two years before, he'd bolted, and rightly so. Joining Cash upstairs perhaps, in the more hospitable bar area. Cash, her boyfriend and occasional fifth team member when his own freelance work as an IT specialist permitted, had been intending to join them downstairs. He'd been gung-ho about it, in fact, intrigued by what resided there. But then he'd spied the dazzling array of ales on tap and swiftly changed his mind, settling at the bar for a pint of Steamship instead. Ruby could hardly complain, it wasn't as if she paid him a wage. And anyway, they were managing perfectly well on their own. Kind of.

"Look out!" Corinna shouted as something flew their way. A wine cork, by the looks of it, only small, but nonetheless everyone shielded their faces and ducked.

An annoyed hiss accompanied the hurling of the cork, and then a shuffling sound, as though someone was dragging their feet along the flagstone floor.

Ruby straightened up. "So, what do you think, team? One spirit? Two? Three even?"

"Spirits…" Corinna stifled a laugh. "Sorry, it's just that whole being in a pub thing – you know, rum, vodka, make it a double…? I'll shut up, shall I?"

Ruby suppressed a smirk too whilst Ness, straight-faced as ever, glanced around her. "There are several spirits here," she answered. "*Mischievous* spirits."

"Mischievous?" Theo mused. "Not angry? Not lost? Not feeling terribly abandoned perchance?"

Ness also shot her a look.

"Oh well, I don't blame them," Theo muttered, at least as amused as two of her colleagues. "There are probably far worse places to be grounded, the stench aside."

The landlord of The Waterside Inn, which overlooked the River Adur in Shoreham, had called them in because of increasing paranormal activity in the pub. Thankfully, it was confined to the cellar. Not so great was that bar staff refused point-blank to go down there alone. As well as sudden temperature drops, and Ruby could vouch for that as it was arctic in several dark corners, there'd been hissing, grunting – the works. There'd also been tinkering with the gas pump, which had been mysteriously turned off several times, causing the beer to go flat and customers to seek more aerated beverages elsewhere. Ness was right. These spirits were mischievous indeed.

"Ruby, do you want to make the address or shall I?" It was Ness asking her, Ness whom she'd met a few years ago, in a similar situation, in the cellars of the Harveys brewery in their hometown of Lewes; another cold, confined and smelly space. Ah, this job, it was all glamour, glamour,

glamour!

"Go ahead, Ness. The rest of us can focus on visualising white light; after all, it might not be a cork that comes at us next time. It could well be a bottle."

All of them joining hands, they formed a circle to draw light straight from source, universal source that is, a means of psychic protection – a spiritual barrier at least.

Ness cleared her throat. "Spirits, we know you're here, we can sense you. We can also suffer harm if you throw stuff at us. Please refrain from doing so again."

At her words the bottles in one of the racks gave a warning rattle, followed by the hint of a giggle – a female voice this time, someone having a laugh at their expense.

"Whilst you may think this is funny," Ness continued, "we don't. Nor do the staff that work at this Inn. In fact, you're frightening them. I'm not sure how many of you there are and I don't know how long you've been here, but this is something of an historic pub, so a fair while I'll bet. The reasons you're grounded aren't clear to me at this stage, but this is not a place to linger. It's time to journey onwards to the next stage of your existence, to go towards the…"

Before she could finish, the already dim light bulb overhead began to flicker.

Ness spoke more acerbically. "That's right, the light."

"Perhaps we should try and single out one spirit?" suggested Theo.

"The ringleader?" quizzed Ruby.

Theo nodded. "Someone's leading this merry little band."

"Merry's the right word," agreed Corinna. "Imagine spending the afterlife continually drunk!"

"No wonder they don't want to leave," Ness remarked. "This is a non-stop party."

"The thing is," Ruby reminded them, "they're being a total nuisance."

"As drunkards often are," lamented Theo.

"I'll try again," Ness decided.

"Atta girl," Theo was grinning again. "Fill your boots."

It was a sigh that accompanied Ness's words this time, rather than a throat clearance. Theo's somewhat relentless teasing did tend to irk her. "I don't sense malevolence here, I don't sense unhappiness. Nonetheless, holding onto the past, to what's been, and what can never be again, that's no existence, not really. Why wouldn't you embrace what's *before* you, the excitement of it, the glory? This isn't the end. On the contrary, there are new challenges ahead; an opportunity to grow, to develop. The light," she tilted her head slightly, clearly expecting the party trick to continue, "is what we call home. In short, it's where you belong; where loved ones are waiting for you. If you're scared, or confused, or just plain bewildered, we understand. Death *can* be confusing. But in the light that confusion will fade. Please, connect with us, talk to us. We can walk with you to the light if you'd like us to."

They were such wise words, full of kindness and hope. Words that sometimes the spirits accepted, and were grateful for even; a bit of guidance when it was needed. There were some, however, who took exception. They didn't want to be told what to do, although that was never the team's intention. They weren't dictators.

As another cork went whistling past her head; as a bottle finally shook free of its rack and smashed to the floor; as a hissing and a grunting resounded in her ears,

Ruby winced. In the cellar of The Waterside Inn, taking exception was the name of the game.

"Project white light," Theo continued.

"No chinks in it, mind," said Corinna, doing a cheeky impression of Theo's usual follow-up.

"Keep it nice and strong," added Ruby, following Corinna's example.

Even Ness joined in. "Let nothing penetrate it."

Except something did: a full can of beer was hurled straight at Ruby's foot.

"Ow!" she yelled, hopping about. "That's it! You've gone too far this time!"

"Darling," Theo interrupted, her 'jolly elf's face' as Ruby often thought of it, rather ashen, "where do you think the best place is to take cover?"

"Cover?"

Theo merely pointed. Another can was on its way.

Spying a handy row of barrels, Ruby shouted: "Everyone, over here!"

As they all ran and hid, Theo groaned with the effort of crouching low, and who could blame her? She was seventy now and as rotund as what was in front of her.

Ruby swore she could hear giggling again. Not just giggling, there was guffawing and snorting too, even a slapping of thighs.

Are they really drunk?

"I think so," Ness replied, catching Ruby's thought, a peculiar talent of hers, which Theo shared. "Or at least they're *presenting* as drunk."

Despite the physical danger they were in, Corinna was still in good humour. "Spirits drunk on spirits? That has *got* to be a first!"

Cash would be clutching his sides too if he'd bothered to come down here.

"Ruby…" said Ness, sounding deeply concerned. In her mid-fifties, she was the second most senior of the team, and if she was worried, there was reason to be.

"Okay," Ruby said, responding to her concern. "I'll take the address this time." Adopting a suitably authoritative tone, she lifted her head an inch or two above the barrels. "Please, don't hurl anything else," she began, "you could hurt one of us, badly I mean, and I don't think that's your intention. *Who* are you?"

Sod off!

"Charming," Ruby sighed, glancing at Ness and Theo. "Did you catch that?"

Both nodded. To Corinna who could sense spirits well enough but not yet hear or see them, she whispered a quick explanation before continuing.

"The thing is, this cellar doesn't belong to you—"

Oops, that had been the wrong thing to say. A roar sounded in her ear.

Of course it does. We've been 'ere longer!

Ruby seized the moment. "How long?"

Longer than them upstairs, blast their eyes!

A hiccup, then a squeal, accompanied the words as if someone had been groped.

"Not me," Theo said when Ruby caught her eye. "More's the pity."

Suddenly, Ness's head jerked. "Molly. One of them's called Molly."

"Hang on…" Theo seemed to hear something too. "Ned, that's another."

"And Joel!" added Corinna.

9

Ruby, Ness and Theo gazed at her in amazement. "Seriously?" Ruby asked.

"Seriously," Corinna replied. "The name just sort of... popped into my head. Wow, that's another first! He's a pirate."

"A pirate?" questioned Ness.

"Yeah, a pirate, a smuggler, it's the same thing, isn't it? I can see him... Well, not see him – sense him, strongly though, as if we've... got a connection somehow. They're all pirates, I think. There's several more apart from those we've named."

Theo piped up. "It makes sense. As I'm sure you're all aware, Shoreham, like so many southern coastal towns, has a huge smuggling history. In fact, Ruby, you grew up in the most renowned smuggling town of all, Hastings." Ruby nodded that this was in fact correct. "I remember reading that pirates pulled off a massive heist here in the mid 1800s. It's quite a story actually, but to summarise, a travelling circus had come to town, and its excited inhabitants flocked to see the show, every last one of them, including the town's coastguards. Taking advantage of the coast being unusually clear, pirates swooped down on a vessel stuffed to the gunwales with tobacco. They used barges to sail the contraband up the Adur to the village of Beeding, where the booty was soon sold and spirited away. Such was the fury of the King's Revenue men, all of Shoreham's coastguards lost their jobs."

When she finished, the clinking of ghostly glasses accompanied a loud cheer.

Theo shook her head. "Well done, boys, well done! You too, Molly, because you were also involved, weren't you? You all seized the day!" Braver than Ruby, Theo rose fully to her feet. "You've had your fun by the sound of it, a *lot* of fun, but it's time for you all to leave. The landlord doesn't appreciate you using his cellar for your carousing. Go to the light, where…" she coughed again, "… your sins will be forgiven."

Sins, you old hag? It's the Revenue what's the sinners! The taxes they put on everything!

A chorus of agreement went up from the motley crew.

"Even so—"

'Even so' be damned! Go on, clear off. We ain't going nowhere.

"But this adventure's over," Theo protested, "surely you're ripe for another?"

Ripe?

Again, there was a gust of laughter, some heckling and some jeering; they were a motley crew all right and they obviously found the opposing gang oh-so-amusing.

I'll tell you who's ripe, that redhead bint wiv yer! Always fancied me a redhead.

Those words, followed by another slap, caused Ruby's jaw to drop. Whoever had taken a liking to Corinna, the youngest member of the team at twenty-two, and her abundant pre-Raphaelite curls, was in trouble with someone – Molly perhaps? That had been a slap across the face this time; a sharp one.

"Look," Ruby began, standing up too, her hands held out before her in a placatory gesture. "We don't want trouble, honestly, we don't. Come on, let's just… talk."

But trouble was what ignited these souls and always had.

Another bottle was seized from the rack and thrown against the wall closest to Theo, bursting open and splattering its contents everywhere.

"Stand your ground!" Theo commanded. "It's only Blossom Hill." Clearly, she wasn't a fan of the brand. "We mustn't show them we're afraid."

"We're *not* afraid," dismissed Ness. "We're bloody annoyed. Or at least I am!"

"What shall we do?" queried Ruby, not only concerned about flying bottles, but whether the noise in the cellar was carrying upstairs and who'd come running down because of it. If it was the landlord, this would put the fear of God into him. Luckily, there weren't many punters to disturb. A quiet Monday night had deliberately been chosen and it was already past ten. In fact, there'd only been an old man *in situ* when they'd arrived, already halfway through his pint and crossword puzzle. She glanced at the doorway again. There was no Cash, no Jed, and no landlord. Whether to be annoyed or relieved about the former, she didn't know. "Theo?"

"White light," Theo replied, "use it like a missile and fire it at the rogues. If they want an all-out Battle of Blossom Hill, let's give it to them."

Corinna was looking askance at her elder companion, her green eyes at once impressed and excited. That didn't last for long, however, as another full can of Carlsberg went whistling past her head.

"Christ," Corinna exclaimed. "That could've killed me!"

"Just fire white light," Theo repeated. "It's as good a weapon as any."

Ruby too was growing more agitated. *Cash, Jed, where are you?* She thought of them as her protectors, but when it came to her and beer, or, in Jed's case, the prospect of a bag of crisps, there was clearly no contest.

The heckling rose by several decibels. The grounded were having the time of their lives, or more accurately, their deaths, the flickering light bulb adding to the mockery.

Where's the redhead? Still in hiding is she? Send 'er out 'ere.

Those that could hear the request ignored it.

"Focus, everyone," Ness advised. "It's their energy against ours, that's all."

The redhead! The redhead! The redhead!

Ruby was surprised to hear that even the females had joined in the chant.

What shall we do? Ruby asked Ness and Theo via thought this time. There was no way she wanted to alarm Corinna further.

Tonight, however, Corinna was more astute than she'd ever been, at least to Ruby's knowledge.

"It's me they want, isn't it?" she said, her voice holding both timidity and boldness.

"No, not at all," Ruby tried to deny, "it's just… a battle of wills, that's all. We'll win. Don't worry. Shit!" An exploding bottle flew up from the floor and cut her forehead. Checking the damage with her fingers, she felt the warmth of blood.

"This is no longer a joke," Theo sounded as angry as Ruby. "They're as outrageous in death as they were in life, the devils."

"We can't even edge our way to the door, it leaves us too exposed," cried Ness. "We're trapped. We're actually trapped."

"No, we're not." It was Corinna, just plain defiance in

her voice now. To everyone's surprise, she sidestepped the barrels and made her way to the centre of the room.

"Corinna," Theo hissed. "Get back here. We said we'd wait it out."

Corinna was having none of it. "I'm spending the night at Presley's," she said, referring to Cash's brother whom she'd been seeing for quite a while and was very keen on, "and I'm already late. This lot might want to party, but so do I. Heaven knows I work hard enough. Besides, they won't respect us if we cower. *This* is what they respect, someone who'll face up to them, who's more than a match, who won't take their nonsense. *I* won't take your nonsense, do you hear? So, you like the look of me, I gather. And why's that? Do you think I'm sassy, a bit of a wench? Well, maybe I am. But you lot, you're hardly gentlemen, are you? Treating us the way you're doing, terrorising us. As for the women amongst you, whatever happened to girl power; to supporting each other? I couldn't be more disappointed in you if I tried."

"Corinna!" This time it was Ruby hissing. "Come back."

Corinna ignored her too. "What are you going to do now, huh? Throw something at me again? Wow, you know how to impress a girl! What big men you are. What brave men. I've always thought of smugglers and pirates as romantic, what with all that seafaring, swashbuckling stuff you got up to. Whenever I've read about you, it's your side I've been on, but actually you're just a bunch of brutes. I'm not impressed at all."

There was silence. If Ruby had to describe it, she'd say a stunned silence.

"Corinna..." This time Theo's voice was more hopeful.

"They're listening."

To Ruby's surprise, Corinna put a hand on her hip and started sashaying back and forth, the other hand flicking her hair in an exaggerated manner over her shoulder. Wearing a floaty black skirt and a black blouse – the Gothic-style attire she favoured – she looked rather swashbuckling herself!

"She's holding them enthralled," Theo whispered to Ness and Ruby.

"They're not the only ones," Ruby whispered back.

"So," Corinna continued, "you don't want to go to the light, you'd prefer to stay here in this dark, damp and dirty cellar? Okay. Fair enough. You were a law unto yourselves in life; be a law unto yourselves in death too. We'll go. We'll leave you to your rollicking ways, not bother you anymore, on one condition. Wanna hear it?"

Corinna had stopped and again she was looking from side to side. It was clear she couldn't see anything and to be fair, neither could the rest of them, but that didn't mean they weren't there. They were, as strong as ever, all that imagined ale, wine and whisky they'd imbibed, fortifying them. Once more, Corinna flicked her hair, her smile as enigmatic as da Vinci's *The Mona Lisa*.

"If you leave the living alone, don't throw stuff at them anymore, don't turn off the gas pumps on the beer, don't yell in their ears or try to materialise in front of them, we and perhaps they, will leave *you* alone. We get it. You're not ready to move on. You like it here. And perhaps, right now, here is fun. You'll go one day, I'm sure of it. You can have too much of anything in the end, but when that will be is up to you."

That landlord hates us.

We hate him too; I'd like to tear his gizzards out!
The girls scream when we blow in their faces.
It's funny it is! A right belly laugh!

Corinna couldn't hear the random remarks her words had inspired, so Ruby ventured forwards too, coming to a standstill by her side. "Do you want to stay?" she asked. "Do you want this... *party* to continue, for a while longer at least?"

Again there was silence, but then someone spoke, a woman this time.

So what if we do? Here suits us.

"Corinna," Ruby said, "they want to stay."

Corinna swung round to face Ruby. "Then let them. Our aim is to help, but only when help is wanted or needed. Sometimes it just... isn't."

"But what if they change their minds or if one or two of them do? What if they become distressed?" Ruby ignored the ghostly gales of laughter her concern caused.

"We keep tabs on the situation," Corinna suggested. "We pop into the pub every now and again, ask a few leading questions. That way we'll know."

Still Ruby wasn't buying it. "We can't lie to the landlord; he wants them gone."

Ness and Theo came forward too, the four of them standing in the centre of the cellar again with the light bulb above them as dim as ever.

"We don't have to lie." It was Theo who answered. "What we can be is economical with the truth. There's a lot to be said for implication." Quickly, she performed a Ness-inspired throat clearing exercise. "Listen up you lot, let's parley good and proper. We understand what you're saying, and we may well take our leave. But, if you continue to taunt the living; if you don't get your drunken antics under some sort of control, you'll not only harm our reputation, you'll attract other people to the cellar – people who may not be as accommodating as us. Instead they'll do everything they can to force you onwards. I'm warning you, they'll come in their droves, and they'll be just as determined as you are. In the end it'll leave you exhausted. The fun that you're having will wear thin. If, however, you let the living be and confine your merrymaking to after-hours, when they've retired to their beds, then they'll believe you're gone; that we've done what we were supposed to do, and moved you on."

There were low murmurs, a growling and a cough. Finally, there came a decision.

From the shadows, a figure emerged, faint, the merest outline, but Ruby got a full impression in her head. He was dressed way above his station, in fancy clothes, breeches perhaps, a waistcoat and a wide-brimmed hat with a jauntily-angled feather in it. He was tugging at a long beard in contemplation. Corinna wouldn't be able to see him, but he was staring at her – the redhead – both lust *and* respect in his gaze.

The man spat on the ground immediately in front of Corinna.

We stand together on this?

"Yes," Ruby assured him. "We do."

There was further pondering, more tugging of the beard.

Hawking up again, he spat a second time.

Then we have an accord.

"An accord?" Ruby queried.

An agreement. A gentleman's agreement, mind.

Ruby nodded in understanding. "Corinna," she said, "could you... spit on the floor in front of you please?"

"Spit?"

"It's to seal the deal, or rather the agreement. They're insisting they're gentlemen after all. I'd do it, but I think it'll hold more sway coming from you."

"Oh, right... okay." Without further ado, Corinna obeyed.

"And that's it?" Ruby re-addressed the figure. "If we're... *economical* with the truth, you'll play by the rules? You won't torment the bar staff any more? I run a spiritual clearance business; we're held in high regard. I don't want that compromised."

A gentleman's agreement is worth something!

As she'd done earlier, Ruby held up her hands. "That's fine, that's great. A ladies' agreement means something too. I was just checking."

Corinna's relieved smile was brilliant, even in the dim light. She couldn't see, but the man had stepped forward, the ringleader, and was sniffing at her longingly.

A scream rang out.

Joel, get yerself back 'ere!

Ruby gulped. It was time to cut and run. All four of them hurried towards the cellar door. Just as they reached it, Corinna hesitated.

"Part of me wishes I could stay," she explained when the rest of the team looked questioningly at her. "They sure know how to have a good time down here in the depths."

That can be arranged, my darlin'...

Joel earned yet another slap on his cheek.

"Corinna, we really do have to go," breathed Ruby.

Theo couldn't agree more. "Best foot forward," she said, picking up pace again. "Let's… erm… break the good news to the overseer of this fine hostelry, shall we?"

Even Ness was grinning as four of them ascended to the light at least.

Chapter Two

THEY emerged to find Cash and Jed indeed propping up the bar. In fact, it looked as if they and the landlord had been having a party of their own – certainly neither appeared at all worried about what traumas Ruby and the team might have been experiencing in the 'depths' as Corinna had dubbed it. The two men were as merry as their ghostly counterparts, which, Ruby decided, was a good thing on the whole. Certainly it made the landlord very obliging when she told him there'd be no more trouble from whatever lurked in the cellar.

"It's gone, is it, the ghost?" he enquired, a definite slur in his voice.

"It should all be quiet from now on," Ruby replied – an evasion of the question; a little white lie told for the greater good, she reminded herself.

The landlord belched before sighing. "Shame really, innit? A pub with a ghost is a lure. Personally, I'd have exploited it, drawn a few more punters in, but my staff are a cowardly lot. They threatened to walk out altogether if I didn't do something about it and good staff are hard to find at the best of times, never mind the worst." He shook his head, swayed slightly. "Could have made a mint running ghost tours."

While Cash nodded in enthusiastic agreement, Ruby

glanced at her colleagues. Their expressions said it all – they'd done the right thing. If the landlord went ahead with such an idea, it could turn nasty down there with bottles flying from their racks and glass fragments not merely brushing against foreheads but embedding in them, deep. As Corinna had said, they'd need to keep an eye on the situation, but for now a plan had been hatched, and her word was as true as Joel's.

The landlord offered the team drinks and they accepted gladly, feeling the need to celebrate a victory of sorts. Ruby in particular for she had news she had yet to break to Cash – to everyone really, including her mother and grandmother. But for now it was news she wanted to hug to herself; to savour. As Corinna was driving her and Cash, she had a rum and coke followed by another. They were hefty measures too. By the time they'd drunk up and were back in Lewes, she was sure she was also guilty of slurring her words.

After dropping them both at Ruby's ground floor flat in De Montfort Road, along with Jed the dog, of course, who'd ridden shotgun with Ruby, Corinna waved goodbye and drove off.

Staring after Corinna while Cash did his best to insert the key into the lock, Ruby reiterated for the umpteenth time how brilliant her colleague had been. "You should have seen how she held the floor against them, Cash. They couldn't take their eyes off her. Not that I could see their eyes, you understand, but I didn't have to, I just knew it. She belongs to a different age, that one, a more romantic era."

"Ah, come on," said Cash, the damned lock continuing to confound him, "the noughties ain't so bad. Not with me

21

and you in 'em; they're romantic enough."

She didn't care how soppy her smile was. "Yeah, yeah, I suppose."

When he had finally succeeded in opening the door, they all but tumbled into the hallway. Jed sauntered past them, probably making his way to the bedroom. As Cash closed the door, Ruby backed him up against it. "I've got a secret," she said.

"You love me?"

"Oh come on, that's no secret. That's blindingly obvious! No, no, no, it's the spirits in the cellar at The Waterside Inn; we didn't move them on."

"You didn't? But you said—"

"No, I was clever, very clever. All I said was that it should be quiet from now on at the pub; to expect no more trouble."

Cash reared back slightly. "I don't understand."

As best she could, considering the amount she'd imbibed, she explained the agreement the Psychic Surveys team had reached. "We struck a bargain!"

"A bargain?"

"That's right. A gentleman's agreement, which apparently a smuggler will live and die by." After a brief pause, she added, "So to speak."

"What if things get out of hand again, if they kick-off? Your reputation…"

Cash had the same concerns as her, but again she explained they'd do their best to keep tabs on the situation. "The thing is, we can't force spirits onwards. So it follows that sometimes we have to get… inventive. I trust Joel, though."

"Joel?"

"He's the leader of the pack. Hey! That reminds me of a song, you know, 'The leader of the pack, vroom, vroom'"

Cash was staring at her, whether amused or bemused, she couldn't tell. "Joel," he repeated. "That's a good pirate name. So, you stand in solidarity with the spirits?"

"Always," she replied, leaning in to kiss him.

Cash's arms tightened around her waist and he started to walk her in the direction of the bedroom. On seeing them enter, Jed performed his usual disappearing trick, probably to reappear in the early hours of the morning, curling up at the foot of her bed, his favourite resting place. Their lips having been locked together for some time, Ruby finally had to come up for air.

"Cash," she murmured, "I've got another secret to tell you."

"That you can't resist me, even when you're angry with me?"

"What? When am I ever angry with you?"

"Ooh, there've been one or two memorable occasions," his voice was a murmur too, husky even and altogether irresistible. But this other secret – the one that was burning away inside – she had to tell someone or she'd explode. Before she succumbed to another kiss, she took a step backwards.

"Cash, wait, listen. I have to tell you… I just have to."

His eyes flickered meaningfully downwards. "Can it really not wait?"

Torn, Ruby thought about it for a moment. "Actually, it can't."

Pushing him onto the edge of the bed, she sat beside him, and flicked on a side lamp. Giving voice to what she'd done would bring it to life, which was a good thing, a very good thing. She'd waited a long time to say these words.

"I've found him."

"What? Found who?"

"My father."

If Cash had looked confused before, it was nothing to how he looked now.

"Your *father*? How?"

"Mum, of course, she told me his name at last. He was in the police force, I've told you that before. He isn't now, he's retired, but with a name to go on and Ness able to pull a few strings with her friend, Lee, who's also in the police force, we got an email address…" Here she paused again. It had been so difficult to know how to word that first email. She'd sat at her desk in her attic office in the Lewes High Street and she'd typed; deleted; typed; deleted. In the end she kept it simple, explaining who she was, how she had found him and enquiring whether he'd be agreeable to striking up a correspondence via email, with a view to perhaps meeting at a later date. It had taken a few nail-biting days, but eventually he'd replied. Peter Gregory was his name: such an ordinary name. So many times she'd tested Ruby Gregory on her lips, but it neither sounded nor felt right. Whatever happened, she was Ruby Davis; always had been and always would be.

Peter said he was surprised to hear from her, but yes, he remembered her mother, Jessica, and, of course, all that had transpired between them. He'd often wondered what had happened to her and the baby, but thought it best not to interfere once the decision had been made to separate. He said he was glad Ruby had got in touch, but that it was wise to take things slowly. They each had their own lives and their own families. This would come as a surprise to them too. It needed to be handled, as he put it, 'sensitively'.

All this she tried to explain to Cash as succinctly as possible, although she suspected that in her rush to get the words out, it was actually quite garbled.

Cash's dark eyes were huge. "Did you tell him about, you know, your abilities?"

"No."

"Did he know what your mum was capable of?"

Raising a demon, that's what Jessica was capable of. Perhaps not a demon as such, rather it was an embodiment of negative energy, something born of dark thoughts and desires; a conjuring designed to impress her lover at the time, Saul, who'd sat with her when she did it, who encouraged her. Neither of them had foreseen the dire consequences of their actions, they'd been drunk instead on the headiness of possibility. Both had been members of *Terra Stella*, a local Hastings group interested in matters of the occult, who'd meet regularly. That's where they'd forged their fateful alliance. All of this, however, had taken place *after* Jessica's relationship with Peter and not before or during. Ruby hadn't yet mentioned her own ability or profession to him, and Peter hadn't mentioned anything about Jessica other than to ask how she was. It was another matter to be handled with care.

Ruby sighed. She'd spent years asking both her mother, Jessica, and her grandmother, Sarah, for the name of her father, an identity, which in turn would confirm her own, and she'd been brushed off. She could remember what her mother used to say, rather irritably at times: *You don't need to know him; your Gran and I are enough.* Certainly Gran, who'd been responsible for the lion's share of raising Ruby due to her mother's subsequent breakdown after the conjuring, had been enough. But with no father or grandfather either, she'd nonetheless always felt the absence of a man in her life keenly. Perhaps it was no more than a longing for some kind of balance; a desire for natural order. It had always just been the three of them, Ruby, Jessica and Sarah – and now there was Peter – or there would be, if she played her cards right.

After she told Cash that Peter was still in the dark regarding her gift, he leant towards her and tucked a few strands of hair behind her ear. It might be the drink – although to be honest, she felt surprisingly sober now after such serious talk – but the unexpected gesture brought a lump to her throat.

"Cash…? Are you okay?"

"Me? I'm fine. I just… I hope it goes okay. Between you and your father, I mean."

"Why wouldn't it?"

"Ruby…" He looked to the side as if trying to perform a conjuring of his own: seeking the right words to say. She studied him while he did this, his chiselled features, his hair that he usually kept close-cropped but which was now growing out – how dark it was; his pale brown skin inherited from his Jamaican mother. His father was English and missing from his life too, having left home when Cash was two and his elder brother, Presley, was four. Fathers. It was a sensitive subject all round.

"Cash," she said again, "I'll be all right. *This* will be all right. From the few emails we've exchanged since I first got in touch, he seems nice, down-to-earth. How I'd hoped he'd be."

"What did he say about his other family?"

"He's got two children, both older than me, a son and a daughter." She winced saying this, knowing that Cash's father, whom he'd traced once, had another family too; two daughters. The fact that she had half-siblings as well was something she couldn't get her head around: the miracle of it. Not that Cash had thought this way about his sisters, or his father. He'd traced him and then he'd… let them go. His father had been kind enough to him, but it was his new family that was clearly his priority, his *replacement* family. 'No one needs that kind of rejection,' Cash had said once, when talking about it. And that was evidently where his concern for Ruby lay. "Cash, look, I'm not condoning what happened in the past between Mum and Peter, but, right now, this very minute, I'm happy, okay? I'm… excited. Okay, I realise my dad and me might never be close, but we might be able to form some sort of relationship. Maybe we'll talk on the phone regularly or visit with each other once or twice a year. Hell, if it comes down to just exchanging Christmas cards, it'll be something. He doesn't live too far away – near Oxford, which is only two hours by car. This sounds nuts, but I'm hoping that what my Mum said is true, that there's nothing psychic about him, that he's just a regular bloke."

Cash took hold of her hands. "Ruby, why does that matter so much? You're proud of what you do; you're out there on the high street. You make a difference to the living *and* the dead. Not many people can say that. Damn it, I'm proud of you."

"I know you are, and I love that you are, but… because of what my mother did, my history is dark and sometimes I think that darkness is inherent. My father being non-psychic… again, it's all about balance. It's not so one-sided." She grew frustrated with herself. "I don't know if I'm explaining this very well."

"I get you, I really do."

"Then be happy for me?"

"I am, Rubes. I worry, that's all."

"About what?"

"That you're going to end up disappointed."

She brought a hand up to his cheek. "Because you were, you mean?"

He was normally so happy-go-lucky, the light to her darkness, but in his expression there was pain, which in turn pierced her. Abandonment, it never quite left you. It stained your soul somehow, left it hollowed out. No matter who came along afterwards, who tried to fill the gap, they never quite managed it. She knew that and he knew that too. "I'll be careful, I promise," she whispered.

He held her gaze for what seemed like the longest time. "So, I'm the first one you've told about Peter? Your mum and grandmother don't know yet?"

"When Mum finally gave me his name she knew what I'd do with it, but no, she hasn't said anything more about it."

"How do you think she'll react?"

"She's made it clear she doesn't want to meet him. He's history and that's how she wants it to stay. Besides, she's still in recovery from her breakdown, although so much stronger than she used to be, thanks to Saul. Funny to think, isn't it, that she and Saul brought each other to the edge, both of them teetering on the brink for so long; and now they've been reunited, they're helping each other to live."

"They know exactly how the other feels, that's why. They can empathise."

Ruby nodded. "And that's true of us in a way, concerning our dads. Cash, I need your support on this. I know it didn't work out for you, but it might for me."

"Yeah, yeah, it might. Of course you've got my support."

Beside her a dog barked – Jed had reappeared and was staring at her.

"And you," she said, smiling down at him. "I need you to stand by me as well."

It was a new chapter in her life. Snuggling up to Cash, his arms tight around her whilst Jed settled himself, she could hardly wait for it to begin.

Chapter Three

RUBY groaned. Was it morning already? She glanced at her bedside clock. Indeed it was. And whose phone was ringing, hers or Cash's? For a moment she couldn't work it out, despite her ringtone being an ethereal tinkling and his, an annoying drone. It was hers, definitely hers. Pushing Cash who was lying on her, half slumped, off and ignoring his muffled protests, she forced herself from her bed – or rather *their* bed. After all, Cash was at her flat more often than his own. They'd even talked about him giving up his flat altogether and moving in with her, making it official. That was definitely the next step; both of them as keen as each other on the idea. Yawning, she looked around. Where was the bloody phone?

Your jeans pocket, Ruby, where you usually leave it.

In that case, it was on the floor where she'd left her jeans, or rather where Cash had left them after he'd pulled them off her the previous night. Yawning again she retrieved the phone, only briefly glancing at the caller ID before answering – *Unknown Call*. Probably work then, despite it being Saturday.

"Hello." Ruby's voice was a whisper at first, only returning to normal pitch once she'd left the bedroom and was in the hallway. "This is Ruby Davis."

"Ruby Davis of Psychic Surveys?"

"That's right. Do you have an issue I can help you with?"

As head of Psychic Surveys, specialists in domestic spiritual clearance, Ruby was actually used to getting phone calls for help at the weekend. Like those in the basement of The Waterside Inn, the spirits followed their own rules.

Heading for the kitchen so she could get some coffee underway, she rolled her eyes when she heard that the caller lived on the Brookbridge Estate.

"We all know there's trouble round here," the caller, Kelly Watkins, stated, "but we've been fine in our house until recently. Typical, isn't it? You think this malarkey is something that happens to other people, and then boom! It happens to you too. My kid's terrified; she's sleeping in our room at night, which, you know… isn't ideal."

The 'malarkey' that Ms Watkins was referring to was, of course, of a spiritual nature. Brookbridge, close to Horam, was built on the site of a former asylum – the Cromer Asylum to be exact, taking its name from the nearby tiny village of Cromer, and nothing to do with its larger Norfolk counterpart. A somewhat grand construction, it was also isolated, perhaps conforming to that old adage: *out of sight, out of mind*. In 1994, the asylum closed its doors and later the land was sold to developers. The hospital buildings were subsequently demolished and replaced by one-, two- and three-bedroomed houses laid out as a housing estate, attractive price tags overriding any reluctance some might have regarding what had been there before. To date only one block remained – a sizeable boarded-up, red brick building that stood on the edge of the estate. Oh, and a more modern medium-security wing, also on the edge of the estate and shrouded by trees, that was still very much in use.

Like many Victorian asylums, Cromer hadn't had the best reputation. Stories of abuse had since surfaced, some of which Ruby knew to be true from the cases she'd dealt with – and there'd been plenty since she'd set up business, hence the eye rolling. It had been quiet there recently, though. This was the first call in months.

"Ms Watkins, could you give me a brief rundown of what's been happening at your house?" Ruby asked.

"Oh, call me Kelly, please," insisted the woman. "Well…" she paused briefly, as if trying to get the facts straight in her own head. "As I said, it's my daughter who's really upset. She thinks there's someone in her bedroom, a woman. And this woman, she sits at the window, she wrings her hands together and she cries."

"Can your daughter see this woman?"

"She says she dreams about her, but even when she's awake she can sense her. The woman's in real distress and so is Carly. Sorry, that's my daughter's name."

"When she's awake, can Carly hear anything in the house? Can you?"

"There's been a sort of thudding noise I can't explain, and the lights flicker sometimes, that sort of thing. Oh, and the TV keeps going fuzzy too, you know, like snow. Saying that, it's a pretty old TV; it needs replacing. Look, you'll know we're not lying the minute you get here. My daughter's bedroom is different to the rest of the house. The atmosphere… it's not the same."

"I'd never suggest you're lying," Ruby assured her. "How old is Carly?"

"Eight."

Young enough to perhaps rule out poltergeist activity. Traditionally, that tended to occur in houses with resident teenagers, the angst of adolescent years and hormones in free fall creating a source of potent energy.

"Would you like me to speak to Carly at some point?"

"If you do, you'll have to go careful."

"Of course. Do you have any other children?"

"Just Carly, although we've reached the stage where we'd like another."

Hence the urgency in reclaiming her own bedroom, Ruby mused, sipping at her coffee. "I can come along for an initial survey today."

"That'd be great," said Kelly, sighing with relief. "The thing is, I have to go shopping later. Would you be able to get here soon, this morning, I mean?"

Inwardly sighing too, Ruby banished any ideas she might have of returning to bed with more coffee and a plate of croissants.

"This morning's fine," she said. She'd go alone. It wasn't fair to disturb Cash or the rest of her team. What she'd do was grab a shower and leave him a note saying where she'd gone, and with a bit of luck he might still be in bed when she returned. After all, this shouldn't take long; it was only an initial survey. A proper cleansing, if needed, could be performed later. "I can be at yours by ten."

Ending the call, she wondered if she could afford a few minutes to fire up her laptop and check her emails – Peter might have been in touch again. *Dad.* Her fingertips brushing the computer's silver lid, she decided against it. She'd check later. Never keep a client waiting. She tried to live by that rule. Even at the weekend.

* * *

Driving onto the estate, half an hour from Lewes, Ruby located Willow Walk easily enough amongst the warren of recently constructed streets, thanks to the genius of the Sat Nav. On her way there, she passed the last original building, the only significant architecture remaining on the estate hidden behind plywood sheets. It was set against the edge of the woods. She'd bet a few of those boards had been torn down or kicked in by local kids, as well as a plethora of would-be ghost hunters, who'd probably dug their way under the high mesh fence that surrounded it. Slightly further on, was an empty patch of land with JCB diggers standing idle. The building that had been there for the best part of a century had been demolished only recently and yet more estate housing would take its place.

She parked outside Kelly Watkins' house and got out of the car. Kelly had said the atmosphere in Carly's bedroom was different to the rest of the house. But what struck Ruby as she stood on the pavement was that the atmosphere on the whole estate had changed. It was late summer and the day was pleasant enough, early morning rain clouds having cleared. Despite this, a shiver ran through her. Something was different; but whatever it was, she couldn't put a finger on.

In a few short steps she was at the front door, pressing the doorbell and listening to its chime. Within a matter of seconds the door opened and a woman only slightly older than Ruby and about the same height stood before her – Kelly Watkins.

"Ruby Davis? Oh, thanks so much for coming round." As she ushered Ruby inside, she added, "I forgot to say, I'm so sorry about calling you out on a Saturday, it's just… I'm getting fed up of it, you know – living with a ghost."

"It's fine, seriously. I get calls at the weekend all the time. And hopefully we'll be able to sort something out; send this spirit to the light."

"The light? Oh right, yeah, I read about that on your website, it's where we all come from or something and where we're supposed to go back to when we die. I like that idea, it's nice. I like that whole holistic approach; it's very with the times. I think most religions nowadays are on the wane, well… in this country at least."

Whilst listening to Kelly talk, Ruby tuned in. Having once studied plans of the asylum, held at East Sussex Record Office, known as The Keep, she reckoned Kelly's house had been erected on the site of the women's block, which was to the east of the campus, as opposed to the men's block, to the west. It gave credence to Carly's hunch that it was a female spirit that resided here; effectively still imprisoned behind the cold walls of Cromer Asylum.

Kelly's voice faded as Ruby made a tentative connection that spanned a century and felt the intense anguish experienced by this woman. Why had she been incarcerated? Ruby knew from prior research that 'insanity' covered a wide range of mental illnesses, some of which could have been treated better by compassion and validation than by locking sufferers away as though they were criminals, at the mercy of nurses and doctors who were also full of contempt towards their charges. *Some of them*, Ruby corrected herself. She was sure that certain staff members back in Cromer's heyday had gone to work there absolutely for the right reasons, but it was never them you read about, or in fact, needed to worry about. It was the ones who'd inflicted the damage, or more to the point, the ones who'd suffered because of the damage inflicted.

"Do you want a cuppa?" Kelly asked. "I must say I expected you to be older, although I've seen the picture of you and your team on your webpage. There's one of you that's quite old, isn't there, the lady with the pink hair?"

Theo – she was talking about Theo. "Tea would be lovely, thanks, no sugar though, I'm trying to give that habit up."

"Me too," Kelly confided, "I've put on a few pounds recently, come out of nowhere they have, so the sugar's got to go. Oh, in case you're wondering, Carly's out at the moment, with her dad. Whilst I make the tea, do you want to take a look around?"

"That'd be perfect, thank you," said Ruby, relieved at an opportunity to get on with the job. "I'd like to start upstairs if I may, in Carly's bedroom."

"Wow, you don't muck about, do you?"

Ruby laughed. "I try not to." There was another thing she needed to know before she set to work. "Kelly, how long have you lived here?"

"A couple of years, that's all. That's how old the house is."

"And when did Carly start insisting there was a woman in her room?"

"Ah, well, that was only a few months ago, about two or three to be exact. Despite the atmosphere in her room, and the reputation of this estate, what's been here before, you know – the nut house – we thought she was playing us up at first. After all, a lot of kids from round this way swap stories at school; they sort of egg each other on, you know? I feel bad about that. Carly's a good kid, she don't lie."

"But before that she hadn't mentioned anything?"

"That's right. I'll tell you what though; it's got far worse over the last few days. If it isn't fixed and pronto, she'll be sleeping in with us 'til she's a teenager we reckon. And if that's the case, she can kiss goodbye to ever having a brother or sister!"

The last few days, Ruby mused, remembering the general feel of the estate, when she'd stood outside Kelly's house. What was it that was in the air? Expectation perhaps? And why would that be? She still had no idea.

Given the go ahead, Ruby went directly upstairs. Straight ahead was Carly's bedroom, and approaching it, all else began to fade; it was just Ruby, the spirit, and the spirit's anguish. It was as though she were in a tunnel, either that or a long, long corridor, which this may well have been once upon a time, leading to the patient's room, or cell, as Ruby couldn't help but liken it to.

What happened? Why were you at Cromer?

Pushing the door to Carly's room open, she was greeted by pink walls, white furniture, and a bed that was suffocating under the weight of fluffy cushions. Despite the typical garishness of a little girl's room, it appeared remote, unreal. What had been there before was far more pertinent.

In the centre of the room she came to a standstill. It was cold, as if the seasons had accelerated and they were already in deep winter. Exhaling, she was sure she'd see her breath before her, but the air remained stubbornly clear.

Rather than speak out loud, she decided to communicate in thought – it seemed the right thing to do, a more gentle approach.

Hello, my name is Ruby Davis, I'm a psychic, someone who can sense or see those who've passed. I can sense a female presence in this room and also that she's hurting – a great deal. This was once a hospital for people who were suffering from mental illness, the Cromer Asylum. Were you a patient here?

Still shivering, wishing she'd brought her jacket with her, Ruby waited. There was no way to push the tide with this one, she realised, no bargaining to be had, and nothing to be frightened of either. This wasn't a spirit prone to violence, of that she was certain. There'd be nothing thrown her way on this occasion. On the contrary, this woman wouldn't harm a fly, and yet still she'd been locked away.

And forgotten about… You were forgotten, weren't you? By those you thought loved you.

There was an intake of breath from somewhere, as if Ruby had touched a raw nerve. Bolstered, Ruby pressed on.

Did no family or friends ever come to visit? Did you… die at Cromer?

Just because her spirit was grounded didn't necessarily mean she'd died here. She could have been released into society but only as a shadow of her former self. In essence, this was where she belonged, or felt that she did.

Tell me your name. Let me help you.

There was a wailing now, most likely only audible to Ruby, at least she hoped so, because the despair in it was terrible to hear. It caused her to shut her eyes, to screw them up tight, to wince. Abandonment was such a curse.

Whoever you are, whatever you did, or more likely, didn't

do, I'm here now. You don't have to stay at the asylum, not anymore. A better place awaits you; your true home. A place where there's no anger and no suffering. You'll be amongst those who'll love and protect you, who won't fail you, not again. Can you see a light shining in the distance? It's that you need to go towards.

NO!

The refusal was louder than the wailing of before. Added to it was the thudding that Kelly said the family sometimes heard. Ruby spun round; where was it coming from? Again, she wondered if Kelly could hear it and would come running. There was another sound now, a more recognisable one – the front door. "Hi, honey, we're home."

It must be Kelly's husband and Carly, returning from their trip. Ruby didn't know what to do – go down to see them and introduce herself to the child, or remain with the woman whose despair was growing. It didn't take long to reach a decision. She couldn't walk out on her; such an action might be misconstrued. She had to stay.

All I want to do is help. There's no peace for you here, not then and not now. Why would you want to stay when that's the case? Don't be afraid of the light. Realise what it is. Your way out of here.

She had no knowledge of how long the woman had been confined, but even so, Ruby would bet she was institutionalised. So many she'd dealt with at Brookbridge were – which could account for the high number of spirits that remained. As afraid as they were of their surrounds, they were even more afraid of being cast adrift. In many ways, and despite any atrocities that had happened to them, Cromer was their anchor. It was better than the nothing they perceived was waiting for them. Ruby didn't blame them; she understood. How could you believe in heaven when all you'd known was hell?

That was the difficulty facing Ruby, one she was trying to figure out how to deal with when the door burst open and a child came running into the room – Carly.

"Are you the lady who can see ghosts?"

The girl was small for her age with hair as dark as her mother's. She was also very obviously awed by Ruby's presence. Ruby began to nod, to say she was indeed that person, when the door slammed shut behind the child. Immediately, the atmosphere in the room changed again; it was crackling with intensity, the pink she was surrounded by, now entirely grey, echoing the original building. Ruby tensed.

"Carly, go, get out of here." When there was no reply, she tried again, doing her utmost to keep her voice level. "Carly, please, you need to leave."

A good kid, as her mother had said, Carly was actually trying to obey, but having begun tugging at the door, she stopped. "I can't. The door's stuck. Why's it stuck?"

Damn it! There didn't seem to be much Ruby could do to help either. It was as if her feet were glued to the floor. Not carpeted, not anymore, it was a cold stone floor with only a threadbare rug covering it. Sometimes this happened; she was able to see what the grounded spirit was seeing – look through their eyes almost; but for it to happen with the child in tow was far from ideal.

The thudding – rhythmic, she realised, *thud, thud, thud* – where was it coming from?

In one corner, by a window that had three bars across it, a figure materialised. She wore a dress of some sort, or a shift, and her hair was short but straggly. It was the woman – her age indeterminate – and she was banging her head against the wall.

"Don't do that! You'll hurt yourself."

The words were out of Ruby's mouth before she could stop them. The woman was a spirit, she couldn't hurt herself anymore, but they looked so real, these grey surrounds, and so bleak too with no comforts of any kind on show.

Torn between the woman and the child, Ruby didn't know which way to turn.

She was confused further when Carly's parents started rattling the door handle, demanding to know what the hell was going on. "Why's the door locked? Who locked it? Let us in. Ruby, Carly, are you okay? Come on, let us in!"

Forcing life into her legs, Ruby hurried towards the woman, whilst at the same time trying to reassure the living. "Things are under control," she shouted. "I've made contact with the spirit. She's not going to harm us; Carly's safe, quite safe. The spirit, she's… frightened, that's all. Please don't panic. Give me a few minutes with her."

The rattling at the door increased, followed by banging.

"Please," she raised her voice higher, "everyone keep calm. I… I've got this."

Hunkering down by the woman, Ruby reached out, touching nothing but thin air. "Please stop. You don't have to suffer like this anymore. I'm so sorry life was cruel to you. I wish with all my heart it had been otherwise. But it's just one life and it's over. Go towards something new, something good. Nothing will harm you in the light. It's love, pure love. Raise your head and look at it, see for yourself."

The Watkins were now issuing threats to call the police.

"Help me," Ruby whispered, growing really quite desperate, "to help you."

Another sound joined the din – something completely different and standing out because of it: the cry of a newborn.

Ruby's eyes widened. "Is that it? Did you have a child?"

The baby's cry ceased, just as the woman started to wail. No longer banging her head, she'd begun to shake – violently.

"A fit? Did you have a fit? Is that what you're trying to tell me? A seizure of some sort?"

There was screaming now, a bloodcurdling sound – such horror in it, but more than that, there was grief. The woman was scratching at her face and tugging at her hair, doing everything, *anything*, to ease the pain that was inside her.

Having to work quickly, Ruby tried to piece it all together.

"You had a baby, a healthy baby, but you weren't healthy; you were prone to fits, epilepsy maybe? It was something like that. Did you… did you have one of these fits whilst nursing your baby? Did you drop the baby? Because of that, did the baby die?"

It took a moment for Ruby to realise, but the woman had stilled, as if listening.

"That's it, isn't it? That's why you were incarcerated. People thought you'd killed your own baby, and you were too grief-stricken, too guilt-ridden to defend yourself. Prison first, but then Cromer, and this is where you died." She looked around her. Were the walls padded? No. By the time this woman had arrived, she may have appeared broken, leading others to think she wasn't a danger to herself or others anymore, but inside she was still raging at what had happened; at all she'd lost.

Daring to hope she was getting somewhere with her, Ruby again pleaded with the woman. "It was an accident, a terrible accident. I'm so sorry you were blamed, that you lost your precious child. But please, let go of your grief, because it's that which continues to imprison you. I know how hard it must have been, I know—"

The woman sprang forward, causing Ruby's head to retract in surprise. Her eyes had manifested fully and they held Ruby's gaze – such fierceness in them. Penetrating so deep that not even Carly or her parents' yells registered anymore, just three words were spat into Ruby's mind – three little words that *seared* it.

You. Don't. Know.

Ruby couldn't begin to formulate an answer to that. After all, this woman was right. She'd had her own life as well as the life she'd borne, stripped from her; she'd been reviled because of an accident, branded a monster and locked away. Ruby had no idea what that was like, or the mental agony that would follow; no idea at all.

Time lost all meaning. Ruby was unable to break the hold the woman had on her; unable to do anything but stare back. She was losing herself, inch by inch, as this woman had lost herself; she was drowning alongside her, in such cold, cold waters.

"You can have my dolly if you like."

What? Who'd said that?

"I'm sorry about your baby, that's sad. But if it helps, take my dolly. I've only just got her, this morning; she's a baby too. I like her, but if you want to be her mummy instead of me, that's fine."

When Carly had run into the room, she'd been holding something – Ruby had barely registered what, but it must have been the doll she was now offering to the spirit – a doll in place of a baby. Would it work?

Finally averting her gaze, the woman turned to look at the child.

"Carly," Ruby whispered, "tell me what you can see."

"Nothing," replied Carly, the doll held out in front of her. "But you're kneeling down, talking to her, so she must be in front of you, right?"

Despite the onslaught of emotion she'd recently felt, by proxy if anything, and that just the tip of the iceberg, Ruby managed a smile. "That's right, that's exactly where she is and she's looking at you, at what you're offering her."

A solution – that's what Carly was offering. Not the doll, not really – a spirit couldn't take something material into the light with them. Regardless of that, it was more than anyone had offered her in a lifetime. The child must have heard every word Ruby had uttered, of course she had, and, as the door finally gave way behind the weight of Mr Watkins, Ruby held up her hands to stay him and Carly's mother. "We've got this," she said. "Believe me, please, we have got this."

Incredibly, Mr and Mrs Watkins did as she instructed, staring at them with wide eyes, just as Ruby was staring at the woman and the child – she the one who was awestruck now.

The woman rose and as she did, she held out her hands too. Gently, she touched the doll, running her fingers over its chubby plastic pinkness.

"Carly, stay as you are," Ruby's voice was barely above a

whisper, "go on doing what you're doing," but the child needed no such instruction.

The woman lifted her hand and touched the child too, stroking her cheek. Carly smiled, as if she knew what was happening and what the gesture meant.

Not taking her eyes of the child, the woman whose name Ruby didn't even know started to back away, through the wall, into whatever lay beyond – peace hopefully.

The child's smile became a beam as the atmosphere changed, but Ruby, still staring at the spot where the woman had disappeared, still reeling from the truth of what had been said, couldn't smile anymore. Instead, she burst into tears.

Chapter Four

THE Watkins, despite any earlier concerns, couldn't have been nicer to her. The fact that Carly had dropped her doll and flung herself at Ruby, in an attempt to console her, probably went some way to softening them. They realised she wasn't a threat, not if their daughter didn't think so, and helped Ruby downstairs where she sat nursing a cup of tea, completely unable to stop the flow of tears.

"I'm sorry," she said, over and over. "This is so unprofessional."

The Watkins, however, wouldn't accept the apology.

"I don't know what you've done," Kelly offered yet another tissue so Ruby could blow her nose, "but she's gone, I know she has. The house feels so different!"

"It's what Carly did," Ruby explained, "she gave her back her faith in humanity."

"How?" Mr Watkins' fascination was clear.

"By one simple act of kindness. Sometimes, that's all it takes."

They'd all gone a bit dewy-eyed at that.

Cash, who'd sent several messages asking what was taking her so long and whether she needed help, texted her again when she finally left the Watkins house and was in her car. Rather than text back, she phoned, still in tears about what had happened.

Immediately, he offered to come and get her.

"What's the point, you'll be in your car and I'll be in mine. Look, don't worry; I'll be back soon. Yes, yes, I'm okay to drive. Honestly, I am. No, of course, I'm not going to crash the car. Will you stop worrying? I wish I'd never phoned you now!"

She didn't mean it and he knew it – she needed to hear his voice, to have his support. He was her rock, as much as the rest of her team; as much as her mother and grandmother; as much as Jed, who'd materialised in the seat next to Ruby, not making a fuss of her – somehow he knew she needed time to process what had just happened – but just *being* there. As she put the car into gear and drove away, she wondered about her newfound father. Would he be supportive too, in the future? Could they support each other? Only time would tell.

Driving back past the last remaining building, she noticed a couple with two kids. The father was talking to his son and pointing at the empty structure. The mother and her other son were busy taking pictures. Voyeurs. This place attracted so many. They came out of the woods, which the building backed into, hoping for what? To catch a glimpse of someone long gone, a tortured spirit perhaps, dressed in rags and traipsing along the corridors, beating at their chest, still in so much torment? Perhaps she was being too harsh. The family in front of her didn't look like bad people; they looked very nice. They just loved a ghost story, that's all; so many did. Better still if it was set at an asylum, it added a certain frisson. Ghosts and madness were fascinating subjects; they brought a gleam to the eye when mentioned, pricked the imagination, caused it to run riot. Brushed to one side was the human cost – the spiritual cost – barely any thought given to the real lives that were torn apart, not always for reasons of madness. Although, could you exist in an environment such as Cromer and remain sane? She didn't think so. There'd be nothing but the madness of others to distract you. Like with a disease, you'd become infected. Asylums fell out of favour from the mid-60s onwards and 'care in the community' was offered instead. A cuddly-sounding term, it was often anything but. She'd once heard it described as 'couldn't care less in the community', which many swore was more accurate. But at least people weren't wrongly locked up nowadays, for reasons of grief, for God's sake, as the spirit at Willow Walk had been – a woman who'd been judged so readily, and denounced. At least that didn't happen as much in these supposedly enlightened times. Not here, not in leafy green England.

Leaving the estate, she headed back to the main road. As she did, she squinted to see into the distance. Was that Ness's car ahead, a Rover? As battered as Ruby's Ford, but just as loved. There was someone in the passenger seat beside her – Theo? She squinted again and Jed also barked, his tail wagging in excitement. After speeding up, she soon had to slow down, thwarted in her attempt to catch up with the Rover as it made a sudden right turn whilst she had to wait at a junction. When she was eventually able to turn right, the car had disappeared. She shrugged. Perhaps it wasn't Ness; her make of car wasn't exactly rare. It could have been anyone.

The further Ruby drove from the estate, the more her mood lifted and she was able to appreciate fully the success of this morning's work, the sheer weight of it receding. She had the rest of the weekend to look forward to, but more than that, the freedom to enjoy it, something she always appreciated but which now seemed like such a gift. Within half an hour she was home where Cash was waiting for her at the door. The speed of her pace rivalling Jed's, she fell straight into his arms.

"Right, that's it," he declared, pulling her inside and shutting the world out, "no more work this weekend. If needs be, I'll take your phone off you."

"Cash, there isn't any need for that, honest."

He reared back slightly. "Ruby, I know what you're like, if you get a call for help, you won't be able to resist; you'll be off like a shot. We've talked about this, remember? About the need to switch off, as much as you can anyway."

"Cash—"

"I mean it. I can see just by looking at you how much this morning has taken out of you. For want of a better word, you look haunted. The team have got my number, so's your mum and your gran. If anyone needs you urgently they can contact you via me. Come on, hand it over and let's just enjoy ourselves."

Breaking away, she dug her phone from her pocket and gazed longingly at it. "What if Peter—"

Again Cash interrupted her. "Peter can wait 'til Monday too."

God, it was a painful separation, but he was right – she needed to take a break, switch off. That woman though, that poor woman, would she be able to get her out of her head? She had to try. Once again, tears threatened. She'd dealt with cases as sad before, as tragic, but this one had turned her into a soggy mess.

You. Don't. Know.

Those words resounded in her head.

It was true. She'd been low, but never that low. Still in the hallway, still holding Cash, she continued to count her blessings.

* * *

Saturday evening was indeed relaxing. Although they'd had an invite to the pub to meet friends, Ruby wasn't in a particularly social mood. Instead, they bought a decent bottle of red, ordered a Chinese and watched a favourite film – *We're the Millers* – on Netflix, a comedy that had her crying again, this time with laughter.

Sunday morning they got up relatively early and headed to the countryside for a walk on the Downs, revelling in what might be the last of the warm weather. After a late lunch at *The Sussex Ox*, Cash managing to fit in three courses to Ruby's one, they returned home. Now Cash was lying on the sofa in the living room, with Jed beside him – not that he was able to see Jed, but he knew he was there, courtesy of Ruby. The pair of them soon fell fast asleep.

She'd been good – really good – she hadn't asked for her mobile once. She'd also ignored her laptop on the kitchen table, but finding herself at a loose end, her resistance waned.

Just a peek – that's all she wanted – a quick catch-up.

Firing up the laptop, she drummed her fingers against the dining table, surprised at how impatient she was. It was a sign of the times, she supposed, that need to be continually plugged in. Going straight to her emails, she was disappointed to see nothing new from Peter. The last correspondence had been eight days ago – the email in which he'd expressed a desire to meet Ruby but also to take things slowly. She'd written back, agreeing to that, but hoping the initial meeting would come soon. They'd also exchanged a photograph of each other, but his hadn't been the best quality; she could discern only the basics from it, not details, like the true colour of his eyes, his height in relation to hers, and how much grey peppered his fair hair. She was so curious to see what he looked like in real life and what characteristics they shared. How would he react when she told him what she did for a living? Should she even tell him? Nerves began to dance in her stomach, despite there being no proposed meeting date on the horizon. When there was, no doubt she'd be a wreck!

Of the other emails she checked, two were related to work, one concerning a case in the ancient city of York, which was being looked after by two Psychic Surveys associates, and seemed to be on the road to success. The other, she couldn't quite believe – it was from yet another resident of the Brookbridge estate, one who'd lived happily in her house for the last five years. Now, as with the Watkins, there was something peculiar happening at her address, something 'far from normal', and as Psychic Surveys were obviously the "go to" people regarding these matters, she wondered if they could pay her a visit – pronto.

Ruby barely had time to construct a reply when *beep!* Another email arrived. Glancing at the door, making sure there was no Cash present, she opened it.

Hi, I'm a friend of Kelly Watkins, who lives in Willow Walk on the Brookbridge Estate, near Horam. I know Psychic Surveys have been called to the estate a number of times and everyone seems to speak highly of you. The thing is…

"Ruby, what are you doing?"

Damn! Cash was awake after all.

"Oh, Cash, hi. I'm just… well, I'm checking my emails."

"I thought we'd agreed, no work this weekend. We're just gonna chill."

"Well, *you've* certainly been relaxing. As you'd dozed off, I thought I'd come in here and have a quick peek—"

In a few steps, he was by her side, one hand reaching out to close the lid of the laptop. "Okay I dozed off, but I'm awake now and raring to go."

Ruby actually winced as the computer shut. She'd been intrigued by those emails from Brookbridge and hadn't yet read the second one fully. Yes, she'd had a regular supply of work there over the last four years, but three cases in the space of a few days? As far as she could recall, that was a first. She was just about to explain, when Cash grabbed hold of her hands and pulled her to her feet.

"Wow," she exclaimed. "You really are raring to go."

"I am! To the pub, The Rights of Man, in fact. We weren't very sociable last night, but tonight I reckon we should ring the changes."

His enthusiasm was infectious. "Who are we meeting?"

"Presley and Corinna are gonna be there plus a few others. Come on, if we leave now, we can get a drink in before everyone arrives."

"Fine, on one condition."

Cash inclined his head to the right. "What's that?"

"You give me back my mobile."

"Ruby—"

"Seriously, Cash! I'm not a kid, just… give it back."

"No checking it 'til tomorrow, though."

"Cash!"

"All right, all right," he relented.

"God, you're a control freak at times."

"Pot, kettle and black, Ruby."

It was a fair point. They were both strong characters.

Following him out of the kitchen, she asked where he'd hidden it.

"Bathroom cabinet."

"The bathroom cabinet? But I've opened that at least twice since yesterday!"

"Which proves my theory."

"What theory?"

"That you can never see what's in front of your nose."

He expertly dodged the swipe she aimed at him, and was in high spirits all the way to the pub – some quality time spent together having put him in a good mood. As tempted as she was to talk about the emails from Brookbridge, she refrained – light-hearted chat was on the agenda, a few laughs and some banter. Besides, the tone of the emails hadn't been desperate and Monday morning wasn't far away; she could tend to everything then. It was a plan she intended to stick with, but when she woke later that night with a raging thirst, she crept from their bed and returned to the kitchen. A cup of chamomile would see her right, and perhaps a little research.

She already knew there was a fascination with Cromer online, plenty of people having blogged about their experiences exploring the abandoned buildings. Most of them had posted photos of their explorations and shivers ran down Ruby's spine as she revisited page after page of what it had been like in the years awaiting demolition. There were windows with cracked panes and thick dusty cobwebs; narrow corridors that ran on and on into the darkness beyond; walls covered in graffiti – *Welcome to Hell*, a popular slogan, and variations upon it. There were benches and broken chairs randomly placed; a hospital bed frame in a similar dilapidated state; a lone wheelchair in a corridor; the floor covered in debris. Continuing to scroll, she found a black and white picture of a woman. Her age indeterminate, her skin was puckered on her cheeks and her eyes… they were empty, for want of a better word. She was holding up a board with her name, Ruby supposed – Caroline Jennings – scrawled upon it. There was also a date – April 1927 – a birth date or the date that she entered the asylum? Who knew? Ruby raised her hand and touched the screen. The woman could have been anyone – she *was* anyone – an individual and yet representative of so many. Those eyes… the look in those eyes…

Withdrawing her hand, she clutched at her tourmaline necklace – an heirloom from her great-grandmother, Rosamund. The stones, known for their protective qualities, were a comfort. An asylum was a hospital; somewhere people went to receive treatment for reasons of ill health – *medical* treatment. But this photo, this wretched photo, reminded her of a prison mugshot – it was the same, no distinction at all. Yes, there had been and still was, a medium-security unit on the fringe of Brookbridge. It was called Ash Hill, if memory served her – a modern low-rise NHS building that had replaced the original. It was where those with mental difficulties who were also criminally inclined were sent. Perhaps this woman had been one of those criminally inclined, perhaps not. She just looked so very sad, reminding Ruby of the mother grounded at the Watkins' house. If Caroline

Jennings wasn't in the secure wing, then the picture suggested all inmates were photographed in a similar way. Perhaps it was necessary for record-keeping, but it was also somehow an indignity.

What they were subjected to at the asylum made Ruby shudder. She remembered a male spirit they'd moved on the year before from the Craggs' house on the estate. He'd been broken, utterly broken, not only for reasons of madness, but because of the treatment he'd received at Cromer. It had been an arduous case, the team having worked round the clock, dealing with so much emotion, sorrow and anger. He'd left eventually and made his way into the light, but it had been traumatic for all concerned. There'd been a few more cases since, and then it had gone quiet… until now.

The chamomile tea was doing the trick. Her eyelids were beginning to droop but by now she was too involved to return to bed. Striking a bargain with herself, she decided she would spend a few more minutes perusing the 'net and then head back to her bedroom to join Cash and Jed, who had no such trouble sleeping. Focusing on facts and figures rather than photos, she learnt there were just over two thousand patients at Cromer at its peak – a figure that took her breath away. *Two thousand?* That was a revelation. Little wonder the site had kept them so busy. The building, the one that still stood, enclosed by green fencing, had been known as a 'rear ward block' – a layout based upon a maze of corridors. On the second floor there'd been private rooms, wards and a nursery, the latter causing Ruby's jaw to drop. On the lower floor there'd been a gym, a dayroom, and another thing she'd previously missed, concerning this particular building anyway – a ballroom, an actual *ballroom*. Added to that, there was a kitchen and dining room, a doctor's office, and an operating theatre. Being to the east of the estate, and the fact that it had a nursery, Ruby presumed it had been home to female patients only, although a ballroom suggested mixed integration. The place was due for demolition, she learnt, at some point this year, but she could find no definite date. The developers had expounded their intention of developing 'a village style community', right now, however, there was nothing quite so cosy uniting the residents of Brookbridge.

The laptop's tile bar showed 4.05 – *the dead of night*, Ruby mused. She'd look at one more site – *Forbidden Places*. Clicking on the page, there, in all its dubious glory, was Cromer Asylum, nearing the top of the list.

It was much the same information she'd read before, although it was glitzed up a little with a liberal sprinkling of words such as 'abandoned', 'decayed' and 'rotting' – emotive words, words designed to get a response – and they had. At the bottom of the page was a lengthy discussion thread containing comments from people who'd actually worked at the hospital during its closing years. These actually helped to dispel some of the drama the page had tried to build up, as they pointed out that the vast majority worked for the good of their patients, and that in some respects it was a 'wonderful' place to be, and 'therapeutic'. They described the wards as warm and airy, and the grounds beautiful. There was a greenhouse apparently, where plants and vegetables were grown, a favourite meeting place for patients and staff alike. Another ex-staff member insisted she'd never felt spooked there, despite the long, dark corridors she'd had to tread whilst on night duty. One person, who'd been treated at Cromer in the early 70s for depression, couldn't praise the staff enough, whilst another, who'd had a breakdown in the mid 80s, described the atmosphere as calm rather than hectic. Others, however, told a different story – not patients, not staff, but those who'd explored the buildings afterwards; who'd sensed horror within its walls, heard screams, and seen dark figures lurking. Ordinarily, Ruby would attribute all this to imagination and wishful thinking, but she couldn't, because she knew from her experience of previous Brookbridge cases that some of it was true; that alongside those who were helped were those who were stamped on.

As she was about to stop reading, a last comment caught her eye, this time from someone called 'Eclipse' – rather an impassioned comment as it turned out, insisting there were still spirits in the remaining building, so many of them, and warning what a terrible thing it would be to destroy it whilst those spirits were still there, as this would serve to confuse and terrify them further. Eclipse claimed to have visited the building several times, becoming distressed by the activity sensed there. Ruby wondered if Eclipse was psychic, but there was no mention of that. Something had to be done about it, Eclipse continued to insist; the spirits *had* to be moved on.

There was something about Eclipse's language style that resonated with Ruby – the use of the term 'spirits' rather than ghosts, and the insistence that they needed to be 'moved on', instead of hunted or banished. Eclipse's concern leapt off the page: 'I feel so helpless! If only I knew what to do about this situation and how to help them. Because the building's due to be torn down, it's a race against time. We need to act quickly! God, I wish I had the answer. Haven't these souls suffered enough?'

Was that the 'royal we' in use, or were there more like Eclipse, who wanted to help the grounded? Again, it was easy to dismiss it as the ranting of a crackpot, but once more, Ruby knew better. The likelihood that several spirits were trapped inside the building was high – very high, and if they remained, one thing was certain: Psychic Surveys would be called out in the future to deal with them as they re-surfaced within a new set of walls. Or, she could deal with the situation right now. Well… not this minute, but soon, very soon. It looked as if she was heading back to Brookbridge in a few hours' time, so even if she couldn't gain entrance, she could at least encircle the building and get a feel for it. She'd never really given it a thought before, but perhaps the time had come to rectify that. Security was lax at Brookbridge, the signs stating CCTV was in operation a blatant lie; in fact the signs were almost as dilapidated as the building itself. No one cared about it. Well, almost no one. She did. Eclipse did.

There was an option to reply to Eclipse, all she had to do was click on an arrow.

Ruby hesitated, but only for a second.

Haven't these souls suffered enough?

The memory of the woman in Carly's bedroom, of Jennings and her hollow eyes, caused her own to tear again.

Eclipse was right; they'd suffered more than enough.

With that in mind, she began to type.

Chapter Five

THE next morning, Cash had already left for an appointment when Ruby received a phone call. *Here we go,* she thought, rushing to answer it. *More work.*

There was certainly no shortage of it at the moment, not in her local area or indeed, in areas far flung, for which she'd assembled an ever-growing group of national freelance psychics willing to investigate for a fee that could only be described as nominal. As much as she'd love to attend each and every case, she couldn't. For one thing, there was the cost of travel; for another, someone had to cover the south, and that was the original team: Corinna, Ness, Theo and herself.

It was Theo who'd phoned her.

"Hello, darling, how are you? Good weekend?"

"Well…" Where should she start? "It was interesting, that's for sure."

"Oh?"

Ruby told her about the Saturday morning visit to Brookbridge. As soon as she mentioned the name of the estate, she expected Theo to sigh and say something along the lines of 'Here we go again', but she did no such thing. Instead, asking for details, her voice was similar to Ness's – solemn.

"So, you're going there again this morning?"

"Hopefully," replied Ruby, "I've yet to make the

appointments, so it'll either be this morning or at some stage this week."

"To carry out an initial survey?"

"That's right." Although as they both knew, an initial survey could occasionally become so much more.

Now Theo did sigh. "Ruby, do you need me today?"

"No… I don't think so. If I do go there today, Corinna or Ness could always come with me."

There was a pause on the line.

"Theo?"

"It's just I have to be somewhere else, that's all."

"No problem."

"Are you sure?"

"Sure I'm sure."

"Oh good, well… lots of luck. I'm at the end of my phone, as you know."

"Absolutely. Theo, is everything okay?"

"Everything's fine, sweetheart. I'll check in again tomorrow."

"I'll speak with you then."

Ruby ended the call and stared at her mobile for a few seconds. That had all sounded very mysterious. What was Theo up to? Then again, as the grandmother of several young children, courtesy of her three sons, Theo had a busy family life, plus she was almost seventy-one, and although still as fit as a fiddle despite her ever-widening girth, maybe helping Psychic Surveys out on a regular basis was proving too much. God, she hoped not! Should she phone back? Probe a little further into the matter? Check if that was indeed the case? Although she was sorely tempted, she decided not to; accused herself of overreacting even. All was well, all was fine, and the team were staying exactly that – a team.

After grabbing a shower, she returned the two calls from the Brookbridge residents, both of them keen for an appointment that day. With a piece of toast stuffed in her mouth, she then headed out the door to her office in the Lewes High Street, which was situated in the attic above a solicitor's. Her car was parked a couple of streets away but before getting into it, she called Ness to see if she'd like to accompany her. There was no reply. Perplexed, she phoned Corinna.

"Ah," she said, on hearing her voice, "third time lucky."

Explaining to a baffled Corinna about Theo and Ness, Corinna replied, "Well, if you need me today, I'm all yours. I'm working the late shift."

Corinna worked part-time in a pub in Ringmer and part-time for Ruby – the day when she could give up work to concentrate fully on Psychic Surveys not quite here yet. Agreeing to pick Corinna up from the flat she rented in Lewes, Ruby decided to bypass the office altogether and go straight there. They'd carry out the initial surveys then Ruby would drop her back home before heading to Hastings to see her mother and grandmother – a visit to them long overdue. She might even stay the night in Hastings, and so had with her a change of clothes and her toothbrush as well as her black bag with all the paraphernalia she might need to perform an holistic cleansing: crystals; oils; sage wands, and that old perennial, salt.

Arriving at Brookbridge halfway through the morning, Ruby hoped they'd be done within two or three hours, after which they could head to the old building. Unfortunately, they were a lot longer. The first house they'd visited was indeed occupied by a spirit – a *terrified* spirit, one whom they couldn't coax out of hiding no matter how hard they tried. That would indeed require a second visit, and possibly a third and a fourth, with all of the team in tow. As for the second house, belonging to the Stem family, it was more poltergeist activity that was the problem – doors banging, books falling off shelves, cups and plates as well, smashing as they hit the ground. Again, the spirit proved elusive – initially. And then it had rushed forwards and smacked Ruby across the face! A spirit blow, whilst not carrying the same weight as a human blow, was nonetheless shocking and Ruby had to fight a knee-jerk reaction of ire. Instead, she and Corinna had sent out wave after wave of love to the spirit, reassuring it all the time – 'it' because neither of them could ascertain whether it was a male or a female, although the fact that the Stems' house was on the west side of the estate where the male dormitories had been, suggested a man. Barely faltering, they talked of the light, describing it as home as they were wont to do, and gently encouraging the spirit to go towards it.

It had taken a while, the time nearing five when they both felt they were getting somewhere. Although Corinna had her bar job to go to, they couldn't just leave, not now that a connection had been made. Corinna realised this as much as Ruby and sent a text saying she'd get to the pub as soon as possible. Luckily, her boss was supportive of what she did and replied telling her to get there when she could, adding 'good luck' before signing off. When the spirit finally went into the light, a little after six, there was an enormous sense of relief all round.

"I wonder what his story was," Corinna said, her skin

paler than usual.

"I wish I knew," Ruby responded. Or did she? Would it only upset her again? "Whatever it was, he's no longer stuck at the asylum; he's gone."

After informing the residents of their success, Ruby and Corinna stood outside on the pavement, inhaling the fresh air of this semi-rural setting. It felt so good. For a while, in the Stems' house, there'd been an unpleasant smell. Not unclean, she wouldn't say that; it was more like boiled cabbage and disinfectant rolled into one – the smell of Cromer perhaps, which had permeated every room and every corridor, soaking into walls, even spectral walls.

"I'd better get you to the pub," Ruby said, looking at her watch.

"Ah, thanks, Ruby and sorry to take you out of your way, I know you're planning to go to your gran's tonight."

"It's no problem, I'm just grateful you could come; I wouldn't have wanted to tackle all that on my own. Shame about the old building though, you know, the last one standing, I was hoping we could go there too."

"Go inside you mean?"

"That or stake out the perimeter. I'm coming back soon, I'll check it out then."

As dusk was beginning to settle, Corinna nodded. "That might be for the best. Even if I didn't have work I'm not sure I'm up for a visit now. Come on, you said on the way over you'd done some research into it. What have you discovered?"

En route to the car Ruby enlightened her. "On one site I was looking at, there was a discussion thread about the building and the spirits that haunt it. It was the usual stuff; there were those who swore blind Cromer was a wonderful, therapeutic place to be, and those who've experienced really unsettling phenomena after its abandonment, saying something completely different. Obviously, there's some play on the cheap thrill aspect, but one person stood out – Eclipse. I don't know what gender Eclipse is, but he or she spoke our language, if you know what I mean. Having visited several times, there's a real concern for the spiritual welfare of the grounded, and a desire to move them to the light. Honestly, Eclipse was literally pleading for help, worried the imminent destruction of the building will cause even more torment and unrest, which of course manifests at Brookbridge and lands in *our* laps."

At the car, Corinna stopped, her expression thoughtful. "It's possible. As much as the grounded might fear this place, they're also used to it."

Ruby agreed. "Eclipse's message was only dated last week. Now, it's obvious there's going to be unrest in that building. There is on the entire estate, and I know we haven't checked it out before – we've had enough on our plate – but every time I've passed it, I've never really felt a pull. Yesterday though, I did. But more than that, I felt a shift in the atmosphere hereabouts; a kind of change. It seems to be more on edge than ever. The case I worked on Saturday morning and these two cases we've worked on today, they've got one thing in common."

Halfway into the car, Corinna turned towards Ruby. "Which is?"

"The families have lived in their houses for a while now, but it's only recently there's been unrest."

Rather than get in the car, Corinna returned to the pavement.

"Corinna?" Ruby queried.

"I want to stand here a while, try and see what you mean."

"Oh right, fair enough."

Ruby came round to join her. By her side, Corinna inclined her head and shut her eyes – trying to tune in, Ruby waiting patiently to hear her verdict.

Eventually, Corinna opened her eyes. "It does feel different. It's almost like an electrical current, isn't it? If you reach out and touch it, there'll be a sizzle."

Ruby smiled. "Yeah, it is like that. I'm wondering if whoever's inside the old building can sense some sort of finality and they're digging their heels in; resisting? I sent a message to Eclipse, by the way, I'm waiting to hear back."

Corinna raised a perfectly pencilled-in eyebrow. "Look, if you do want to find a way in there tonight, I can always try and fob work off some more."

Ruby was tempted but eventually she shook her head. "It's not fair to take advantage. Besides, I don't want to arrive in Hastings too late, Gran's been a bit frail recently, she prefers to eat early and go to bed soon after."

Immediately, Corinna was all concern. Laying a hand on Ruby's arm, she said, "I'm really sorry to hear that. I hope she's okay?"

"She's eighty, she's slowing down." Ruby had to swallow hard. God, she was emotional lately. "It's to be expected, I suppose."

"Yeah, yeah, it is. Even so, if there's anything I can do."

"Thanks. Come on, you're right; we've done enough for today. I feel exhausted. How you're going to cope with a shift tonight I don't know."

"I'll cope just fine. Presley said he'd come in to prop up the bar, so it'll be fun."

"It's going really well between you two, isn't it?" Ruby had lost count how many times she'd asked Corinna this question – a lot, but she liked hearing the answer.

"Really well." Corinna almost swooned as she said it, causing Ruby to smile again. "Those Wilkins brothers are something else, aren't they?"

"I think so," Ruby replied, finally getting in the car.

Having dropped Corinna off, Ruby put her foot down to get to Hastings as soon as possible. Parking in the free zone, she made her way on foot to Lazuli Cottage in the Old Town, looking forward to a girls' night in with her family – playing a board game perhaps, or just chatting as they ate and drank. Knocking on the door, which she tended to do rather than dig around in her bag for her key, it was opened straightaway – not by Sarah, as was usual, but a smiling Jessica.

They hugged before going through to the kitchen where Sarah was sitting. She started to rise so that she could hug Ruby too, but Ruby insisted her grandmother stay put, and bent to hug her instead. She'd described her as frail to Corinna, and frail she was, but only in body, Ruby reminded herself, not in spirit.

"How are you, Gran? Shall I put the kettle on, make us a cup of tea?"

The fact she had to ask was testament enough to how Sarah was feeling lately. There was a time when the kettle would be boiling as soon as Ruby entered the house, her grandmother always aware when she was on her way, even if she hadn't called beforehand to let her know – her highly developed intuitive powers in action.

To accompany their tea, Jessica had placed some biscuits on a plate, not Sarah's homemade shortbread

66

which Ruby, like Cash, adored – but shop-bought. Sampling one, it was nowhere near as delicious, but if Gran hadn't felt like making any lately, Ruby wouldn't complain; shop-bought would do just fine. Setting down the pot of tea, Jessica warned Ruby not to overindulge in biscuits because dinner would be ready in an hour. Ruby could smell the lamb roasting in the oven, and the rosemary and garlic that garnished it. As she poured the tea, she told her mother and grandmother about her day.

"Strange about Brookbridge," Jessica commented, nibbling on a biscuit too.

"It is, isn't it?" replied Ruby. "The whole atmosphere seems to have changed lately. I said to Corinna that maybe it's because the last building is due to be demolished soon and it's stirring things up."

"Maybe," mused Sarah, her hands shaking slightly, Ruby noticed, as she brought her cup to her lips. "It sounds like draining work though, darling. Make sure you take care of yourself too; protect yourself adequately."

"I will… I do," Ruby assured her grandmother, reaching across to give her arm a quick squeeze.

Having finished her tea, Jessica got up to carry on preparing dinner. Alone at the table with Sarah, Ruby checked she was okay. "You seem tired, too."

There was a smile in Sarah's silvery eyes. "Of course I'm tired; I'm old!"

"You're not, not really, not by today's standards."

"By *anyone's* standards. But please, don't worry about me." She glanced at Jessica, who had her back to them, humming a tune. "I'm in good hands."

Again, the miracle of that amazed Ruby. Despite the fact that they had all lived under the same roof for so many years, her mother had been lost, cut off from them, from Saul, from everyone she'd ever known; trapped in a world of shock and misery. It had taken finding Saul again, and confronting the horror of what she'd conjured, to break free of the reins that kept her in such a dark and miserable place. There'd been no physical walls to constrain her, but the walls of the mind were as strong as any built of bricks and mortar. It had taken thirteen years for Jessica to recover. If it weren't for her grandmother holding them together as tightly as she did, there would be no Davis family. And now it was their time to look after Sarah – to fill *her* shoes.

After a pleasant evening, transferring to the living room after dinner to chat some more, Sarah bid her daughter and granddaughter goodnight and went to bed. Alone with Jessica, Ruby decided the time was right to reveal that she and Peter Gregory had been in touch. She still felt reluctant to talk about him in front of Sarah, worried that somehow she'd view her search – her *longing* – for another family member as some kind of betrayal. Her mother, however, might be interested to hear how things were progressing. As succinctly as she could, Ruby told her about the exchange of emails. Jessica listened intently, her expression barely altering.

When Ruby had finished, there was silence. At last, Jessica began speaking.

"It all sounds positive, Ruby, and I wish you luck, I really do."

"Mum…" she took a deep breath, "I know Peter left you when you told him you were pregnant; I know he was married, that he had children already—"

"He had children?"

68

"Yeah… a boy and a girl."

"I had no idea."

"Oh God, Mum, I'm sorry! I just assumed…"

"It's fine, it's… I never asked. More than that, I never wanted to know."

Ruby swallowed, felt unsure suddenly. "Look, if you think I should stop—"

"You're not going to stop. You're curious by nature, that's what makes you so good at your job. And you've come this far. Darling, I understand your curiosity. When I gave you his name, I didn't doubt for one minute you'd find him. In a way, it was my blessing." Jessica sighed and shook her head somewhat ruefully. "It was all such a long time ago. The man was a liar and a cheat, but then again, so was I."

"If you were, you're not like that anymore," Ruby pointed out. And the same might be true of Peter. "What I'm trying to say is… did you love him?"

Again, there was silence – Jessica digesting perhaps what she'd just discovered. After a while she nodded. "Yes, Ruby, I did."

Rather than continue to elaborate, Jessica did as Sarah had earlier; she stood up, declared she was tired and left the room, leaving her daughter to stare after her.

Chapter Six

RUBY drove back to Lewes the next morning, climbed the three flights of stairs to her office in the gods and settled herself in her beloved captain's chair. One of the first things she did was send an email to the Bradleys, who occupied the house of the elusive spirit at Brookbridge. She explained that, in her opinion, more visits might be required to build up trust with the spirit, and assured them that the costs incurred would be kept to an absolute minimum. It was the welfare of the spirit, as well as the Bradleys, that was of paramount concern to Psychic Surveys, and to that end, they'd do everything they could to achieve it.

Having sent the email, she checked her inbox. Before she did this, she had to take a deep breath – hoping, always hoping…

Scanning the page, there it was; what she'd been waiting for. Hurriedly, she opened the email – her hands shaking as she tried to control the mouse.

Hello, Ruby, I hope you're well. Over the last few days I've had a think, in fact, I haven't done much else except think about our correspondence. I've concluded it might be a good idea to meet sooner rather than later. It's not easy getting to know each other via email. Why don't we meet in Windsor? That's halfway between Lewes and Oxford. I know a nice pub there. The Red Lion. I've included the link. Peter

For a moment Ruby could only sit and stare. A meeting? He was suggesting a meeting, and sooner rather than later? How soon? Her diary was to the right of her and she glanced at it: her schedule was fairly hectic, but some things could be re-arranged or handed over to the rest of the team. They'd understand and support her. She was going to meet her father for the first time – Peter Gregory – a man her mother had been in love with. It was important, as it would be to anyone she presumed, to feel she'd been conceived in something akin to that emotion, even if it had been one-sided. And maybe it wasn't; maybe Peter had loved Jessica too. She would never know the full story, *his* story, if she didn't take this first step.

Flexing her fingers, she typed an eager reply. *Hi, Peter, I'd be so happy for us to meet. Any time that's convenient for you is convenient for me. Just name the date!*

A minute or two after pressing 'send', her email pinged again. Could it be him, replying so soon?

It wasn't, it was Eclipse.

Ruby, hi, thanks so much for contacting me. I've looked you up on the net and wow, I can't believe I didn't know about you before today! It looks like we share a lot of the same values. I am NOT someone interested in ghost hunting or giving myself a scare. What I'm interested in is helping trapped spirits to move on. I don't claim to have particularly developed psychic skills, but honestly speaking, I think anyone with a shred of sensitivity who's explored the last remaining building on the Brookbridge estate would be able to feel the despair within its walls, human despair, all those tortured souls still suffering. I can't stop thinking about them. I want to help, but like I said, I'm not psychic, intuitive perhaps, but that's not enough to make a difference. As you've got in touch with me, I'm guessing you may be interested in hearing what I have to say? I can get us into the building easily enough. I know a way. Don't worry about the warning signs, or the security cameras, they're fake. That building's as doomed now as it was then, so why not let people go in and tear it to pieces? Anyway, what I was wondering was, would you like to meet up to discuss this face to face? I'm not far from Lewes so I could come to your office. Either that or I'll meet you at Brookbridge. If you prefer Brookbridge, after dark is probably better and wear loads of warm clothing. It doesn't matter what the weather's like, it gets really cold in there! Timing really is important. That building needs to be emptied before it's torn down. Let me know. Eclipse

Ruby sat back in her chair. What a morning it was turning out to be; two meetings on the cards with two very different people. As for Eclipse, she still had no idea whether it was a man or a woman she was corresponding with; there'd been no clue in the email, not as far as she could see. She wanted to meet Eclipse though, preferably at her office first, although as had been pointed out, timing was critical. So this was something else to fit in this week, hopefully.

As Jed materialised before the Calor gas heater, looking slightly miffed that it wasn't lit, Ruby got down to business. Next on the agenda was checking in with Ness, Theo and Corinna, regarding their availability during the week. She hadn't actually spoken to Ness for a few days, which was far from usual, so she tried her first.

As on the previous day, the phone rang and rang. Was it going to remain unanswered again? Even if it did, her call would register and normally Ness would phone her back. Just as Ruby was sure it was going into answerphone, Ness did indeed pick up.

"Hi, Ruby, sorry about the delay, how are you?"

"I'm fine thanks, how are you?"

"Okay."

Okay? She didn't sound it. Not wanting to tread on her toes, however, to pry – Ness valued her privacy – Ruby explained why she was calling, imagining the look on Ness's face all the while – such a serious look. "So, really, what I'm doing is checking your availability this week."

There was a slight pause. "Ruby, something's come up. A private case."

"A private case?" Ruby repeated.

"Yes, it's… Sorry, I really can't say anything more than that, not right now. It's confidential."

"Oh, it's work related to the police?"

"In a way."

Ruby didn't press further.

"It's odd about Brookbridge," Ness continued.

"You can say that again. I was wondering if it's something to do with the imminent destruction of the final hospital building."

"Perhaps."

Despite such a non-committal response, Ruby felt the need to elaborate. "At the moment, when I think of Brookbridge, I imagine a saucepan on a hob. At first it's simmering away, but the heat's building, the lid's beginning to rattle: a warning sign. If nothing's done, if it's just ignored, what's inside that pan is going to blow to kingdom come. Do you know where I'm coming from?"

"I know exactly. And we're here for you, it's just… we have to work around this other case, that's all."

"We?" Ruby questioned.

"I've asked Theo to join me."

"Oh right." Theo hadn't said anything about that when she'd last spoken to her. *Because it's confidential, Ruby, remember?* Of course, and, even though she was even more curious than before, she mustn't question further. After all, she was the only full-time member of Psychic Surveys, the rest were all freelance; they had their own work – Corinna as a barmaid and Theo and Ness with private cases that they sometimes took on – she knew that. And her current workload wasn't too onerous, although experience had shown that could change in a heartbeat.

Ness had picked up on Ruby's thoughts. "Ruby, we're not abandoning you."

"I know you're not—"

"Psychic Surveys is our priority, but, if you are able to manage at the moment, this case is something I'd like to continue with."

"You *and* Theo?"

"Both of us."

"Okay."

"If anything changes, call me."

"I will."

"Ruby," Ness clearly saw fit to remind her. "We're here for you."

"I know. You always have been."

Despite that, as she rang off, Ness's use of the word 'abandoned', stuck.

* * *

Just before lunch, Ruby sat back, satisfied with the

morning's work. The case of the elusive spirit had been
passed on to Corinna, who said she'd rope Presley in as
well. Like Cash, he had an avid interest in the paranormal
and was willing to help out when he could.

With that case delegated, she'd made a follow-on call to
The Waterside Inn, checking with the landlord that all was
still peaceful at the pub. The landlord had assured her that
normality had been restored and, although the staff still
tended to visit the cellar in twos and threes, overall they
were much happier. His words had caused Ruby to smile –
that gentleman's agreement was holding fast.

Having also replied to Eclipse, she made an
appointment to meet the next day, which would give her
this afternoon to catch up on admin. She already kept
notes on each and every case, but she'd begun the task of
cross-referencing them, noting similarities where they
existed and adding information from research done by
others who'd experienced anything similar. Some case files
were bulging with these detailed notes, but she was
enjoying the process, and felt it was valuable, not only in
increasing her own understanding of the paranormal
world, but also as a future reference to others. Again, she
had to smile to herself. She was following in the footsteps
of her great-grandmother, Rosamund Davis, who had been
very well respected in certain circles during her lifetime.
She'd written reams and reams on the paranormal, and had
published papers that weren't scorned but held in high
esteem. During Rosamund's time, spiritualism was in
favour. It had fallen out again, but now it was back,
accepted by more and more people, but not as a parlour
game, hobby, or an interest – it was something more real
than that. Ruby hadn't read *all* of Rosamund's work, but a

fair bit of it. In it she recognised the passion she herself felt for the grounded. They were alike in many respects. It was Rosamund's research that had helped in the understanding and defeat of Jessica's conjuring, which Rosamund referred to more plainly as a 'thought form'. Sometimes, if focused on, such forms were able to bridge the gap between their plane and ours, and manifest, growing in substance when fed a diet of fear. Ruby was grateful to Rosamund for giving them that insight – it had saved them. If there was anything more to learn regarding the non-human, however, she'd pass, certainly for now. Her focus was on that which was entirely human, or at least had been once – spirits who were distressed, confused or frightened – and moving them towards the light; hence her enthusiasm for meeting Eclipse, someone who shared that goal.

Taking time out briefly to make a fresh cup of coffee and munch on a sandwich she'd grabbed from a petrol station on the way back from Hastings, she sat at her desk again, and continued to make notes. Currently, she was adding to those on Old Cross Cottage, an ancient cottage in a picturesque Dorset village that she'd stayed in earlier in the year with Cash, in which very unusual events had occurred.

Halfway through the afternoon, her mobile rang. Her eyes still on the screen in front of her, she reached blindly over to answer it.

"Hello, Psychic Surveys, how can I help?"

"Psychic Surveys?" the voice queried – a *male* voice.

"That's right, this is Psychic Surveys, specialists in domestic spiritual clearance and I'm Ruby Davis. Can I help you at all?"

"Specialists in *what*?"

Ruby frowned. Who was this? "Domestic spiritual clearance," she repeated. "I'm assuming as you've phoned this number, you might already know that."

"No, I had no idea."

There was a pause on the line – a heavy pause, causing Ruby's frown to deepen. She was about to break the silence, when the caller spoke again.

"I'm Peter Gregory."

"Peter?" Her free hand flew to her mouth; the other almost dropped the phone. Peter Gregory – her father. This was *not* the way she wanted to break the news to him about her profession. Why oh why hadn't she thought he might phone? After all, they'd shared mobile numbers in a previous email. She also cursed herself for not checking the caller ID; if she had, his name would have flashed up. "I… oh my God, I didn't expect… I'm sorry. I sound so… Oh Christ! I don't know what to say. I just… "

Peter began apologising too. "*I'm* sorry. Perhaps it was wrong of me, phoning out of the blue, I should have emailed you again, prepared you."

Part of her stunned brain was processing the sound of his voice. It wasn't particularly deep, but it was certainly pleasant. It wasn't posh either, although each word was enunciated properly. It was a nice voice, an ordinary voice, easy on the ear. She liked it. Realising she was spending too much time analysing, she forced herself to speak again, properly this time and not just in snatches. "It's lovely to hear from you, a wonderful surprise. Erm… how are you? Are you well?"

"I am, thank you. That's a very interesting profession you have, young lady. I didn't realise."

Ruby couldn't help but smile at being called a 'young

lady' – it was such a 'Dad' thing to do. Or at least she imagined it to be. "Oh that," she said, adopting an airy tone, "well, yeah, yeah, it can be. Gosh, this really is such a surprise. It's our first phone call." Damn, couldn't she think of something less twee to say? *Why* are you phoning would be a good start. Without actually asking, she willed him to answer.

"As I probably implied, I've had enough of emails. I thought we should talk, before… you know, we meet."

"Sure, good idea. It's lovely—" *Stop repeating yourself!* "Are you having a good day?"

"My day's been fine so far. What about yours?"

"Busy."

"With the spirits?" Was that a tease in his voice, or a slight edge?

"With admin." It wasn't a lie, not really, but she thought it best to play down saying anything further until they were face to face. "I've got so much of it."

"Is that interesting too?"

"Not really. You know what admin's like; laborious at the best of times."

"I do know what it's like. I certainly had to plough through my fair share of red tape when I was in the Force. It was one of the reasons I left."

One of the reasons? What were the others, she wondered.

"It's a necessary evil, though, eh?" she replied.

"It is. It is."

There was another pause, one that felt as heavy as when she'd been on the line to Ness.

"Look," he said finally, "the reason I'm phoning is about our meeting. It just so happens I've got a free day tomorrow. I know it's short notice, but—"

"Tomorrow's fine. It's only lunch, isn't it? And I can spare the time."

"Do you mean the spirits can spare you?"

That was a definite tease. "Yes, yes, they can." They'd have to. She was going to meet her dad for the first time. That's what couldn't wait. It had been too long already. "About what I do, I can explain when I see you."

"I'd like that." No tease now, he'd grown serious. "I can be at The Red Lion by one o' clock. Is that okay?"

"One o' clock is fine."

"Good. I'm looking forward to meeting you, Ruby."

"I can't wait to meet you too."

"Until tomorrow then?"

"Until tomorrow."

After the call, Ruby sat in her chair in what could only be considered a state of abject shock. The minutes passed, plenty of them – almost a full half hour – the world around her fading, even Jed, who'd been staring at her askance and in amusement from his position in front of the Calor gas heater whilst she'd been breathless on the phone. Slowly the walls re-materialised along with her piles and piles of books stacked up against the walls, the desk in front of her, cluttered as usual with all manner of papers and more books, and Jed, still askance. Tomorrow was when she was supposed to be meeting Eclipse. That would have to be delayed. Or… she considered for a moment… it could be brought forward. Maybe she could meet whoever Eclipse was this evening, even though she was supposed to be meeting Cash. Cash could come with her, but then again he did have band practice with Presley – *Thousand Island Park* were due to play a gig in Lewes soon at The Lamb, and, as their drummer, he still had a couple of songs to perfect – so theirs was going to be a late meeting anyway. She could be done with Eclipse by then.

Dashing off an email to Eclipse marked *Urgent*, she guessed she'd soon find out.

Chapter Seven

AS soon as Eclipse's email came bouncing back, Ruby phoned Cash. He immediately offered to skip band practice and go with them to Brookbridge, but she told him not to; the gig wasn't too far off and he needed to get a handle on the entire set of songs they were playing. Besides, Presley would be furious with him if he skipped it.

"But you don't e ven know if Eclipse is a man or a woman!"

"It's okay," she said, "whoever it is has assured me they'll be wearing a pink carnation and carrying a copy of *The Sporting Times* under their arm."

"The Sporting Times?"

"It's a joke, Cash! I remember hearing it once on a comedy sketch, that's all."

"Are you actually going inside the building?"

"That's the intention, yes."

"But what if you get caught?"

"Who by?"

"The police!"

"Cash, it's fine, it's okay. I've been through all this with Eclipse. The only thing we have to worry about is the grounded spirits. That's our concern."

"Eclipse," he muttered, "what kind of a name is that?"

Ruby raised an eyebrow, Cash was named after Johnny

Cash and his brother, Presley, after Elvis; they were hardly common names either, she told him.

"My name's nowhere near as hippy!"

"Look, I'm sure it's a pseudonym," she appeased, "a forum handle."

"Yeah, yeah, I suppose it is. I can't believe you haven't asked about gender yet."

"Perhaps I like the enigma of it?"

"Ruby!"

"Oh Cash, I thought it rude to ask, okay? *Hey, by the way, are you a man or a woman?* Maybe… Eclipse is gender fluid. That's a thing nowadays, isn't it? People don't like to be defined and I don't blame them. I think it's a good thing, a *progressive* thing. Anyway, I'm going to find out gender, age, height, eye colour and maybe even shoe size soon. That's good enough for me. Besides, there's something else I want to tell you. That I'm *dying* to tell you."

"Oh? There's more?"

"There is, and it's big news. *Very* big news."

"Ruby, stop being such a tease."

Laughing, she told him that her dad had phoned, that she was meeting him the next day – Wednesday. Saying the words out loud almost made it believable. The brief silence that ensued signalled Cash was just as stunned as she was.

"Blimey, and this is the *second* thing you've told me – I thought it'd be the first!"

"I'm sorry, I'm guess I'm still trying to process it."

"Wow! I can't imagine how you're feeling."

"On cloud nine, but nervous, dead nervous. I don't know how I'm going to manage to drive tomorrow."

"Do you want me to drive you?"

"Oh, Cash, would you? I wasn't hinting by the way, just being honest."

"I know and yeah, it's fine. The beauty of being self-employed and all that."

"It has its perks," she replied, laughing again. "Thinking about it, I should really go into the pub alone, it being our first meeting, so actually that might not work."

"Ruby, I'm not suggesting I go in with you! I'll bring my laptop, work in the car."

"Really? Is that all right? Are you absolutely sure?"

"Sure I'm sure. It's fine."

As at the Watkins' house, Ruby suddenly felt overcome with emotion.

"Babe, what's the matter? Are you still there?"

"Yeah, I'm here. I'm just… Thank you, Cash, for offering to drive, for being there for me. I really appreciate it." Jed had come over to nuzzle at her. Instead of crying, she forced herself to laugh. "And you, Jed, thank you too."

"Of course I'm here for you," said Cash. "But this Brookbridge business, going to meet a total stranger at an abandoned building, it's not on."

"Look, Cash, I'm not stupid, I've thought about the dangers involved. I've got you on speed-dial as well as the rest of the team plus I've asked Kelly Watkins who lives really close by if she'd be on standby too in case of an emergency. She said yes. I'll meet Eclipse on the street in front of the building first, in plain sight. Any suspicions and I'll hightail it."

"Kelly's on standby?" Cash checked.

"And her husband. They can get to me in minutes."

"I'd prefer seconds."

"Cash, I think Eclipse is all right; we're singing from the same hymn sheet."

"You hope."

"It's my instinct. Besides, I'm not going to do a thorough investigation, not tonight, I just want to get a feel for what's going on, that's all."

He sighed. "There's no stopping you sometimes, is there?"

"I won't take any chances, I promise."

"Just stay in touch."

"I will."

"And Ruby?"

"Yeah."

"Make sure you are quick, okay? I'll see you at home."

Their home, the flat in De Montfort Road. Not officially, not yet. But it may as well be.

* * *

As Ruby drove into the Brookbridge estate, the day was definitely on the wane. She parked her car outside the Watkins' house before walking the short distance to the fenced-off building. The beginning of September, it seemed any summer warmth had finally departed, the chill in the air a sign of what was to come. *To be endured* thought Ruby, but not unhappily. Certainly, autumn and winter in England could be miserable at times with day after day of grey sky, but there was a flip side. It was the season for jeans and boots, her preferred attire. It was also the time to snuggle up with your man and a good film in the evenings with a bottle of spicy red on the go as

84

opposed to a chilled white. Yes, she decided, there were definite upsides, the prospect of which created a feeling of contentment in her stomach. Life was coming together – in ways she expected and in ways she had not dared hope for.

Excitement and apprehension causing her pace to quicken, she approached the abandoned building. As she'd told Cash, she'd agreed with Eclipse to meet at the front of the building, and it was here she waited, her phone secreted in her jacket pocket, staring into the distance to see if she could spot anyone.

"Ruby Davis?"

She spun round, coming face to face with the name's bearer at last – a man, a tall man, with blonde hair tied back in a short ponytail and ice-blue eyes. Rugged, handsome and Nordic, were all words that sprang to mind. Dressed in a patchwork coat and jeans, he was also, as Cash had feared, hippyish – but Ruby didn't mind hippyish; she quite liked hippyish. Hippyish felt safe.

"Eclipse?"

"That's me," he confirmed. "It's really good to meet you."

About the same age as Ruby, twenty-six or twenty-seven, maybe a bit younger actually, he moved towards her and held out his hand. She proffered hers too and as he grasped it, she registered the warmth of his skin and the firmness of his grip. Just as her emotions were in a heightened state, so were her senses – everything about him as vivid as his coat. Releasing her hand, he took a step back.

"That picture on your website doesn't do you justice."

Ah, he was a hippy with a smooth tongue, now that was

something to experience.

"I didn't know what to expect with you," she confessed. "Whether you'd be a man or a woman. What's your real name?"

"It's Eclipse," he said, his wide smile nothing less than dazzling, "my parents, they were a bit out there, you know? Actually," he quickly backtracked, "they were very cool, my mum and dad – very open-minded. Not religious people, but spiritual."

"Were?"

His smile faded. "Yeah, that's right. They're gone now, it's just me and my sister, Luna."

"Luna? That's such a lovely name."

His smile was back. "I hope you like Eclipse too."

"I do. Very much."

He turned to face the building, and so did Ruby, glad of having something else to stare at.

"Well, there she is," he said, "due for demolition very soon."

"How soon? Do you know?"

"It can only be weeks. That's the word on the vine."

"What vine?"

"I've got a friend that works for Rob Lock, the site owner. He told me."

"Friends in high places, eh?"

"They can come in useful."

"Is he a… sympathiser?" She didn't know what else to call his friend.

"Yeah, he is, and he knows as well as I do, erm… as you do too, about the activity on the estate. You've got to feel sorry for the poor bastards, haven't you?" he said, meaning those in the building.

"Have you done your research on the place?"

He turned towards her, the blue of his eyes so intense. "Oh yeah. I've spent a lot of time researching Cromer. The original asylum was split into two. On one side was where the women were housed and on the other were the men. This building is one of the largest, but it's also unusual 'cos as well as a mixed dayroom, it had both female and male wards under one roof. There were also private rooms, which were more like cells. But get this; it had a ballroom! Weird, huh? Freakiest of all, though, is the nursery. Can you imagine babies in this place?"

"A nursery for the babies of the women incarcerated because they got pregnant outside of marriage?"

"I guess," answered Eclipse. "And those babies, some of them spent their entire lives in the asylum, the only reason being they were *born* here." He shook his head as did Ruby, both of them contemplating such a dark fate. "Did you know," he continued, "that in Cromer, like in loads of other English asylums, the discharge rate was only thirty to fifty per cent? So many who came here never got out."

There was anger behind his words, anger that Ruby responded to. "Why were there both male and female wards in this block?"

"As far as I can make out, some of the patients were old, some of them young mothers, of course; but most, well... most I think were lobotomised. They had no interest in anything, certainly not each other. They were like... vegetables."

"Or the walking dead," Ruby offered.

"Yeah, real life zombies. In the doctor's office – the desk is still there, a tall cabinet – and, get this, a pair of spectacles, honestly... they're just lying in one of the desk drawers, untouched. From what I can make out, people, you know, voyeurs, don't hang around in the doctor's office, and they don't tend to hang around in the operating theatre either. That's still got a gurney in it as well as some ancient-looking gear, although most of it's been smashed up. Stuff's been nicked from there – syringes, bowls, that kind of thing – but you'll find it abandoned in the corridors, people dropping it on their way out in a sudden change of heart, like it suddenly hits them that no one needs shit like that, not even the most ghoulish of bastards. The walls are full of graffiti; no doubt you saw it on the *Forbidden Places* site. It's…" and here Eclipse paused, lifting his hand to his temple to knead the skin there, "disturbing, like… sick. I can't see spirits, not like you can, but sometimes I can hear moaning and crying, far-off sounds being carried towards me on a breeze, or sometimes blasting by in an instant. It happens even when the air outside is as still as anything; when these trees that surround us are completely still. This building was shut in 1994 and the first time I came here was in 2009 when I was sixteen. Initially, I was coming back all the time, like kids do, but there was a time I didn't come. I never forgot it, though, and lately it's been on my mind more than ever. I feel bad for the people grounded here. I've sat in that building, on my own, in various rooms, sometimes all night, trying to get someone, anyone, to communicate with me. I've done my best to let them know they're not alone; that I want to help however I can. I'll admit, sometimes the atmosphere… it can like close in on you, and I've had to get up and leave. That's happened several times actually and believe me, I'm not easily scared."

She did believe him – wholeheartedly. It's not many

who'd volunteer to hold a lone all-night vigil in a building of this type. Even she'd think twice about doing that. She'd want her team with her, at least one of them, or Cash, injecting humour into an otherwise humourless situation. And Jed, she'd definitely want him – where was he? Was he going to show up this evening? There was no sign of him yet, which in a way was reassuring. It showed he trusted Eclipse, that he didn't consider Ruby in any danger – imminent danger anyway. Despite this, she explained to Eclipse the precautions she'd taken, and that she had friends who lived a few streets away, who'd come running if she needed them or hadn't checked in by a certain time.

"I'm not going to harm you, I promise," Eclipse declared.

"It's just so you know."

He nodded. "Of course."

Eager to get back on track, she asked him to explain what happened when it got scary inside.

A frown darkened his otherwise golden features. "Nothing, not really, that's the thing. A few more bangs and cries than normal perhaps, but a door banging in the wind or a loose piece of guttering can explain that stuff. Some of the cries too, they must be from animals in the woods behind us. We have to remember where we are and how rural it is, or used to be. Yeah, I know all that, I accept all that. I look for a logical explanation first, but sometimes logic defies me. Like I said, it's more the atmosphere and how heavy it gets, how I feel inside too – the effect it has on me emotionally. The reason I have to get out is because I just can't take it anymore."

Ruby understood, completely. "I think you do have

mediumship qualities, Eclipse, but perhaps you're at the start of the journey. Empathy is the key and you certainly seem to have bags of that. Has it always been like this for you?"

His smile was shy. "I think it could be said I'm sensitive by nature. I just... yeah, feel for others, you know, those who've been shat on by society. Tearing down those walls, it's like leaving them naked. It won't represent freedom; it'll cause more terror and more confusion, because the walls they've built in their mind, that they can see, will still be there, as strong as ever." He sighed heavily. "God, I can't believe I didn't know about Psychic Surveys. Where've I been living all this time; under a rock?"

"You know about me now," she said, her smile widening.

"But what about costs?" he questioned. "I mean, I can pay something for your time. Don't get me wrong, but I work in a record shop in Bexhill; I don't earn loads."

Ruby waved a hand in the air, embarrassed by talk of fees. "I'm not going to charge anything. This isn't going through Psychic Surveys, this is a private case."

"A private case? What, yours and mine, you mean?"

"Yours and mine," she said, holding out her hand again so that they could shake on it – it was another 'gentlemen's agreement', a promise made. "Besides, I contacted you, remember, so, really, no talk of money."

Retrieving her hand, she turned back to the building, as did he. For several silent moments they stared ahead, at windows covered in plywood, at a shell that was far from empty, and at a sky that was now fully dark.

"Are you ready?" Her eyes were still on Cromer's last bastion.

Digging around in his coat pocket, he retrieved two torches and handed one to Ruby. "Yeah… as ready as I'll ever be. Let's do it."

Chapter Eight

AROUND the back, at the edge of the woods – the *dark* woods, in their own way concealing as much as the building in front of them – there was a place in the chain link fence where the mesh was torn slightly. Eclipse lifted it as far as it would go whilst Ruby hunkered down, having to crawl through on her hands and knees. Once she was on the other side, she returned the favour, the wire cutting into her skin. As soon as she could she retrieved her hands to rub at them.

"You all right?" Eclipse checked.

"Fine," she assured him, not wanting to make a fuss.

"There's a low window, just over here, we can get in that way. Don't worry about the window, I cleared the frame of glass a while ago."

Eclipse hopped through first, making it look so easy. Ruby struggled, her jacket snagging on a piece of splintered wood and having to be unhooked, something she tried to do herself, swearing a good few times whilst she was at it. Again, Eclipse helped her, releasing the snag with very little difficulty and certainly no swearing.

"Thanks," she mumbled, her cheeks flaming.

With no sun or moon daring to intrude, it was darker inside than out. Ruby shone her torch around, although its reach was not as impressive as she hoped.

"What is this room?" she asked.

"It's a utility room. You see over there, there's still a sink and an old counter."

So there was – a vast sink, at least triple the width of hers, and far deeper. The walls were tiled in a brickwork pattern, and below her feet, covered in detritus, were ceramic tiles. She inhaled. It smelt as sour as the cellar of The Waterside Inn, and the atmosphere was leaden. Quiet too, so quiet. Visualising white light, she surrounded them both in it. Cash had asked her to keep her phone on and she did, on vibrate. A loud ring in the midst of this would be too startling.

"Where do we go now?" was her next question. It was handy having someone who knew the layout of this place to guide her.

"I'd like to show you something that's in the doctor's office. That and the theatre are both on the ground floor, although right down at the far end."

Ruby gulped. He didn't muck about, this man. He aimed straight for the jugular. Asking her to follow him, she duly complied, shining her torch directly in front, in case she caught her foot on something and tripped over.

In the corridor, she was mostly aware of the walls and how narrow they felt. There were probably crude depictions adorning them, but she couldn't look; she really needed to keep the ground in front of her illuminated, and she needed to keep up with Eclipse.

Despite focusing so intently on the way ahead, she spied a door to the left. "What's in there?"

"The gym, although don't expect to see any equipment, it's all been stripped. It's just an empty room now."

Making her way over to it, she stood in the doorway –

he was right, it was void of all but darkness. Ahead, she could make out another door.

"That's the dayroom," he explained.

"The dayroom? Actually, I'd like to have a proper look in there before we head to the theatre, just so I can acclimatise myself. Is that okay?"

"Acclimatise? Shit, sorry. I'm used to this building. Sometimes I forget—"

"It's fine, honestly. I'd just like to take it a bit slower, that's all. There may be a huge spiritual presence here, but even so, it can take time to tune in."

He peered at her intensely. "Have you picked up on anything?"

"Surprisingly no, but like I say it's not the immediate process some people imagine it to be. Of course I can feel the weight of the atmosphere, just like anyone would be able to, but spiritual contact – there's been none of that yet."

Eclipse went from fascinated to sombre. "*Yet* being the operative word."

Walking slightly ahead of her, he pushed the door open to the dayroom. It swung on its hinges, the creaking reminiscent of the old Hammer Horror films in which a thousand doors had done the same. She entered after him, receptive but cautious. Within madness, boundaries were often blurred. These patients had been disturbed in life, for a variety of reasons, such behaviour perhaps continuing in their spirit form. She mustn't fear it, though. She had to try and understand it, remembering that at the core of each and every one of them was something that remained untouched by the human experience. Whatever they'd been, whatever they were currently, they'd be magnificent

94

again in the light. An idealistic view perhaps? There were plenty who'd say so and understandably. But it was a psychic's view too. You couldn't do this job – you *shouldn't* – unless there was a willingness to believe that. And she was willing, despite her experiences and actually, because of them. No matter what acts someone had committed, there was always a way back; a chance to evolve.

The dayroom was large – cavernous – and so black around the edges.

"It would have been handy to have taken advantage of the daylight," she mused.

"I agree, but there are too many people around then. The police…"

"I thought you said no one cared."

"Yeah, but if the police have got nothing better to do, they might mosey on over if a resident complains."

"True."

As her eyes adjusted, she could make out random items of furniture. There were chairs, those of the stacking variety, just a few of them, scattered around. One wall seemed to be covered entirely in a mural. She edged closer to it – more graffiti; quite brilliant actually, if predictably demonic, its various depictions of hell reminiscent of Dante's *Inferno*. As good as it was, it dismayed her. This kind of thing encouraged people to feed on fear, to gorge on it, blinding them with fantasy rather than reality.

Eclipse had edged closer. "Anything?" he asked, still full of curiosity.

"Not really, it's all very subdued, which could be relevant actually, considering what you said earlier."

"Oh yeah, before drugs became more widely-used, lobotomies were regarded as a miracle cure."

"When was this? What decade are we talking about?"

"The early 1940s. During that time, surgeons in the UK performed more lobotomies than in the US, proportionately speaking. I think at its peak, more than one thousand operations a year were performed."

Ruby was aghast. "Really? Christ!"

"Yeah, it was seen as a better alternative to incarceration, a kind of way out, if you like, although actually it backfired, and a lot of people weren't released because any ability to function socially post-op was out the window. And yet, you know, they still continued. It was a quick procedure, yeah? It took around five to ten minutes. On and on they went, experimenting and perhaps in a way, making life easier for themselves. The patient might not be fit enough to re-enter society, but at least they wouldn't give any more aggro behind closed doors."

"Eclipse, you've really done your homework, haven't you?"

"There's another reason why I'm so interested," he confessed. "It's not entirely because I'm such a sensitive soul. It's 'cos of my grandmother too."

"Your grandmother?"

"That's right. My gran, Susannah Barrett, had a condition, bi-polar we reckon, although there was never any formal diagnosis, and because of it, she was locked up. My mum was really young when it happened, barely a teenager and it left her broken-hearted. Despite her illness, my mum loved her mum, but the situation was out of her hands. The tragedy of it was felt down the generations; it affected our lives too, mine and Luna's, and not for the better. My grandmother was released eventually, but apparently she was nothing like her former self."

"She'd had a lobotomy?"

"Yeah, and so much brain tissue had been destroyed she was, like we said earlier, a zombie. It wasn't here; it was up in Manchester. Nothing remains of the original asylum. It's a housing estate, like this one. Looking at pictures of how she used to be, really vivacious you know, it was all so…" Eclipse took a deep breath, "…unjust. I hated that she'd suffered, and that we all suffered too. And I hate that these souls in here are suffering. It should be over, but it isn't. I want it to be over."

"We're here now, aren't we? We can do something about it."

"I really hope so."

"Shall we… erm…" she had to be brave, she *had* to be, "go through to the doctor's office?"

"So there's nothing here?"

"I'm not picking anything up at the moment."

"Okay."

He'd warned her the corridors were long and he was right, they were endless. *Where the hell is it?* The building was a large one, that couldn't be denied, but it still seemed disproportionately bigger inside, as though they were in some kind of Tardis. A loud bang coming from the room they'd just left made her cry out.

"What was that?" she whispered.

"It could be anything, a door caught on the breeze maybe? Like I said, that happens often. Do you want to go back and see?"

Before answering she stood stock still, barely breathing. There was no more noise. "Let's carry on."

The further down the corridor they walked, passing a stairway on their right, and more doors, some open, some closed, the more Ruby could smell something – not mould or damp, traditional odours of neglect, but something more akin to bleach or a cleaning fluid of some kind. Was it an echo from the past?

Curious, she asked Eclipse if he could smell anything.

Eclipse sniffed. "No. Can you?"

"Yeah, there's a slight tinge of something." So it *was* an echo, the past beginning to collide with the present, at least to the one of them that was psychic.

"This is the doctor's office," Eclipse said, and Ruby noticed him swallow.

"You've been in here before?"

He nodded.

"By yourself?"

"Yeah. Madness must run in the family." When Ruby made no reply, he looked contrite. "Sorry, bad joke. I'm not like my grandmother; I don't suffer from bi-polar or any other condition. Many people consider me relatively sane."

"It's just jokes like that, in these surround—"

"I'm sorry," he said again, and it was obvious he meant it. There was sadness in his voice too, so much sadness that Ruby guessed a bit of humour every now and then was his way of dealing with the weight of his own history. As coping mechanisms went, it was a good one. Everyone needed a method of release.

The door to the office, like some other doors in this building, was hanging off its hinges, a glass panel within it completely shattered. Edging his way past, Eclipse walked in without any problem, but for Ruby it was a different matter. The door might as well have been closed, or bricked up, because that's what it felt like was in front of her – a wall of emotions, terrible emotions that engulfed her as a tidal wave might. *Deep breaths, take deep breaths, Ruby. Breathe.* She did her utmost to obey the self-administered instruction, forcing her feet into a room that was furnished, as Eclipse had said, with a desk and a filing cabinet. To her surprise, Eclipse went straight over to the filing cabinet and pulled open a drawer.

"When I first came in here," he explained, with his back to her, "there were patient notes and photographs all over the floor—"

"Photographs?" Ruby managed to utter. "I've seen a photograph of one of the patients on the Internet – Caroline Jennings. Not on the same site where I found your details; another site devoted to Cromer. God knows there are enough of them."

"Yeah, don't I know it, although more people tended to come here when there were more buildings. Now there's just this one, they don't so much. They come and they take photos, regarding the patient notes they take photos of photos and then they, well… drop them to the floor again and walk all over them. There are boot marks on virtually every one. Every time I come here, I make a point of picking these papers up, reading them, then filing them away – in here. I've even been able to match photos and case notes together. The ones that weren't torn up."

"Why didn't you remove them entirely?" Ruby asked, curious.

"To take them where? Home? No, I don't want them in my home, they're too… unsettling." At his words, Ruby nodded, it was fair enough. "I've taken photographic records though, of everything I've found, and of course, as you probably know, there are records at The Keep, but this is where the originals are, and sure, yeah, they've been disturbed by others, but like me, no one wants to take them anywhere. These photos, these *lives*, are just too real for most people to deal with. When you're in this room, none of it's quite so funny anymore, and so, in the end, they leave well alone."

Ruby crossed to the filing cabinet too and shone her torch on the bundle inside. "They look like convict photos, don't they?"

"Because that's what they were, in the eyes of those who considered themselves normal; those who never pushed against the boundaries of society, who never had cause to."

"So, all of this, you've got photos of?"

"Yeah, on my phone." He paused. "You don't want to touch them either, do you?"

He was right, she didn't – the emotions coursing through her, emotions that belonged to so many others as well as her own, were hard enough to deal with. What she'd seen was enough – so many eyes staring up at her – *dead* eyes, both in a literal and a metaphorical sense. She had to turn away.

"Eclipse, I don't think I can stand much more, not tonight."

"You'd rather leave the theatre for another time?"

"I think so."

He was reluctant but he agreed.

"Can you send me the pictures you've taken, though? I'll… look at them tomorrow if I get a chance, or more likely the next day."

"Sure. Look, Ruby, I realise this must be hard for you. Mental illness *is* hard—"

"I know, okay. You don't have to keep saying." Her

voice was harsher than she intended, something that surprised them both. "There've been problems in my family too, so I understand about the ripple effect. Maybe that's why I'm feeling the way I am." Damn it, she was going to start crying again if she wasn't careful. "This… it's intense, okay. I can deal with it, but perhaps in small doses, at least until I've had a chance to process it. At the moment it's equal to an onslaught. There's so much that's residual here as well as actual. It's awful. Oh God, it's just awful!"

Staggering slightly, he caught her, just in time. She would have fallen otherwise. Her hands were up by her ears, covering them. "The cries, can you hear them, the screams, the wailing, the banging, the crashing? Eclipse, can't you hear it?"

Of course he couldn't, it was only in her head; deep down she knew that – and it had happened so suddenly, as though a radio on mute had been turned to full blast. It was an assault, but what was the intention behind it? To harm, to scare, torture her even?

She was only thankful this man had his arms around her; that she wasn't alone. "Eclipse, get me out of here. Please."

He'd grasped the sudden seriousness of the situation. Still with his arms around her, he started to move them forwards, both of them shuffling at first, towards the door – the broken door with its shattered glass – after which there was a long, dark corridor to negotiate before any hope of freedom. Hardly daring to look, she kept her eyes half closed, the din in her head as loud as ever. The wails held such torment! Torn from those whose lives had been torn too.

"We have to hurry," she whispered, her voice choked.

The walls either side of her, narrow, claustrophobic even, appeared to writhe. Why? What was wrong with them? She had to look, there was no escaping it – they were just too close. Shapes; blackened things; husks – it was those that lined the walls; hundreds and hundreds, thousands; as much a part of the building today as they ever were in the past. Again, Eclipse seemed oblivious, his grip still tight, intent on fulfilling her request and getting them out of there. Thank God he was oblivious! This was the sort of thing that could drive a person to madness. Hands, misshapen and claw-like, broke free of the walls, reaching for them. She flinched, pressed herself further into Eclipse, forgetting for a moment to visualise white light; to strengthen their shield. *Don't forget, Ruby, you can't, not in here.* Summoning up the strength from somewhere, she imagined bolts of white light and fired it at them, not as a weapon meant to harm, rather she was trying to pierce their armour with love; something they obviously didn't know how to deal with. Nothing was absorbed. Nothing.

Halfway down the corridor were the stairs they'd passed earlier, leading upwards to the wards, the cells and the nursery. Like the theatre, she hadn't explored them yet; she hadn't even touched upon the worst of it. How would she react when she did? How could she bear it?

"We're there, we're almost there," Eclipse was busy assuring her, but 'there' seemed so far away. Her head was going to explode with the pressure building inside it, she was certain; the misery that was being heaped upon her too much to endure. Despite his arms around her, Ruby sank to her knees, right there, in the corridor of the abandoned asylum, caught between the writhing walls.

"I can't stand it," she tried to explain. "I just can't."

What would he do? Leave her there whilst he went and begged for help? Or would he forcibly get her out, dragging her by the arms? What did she want him to do? She didn't know. It was impossible to think rationally above the internal cacophony.

He was pleading with her, she knew that much. He was frightened now. She registered that too. But she could do nothing about it, nothing at all. She was helpless, as scared as him. She'd underestimated the hell of madness, of being *perceived* as mad. Would he do it? Would he leave? She didn't know him, not really, nor how he was likely to react. If he left her... Christ, if he left her...

A barking brought her back from the edge, Jed having materialised at last and snarling at the walls, as they were snarling at him. In her mind's eye Ruby imagined row upon row of chipped and blackened teeth bared at Jed and him baring his teeth just as ferociously. A wild gesture. Feral. At the same time that Jed appeared, she found herself being lifted upward. Eclipse had no intention of leaving her.

"It's okay, Ruby," he was muttering, "I've got you. I'll get you out of here."

As though she were no burden to him at all, he broke into a half-run, a half-stumble. Her feet barely touching the ground, he was virtually carrying her. Jed stayed where he was, standing between them and whatever else was in the corridor – another shield.

"Jed," she called, concerned for him, but her voice was weak. Quickly, she transferred to thought. *Jed!*

But, like the smugglers she'd recently dealt with, he was

103

a law unto himself, coming and going as he pleased, obeying his own rules. *Where do you go when you're not with me, Jed? Who else do you protect?*

Or was she his sole charge?

Jed, come on!

Eclipse put her down at the window of the utility room, and she bundled her way through with no snagging of the coat. He followed. Taking her hand, he dragged her from the building. Both of them crawled under the fence and sped on, not stopping until they were at the edge of the woods where Eclipse doubled over, panting. Ruby was panting too, aware that the sounds in her head had died down. Apart from their breathing, it was silent again.

When at last he was able to speak, Eclipse lifted his head and looked at her. "Who's Jed?" he asked, frowning.

Chapter Nine

ECLIPSE accompanied Ruby to her car, sitting in the passenger seat whilst she slid behind the wheel.

"Jed," she explained, "is my dog."

"Your dog? There was no dog in there."

"There was, towards the end."

"But—"

"He's a spirit dog, an attachment if you like. I first met him at a house cleansing about three years ago. Instead of moving on, he… well, he's a part of the team now. And a very valuable part too." She bowed her head and took a long breath outwards. "I don't know what I'd do without him."

"A spirit dog? Shouldn't he be in the light?"

"Eclipse, I'm not a magician, I can't control Jed, okay? He comes and he goes, but I think when he's not here, that's exactly where he is, in the light."

Instead of taking umbrage at her sharp tone, he softened. "Ruby, what happened to you in there? Tell me."

How could she find the words to explain what had happened? She looked at him; at the earnest expression in his eyes.

"It was like being a thousand people at once," she finally answered.

"A thousand mad people?"

"A thousand *ill* people."

He was immediately contrite. "Yeah, of course. What am I thinking? I can't imagine—"

"Which is a good thing, believe me."

"I do, I actually really do."

"Although… it's strange; their emotions may have been in my head, but it was as a collective, a mass, I couldn't distinguish one person from another and so… I can't imagine the *uniqueness* of each experience, nor the depth of it."

You. Don't. Know. Those words still rang true.

"Look, Ruby, shall we go for a drink? Try and get our heads round this."

"A drink?" She checked her watch. They'd only been in the building for half an hour, maybe slightly more. It wasn't so late. She could have a drink and still be home before Cash. But… it was a big day tomorrow, a *momentous* day; she needed some down time, a chance to recover; to feel Cash's arms around her instead.

"I can't come for a drink tonight, for various reasons, but are you okay? Not traumatised from anything that happened in there?"

He shrugged, that bright smile back on his face. "I didn't experience anything out of the ordinary, not today."

"Nonetheless, there's unrest brewing on this estate, I've thought that several times lately. And in that building particularly it's rife; that ripple effect in action again. I've had several calls from Brookbridge in the last few days, and I wouldn't be surprised if there are more to come. This sense of something brewing is very real; it can be felt by anyone I should think – dead or alive. And you could be right, it could well be because the last building is due to come down. The majority of spirits may hate this place but they're attached to it – deeply – they're institutionalised. That's what we're up against here. Spirits of the most resistant kind."

Eclipse was nodding avidly. "It makes sense, yeah, it all makes so much sense."

"I'm glad you think so." His enthusiasm raised a tired smile.

"I know it was difficult for you in there, but you will come back, won't you? You won't just… leave them?"

"Of course I'm coming back. But I want my team with me."

"You said this was a private case, yours and mine."

"I'm not talking about excluding you, Eclipse, but I can't go in there again without my team, not now that I know what we're up against. I need their skills, their experience, and their knowledge. I'm not strong enough to do this on my own."

"You won't be on your own."

"I think you know what I mean, without the help of my fellow psychics. I've made the mistake of excluding them in the past and I was wrong. Together we're stronger."

"Is it still no fees applicable?"

"Of course there are no fees! How many times do I need to remind you, it was me who approached you."

"Perhaps I should be the one who charges then?"

She laughed. "You can try."

Eclipse smiled too. "You sure your team won't mind me tagging along?"

She thought of the Wilkins brothers – both Cash and Presley. "Don't worry, they're used to tag-alongs," she replied, but not without affection.

"So what's the plan from hereon in?"

Retrieving her mobile so that she could send texts saying she was all right, she explained what she had in mind. "I'll talk to my colleagues this week and get back to you. Two of them are working on a case of their own at the moment; another has a part-time job in a pub, and so we have to bear that in mind and work around them. We need to do more research too. Those photos you have of the patients and whatever medical notes you've photographed, don't forget to send them to me."

"I won't," Eclipse looked in the direction of the building they'd only recently left. "But remember we're running out of time."

"It'd be handy to know how much time we do have, though. Your friend that works for Rob Lock, can he do some digging for us and find out?"

"I'll ask. So… hopefully, I'll see you soon?"

"Oh yeah, Eclipse, you will. Very soon."

* * *

"Damn!" The nightmare propelled her out of sleep. Although she had visualised plenty of white light before turning in, writhing walls and clawed hands had still managed to make an appearance. Cash was snoring gently beside her, Jed, however, was sitting upright at the end of their bed and staring at her. *Can't sleep either? I don't blame you.* How she wished she could give the furry mutt a cuddle – what a shame her arms would pass straight through him if she tried.

Lying back down, she screwed her eyelids shut – would she be able to rest again, or was that a vain hope? Damn again if it was the latter – she'd meet her father, a few hours from now, a bleary-eyed and haggard wreck and he'd wonder what the hell he'd sired! That wry sentiment making her smile at least, she turned on her side and cuddled Cash, relishing the warmth of his body and how smooth his skin was. She'd told him earlier what had happened, not all of it, not the lurid details; he didn't need those images plaguing his mind as they were plaguing hers, but the general gist of it. He'd raised an eyebrow that Eclipse had turned out to be a man.

"Ruby," he'd said, "I've said it so many times, what you do is dangerous. I don't particularly mean in a spiritual sense, but in a practical sense. You went into a derelict building with a man you didn't even know. Okay, you weren't harmed, but you could have been. What *could* have happened doesn't bear thinking about."

"The minute I saw him, I knew he was okay."

"Ruby—"

"And I'd taken precautions, you know that."

"Eclipse," he'd mumbled. "I mean honestly, who calls their kid that? I expect he had a goatee beard."

"He didn't."

"Long straggly hair."

"Long but not straggly."

"Some kind of colourful coat."

Ah, she couldn't defend her newfound friend on that score.

"So," he continued, "the place is haunted; in fact, the whole estate is a bit dodgy at the moment. What are you going to do about it? What's the plan?"

"The plan is to research and then return."

"With Eclipse?"

"With him and the team. It's not a paid job, but I want them with me if possible."

"What about me?"

"Of course you, if you want to."

"That's a lot of us."

"It is, and I'd rather we had permission from the site manager to go in there, rather than breaking in under cover of the darkness. Although if that's what it comes to, so be it. Eclipse knows someone who works for Rob Lock, the site owner; he's working on getting him to find out a demolition date. Once we know that, I'll approach Mr Lock as Psychic Surveys, and ask for permission."

Cash pulled a face. "That's another risk right there. A site owner can't just allow people into a derelict building, not knowingly anyway; there are all sorts of health and safety issues involved. And this Rob Lock, he might not be prepared to turn a blind eye."

He had a point – it *was* a risk going the professional route, one that might be too big to take. And so she'd be forced to sneak around. With Psychic Surveys, she'd dragged psychic talent into the open and kept it there, on the high street, loud and proud, a business as essential as any other, and expanding, slowly but surely. Work was always steady and her reputation was excellent. To be reduced to such furtive measures at Cromer irked her – but it would irk her even more if she got banned from the site.

With all this mulling, all this cogitating, there was no way she was going to be able to go back to sleep. That chamomile tea she had in the cupboard was calling to her – that and a bathroom trip. It was 4.30 am. If she drank the soothing tea and gazed at her computer for half an hour or so, surely her eyes would droop and she'd be able to return to the land of nod before the alarm went off at eight. God, she hoped so. Leaving the comfort of her bed at an ungodly hour yet again, she made her way to the bathroom. Staring at her reflection in the mirror whilst washing her hands, she thought how pale she looked, pale and… something else.

Like a thousand people at once?

That's what she'd said to Eclipse, trying to describe how it had been in the asylum, a feeling that hadn't quite gone away. Behind the green of her eyes were the eyes of so many – strangers to her – and yet, were they really? Wasn't everybody connected in some way? Certainly everyone was in this world together, in the shit together. Was there such a thing as someone else's war? This battle, the one that the patients at Cromer still waged, was hers too – hers and Eclipse's. She'd made it so.

A few minutes later, a cup of steaming tea beside her, her laptop providing a glow in the dim kitchen, she clicked on her emails. Eclipse had sent the photographs and slowly she scrolled through them – pictures of men and women, young and old. There'd been children at Cromer too, children *born* there – but these were all adults. She read their names, such ordinary names: Ronald Brown, Stephen Evans, Sarah Carstairs, Annie Gibb, Doreen Hughes, Melissa Bates, Mary Wilson – the women far outnumbering the men in this selection. Not that that surprised Ruby. When she'd first been called to Brookbridge, she'd started reading about mental health in a bid to understand it and had found a paper on female institutionalisation in the nineteenth century. What she'd discovered was astounding. Women were frequently admitted to asylums during this period for the slightest of reasons – for not accepting a marriage proposal from someone eminent; for PMT, otherwise known as 'insanity attacks'; for having more than one sexual partner, or for not having sex at all, for being 'frigid'. Men were admitted too, she wasn't denying that; she'd dealt with the spirits of male patients several times over, but it was women who seemed to be more susceptible. In the nineteenth century there'd been no standardised diagnosis of madness, rather it was left to the discretion of the doctors to decide who should be admitted or not. Reading through some of the patient notes that Eclipse had sent, this hadn't changed dramatically in the early twentieth century. One patient, Agnes Jones, was considered 'unruly', and, in order to constrain her she had been placed for long periods of time in what they called a Restraint Chair, sometimes with a hood over her head. Ruby's eyes widened as the words sunk in. *What the hell is a restraint chair?* She could google it, but she didn't want to, not at this hour, adding to the already terrible images in her mind. Just reading about it, *envisaging* it, complete with straps and hooks, was enough.

Another patient, Mary Wilson, was deemed to be suffering from psychosis. Ruby remembered seeing a picture of her and matched up the photo with the notes on her screen. A young woman, aged twenty-four; hysteria and hallucinations were amongst her symptoms, no reason for them given, no background information, no attempt to understand – the notes merely concentrated on what she was at the time – ill.

Reading further, Ruby took a sharp intake of breath. Mary was one of those who'd been lobotomised, the operation recorded as successful. If so, then when had she been released? The notes were severely tattered in places, and subsequently some words were illegible, but right at the end she could make out a date – 1943. Mary had died, at the asylum, aged twenty-six, her treatment not so successful after all.

Ruby glanced at the clock, it was 5.10. She'd give it ten more minutes, and then go back to bed; try and find some escape from all this, although 'this' was helping her to understand the experience of individuals at least, as opposed to the mass she'd encountered. The tea had remained untouched and was now barely warm, but she finally began to sip it without taking her eyes from the screen. Clicking on another photo of patient notes, she zoomed in. These belonged to Rebecca Nash – a girl who was barely out of her teens, and who'd lived beforehand with her mother in Angmering, Sussex. Her illness: she could hear voices. Ruby shrugged. Perhaps she was schizophrenic: wasn't that supposed to be one of the principal indications of that illness? Oh, and auditory hallucinations, Rebecca had been suffering from those as well. As with Wilson's notes, a few sentences were illegible due to deterioration, the ink faded rather than the paper crumpled or torn. Rebecca's birth date of 18th December 1921 was recorded in a box at the top right of the paper, so it was apparent that these notes would have once again been written sometime in the 1940s. According to the doctors, Nash could sometimes be violent, lashing out at nurses, her language described as profane. She'd endured the restraint chair too, and solitary confinement – over and over again, it seemed. She was often considered to be in a distressed state and also dangerous. Other treatments included continuous baths to calm her when agitated – Ruby had yet to find out what a continuous bath actually meant, but it didn't sound healthy – and, insulin shock treatment. Again she needed to know more about that. None of the treatments seemed to improve Rebecca's health; if anything they would make her protest further: 'I'm not lying, I'm telling the truth. I do see people. I hear them. They're always with me, always. They won't leave me alone. They want me to help them, you see? They're lost. Confused. And that's all I try to do, help them.'

Reading the transcript – actual words recorded from the mouth of Rebecca Nash – caused Ruby's jaw to fall open. The mug that she held in her left hand also jerked, spilling the last of its contents over her and the laptop.

"Shit! Shit! Shit!"

Immediately, Ruby jumped up and rushed over to the sink to grab a cloth, not to dab at her clothes but to save the laptop. As she did she sent the chair behind her crashing to the ground, the sound in the otherwise silent kitchen, deafening.

"Shit!" she swore again, bending to pick it up just as Cash raced into the room, Jed at his heels.

"Ruby, what the hell?"

"Oh Cash, sorry, I got a bit of a shock, that's all."

"*You* got a shock?" he all but accused.

Trying to explain, she pointed to the computer that Jed was now sniffing at, his ghostly nose at one point nudging the keyboard – his interest in what was on screen as keen as Ruby's.

"Those are patient notes, from Cromer – notes that were left on the floor and trampled on. Eclipse took photos of them and sent them to me."

"And?" said Cash, still with a frown on his face. "What did you find?"

114

"That one of the patients was called Rebecca Nash; that she was there in the 1940s. Whether she died there I don't know yet, but back then, so few got out."

"What was wrong with her? What illness did she have?"

"That's just it, Cash. I don't think she had an illness. I think Rebecca was psychic."

Chapter Ten

ON the day that Ruby was meeting her father for the first time, she should have been filled with nothing but the urgency to dash to Windsor. But, after a night of Rebecca Nash and all those she'd read about – the faces she'd seen staring up at her, beseeching her almost – she also wanted to hurry back to the asylum to help those souls, just as Rebecca had wanted to help them. At least she had the freedom to do that. She didn't run the risk of torture, of being locked up for her efforts with the key as good as thrown away. Had a lobotomy been performed on Rebecca? It was likely. Even if she'd got out of the asylum, it would have been as a shadow of her former self.

As sympathetic as Cash was, he had managed to persuade her back to bed and she'd fallen into a fitful sleep that was also filled with shadows. When the alarm clock rang, she'd lain still for a while, with Cash's arms around her and Jed by her side, once again thinking how lucky she was, but more than that: how *un*lucky others had been.

Although she'd wanted to do some more research into the asylum and the exact methods of treatment they used, Cash assured her they could do that en route to Windsor. "Right now, you just need to have some breakfast and get yourself ready to meet your dad, okay? Get yourself all psyched up."

"Psyched up?"

He grinned. "If that's a pun, it was unintended, honest."

She'd decided to drive after all, needing that focus, so it was Cash who sat in the passenger seat with his iPad. They'd hardly left Lewes when he was online. A 'restraint chair' was exactly as she'd imagined, but what she didn't know was that prior to 1933, the hours that someone could spend strapped to the chair were uncapped. It was only after 1933 that the New York State Department of Mental Hygiene ruled that a patient couldn't spend more than two hours in continuous restraint or three hours in seclusion – guidance that was accepted in England too – in theory.

"I'll bet there were those who broke the rules," declared Cash. "After all, who was going to tell? Back then, authority meant a lot more than it does now. Doctors were like gods, weren't they? It was their way or the highway. It also says here that before 1933, iron handcuffs were used to restrain patients having an 'episode'. *Iron handcuffs*, Ruby!"

Ruby kept her eyes on the road but his words caused her breath to quicken slightly. Poor Rebecca. Poor all of them. "Cash, it said in the notes that Rebecca also received continuous bath treatment and insulin shock therapy, what are they?"

"Hang on." There was a minute or two of silence before he started speaking again. "Here we go, hydrotherapy was a popular treatment in the early twentieth century and continuous baths were when a patient was placed in a canvas hammock in the bath and then covered with a canvas sheet with just their heads poking out. Fresh water was then poured at approximate body temperature into the bath, whilst the old water drained away. This was supposed to have a calming effect."

"Oh okay," Ruby said, relieved. "That doesn't sound so bad."

"Maybe not, until you realise continuous baths could last for several hours or even days."

"*Days?*" Ruby all but spat the word.

"That's right. Other hydrotherapy treatments include Scotch douches, where patients were blasted with alternating jets of hot and cold water, and then wrapped in packs of sheets that had been dipped in varying temperatures of water, remaining in them for several hours. Ruby, these treatments were thought of as help, not torture, at least by some."

"Sounds pretty torturous to me. Okay, what about this insulin business?"

"Ah, now this is interesting. It was believed that patients with schizophrenia and who were also diabetic, improved psychologically after a coma."

"A *coma?*" Again, Ruby was stunned. "An induced coma, you mean?"

"Yep. Coma was induced by the injection of a large amount of insulin, although it says here the methods of administering the treatment were varied, and there were no real guidelines for doing it. The patient would suffer epileptic seizures an hour or two after injection and before the onset of coma. After they'd been in a comatose state for about an hour, the patient would be brought back by an intravenous injection of glucose. The patient would then undergo this treatment another thirty to forty times over a set period, after which they were supposed to be much improved."

"Improved my arse! It sounds horrific."

"The treatment was abandoned in the mid 1960s apparently and replaced by tranquilisers – a much easier option I should imagine, for the doctors anyway. Less work involved. Drugs have replaced ECT too, electroconvulsive treatment – you know, where they attach those wires to your head and turn up the voltage."

"Yeah, I know. God, Cash, if I'd been born then, that could have been me, you know, suffering such a terrible fate. Not only would the odds be stacked against me and my mother – because I was born outside of marriage – add our abilities on top and voila! You've got all the ingredients for a long stretch inside, possibly a lifetime."

"Thank your lucky stars you were born a lot later then."

"I do. I'm *really* thankful. I'm wondering if Rebecca was eventually lobotomised."

"Ah, lobotomies," said Cash. "Let's see what I can find out about them."

Ruby was about to stop him, to say she'd heard enough, but one benefit of this research was that it was keeping the nerves at bay regarding Peter, giving her something else to chew over other than their imminent meeting. With that in mind, she let Cash continue. She had to know this stuff anyway, if she were going back into the remaining ward block. Ignorance was not an option, no matter how damned blissful.

"Lobotomies," he continued, "were hailed as yet another miracle cure. Yep, it really sounds it! Inserting a spike into a person's brain and giving it a good wiggle."

"It goes back centuries though, doesn't it? Wasn't it ancient practice to drill holes into skulls in order to release evil spirits? I remember learning about that in school."

Cash nodded. "Yeah, yeah, me too. It was called trepanning I think."

"So, come on, what about more modern practices?"

"The first operation was performed in the US in 1936, then from the 40s onwards it was in wide use in the UK with around one thousand operations per year."

"Eclipse quoted similar statistics."

"Oh, did he?"

"Uh huh."

"How come he knows so much?"

Ruby explained about his grandmother.

"Oh right, so he's quite the expert."

His slightly frosty tone caused Ruby to frown. "Well, he has a personal interest, for sure, but he's also a very compassionate man. The plight of his grandmother, of those like her, it moves him. He wants to do something about it. Make a difference."

"But he's not psychic?"

"He couldn't see what I could see in that building, or feel it, that's for sure."

"So you won't be asking him to join the team?"

Again, she looked askance at him. "This isn't an official case, I've told you."

"Just asking. I'm looking forward to meeting him; checking out his goatee beard."

"He hasn't got one, I've told you that too."

"So you have," he replied, returning to the article on screen.

"The most prolific lobotomist in the country, and indeed the world, in the twentieth century, was the neurosurgeon Sir Ralph Gould. Based in Wimbledon, he was believed to have performed over three thousand lobotomies. Woah!" Cash paused for a minute to digest that information. "That's impressive."

"Impressive?" queried Ruby.

"*Ghoulishly* impressive," Cash amended. "It says here that often he would travel across the south of England at weekends, performing smaller leucotomies— "

"Leuco-what?"

"Hang on, let me look to see if there's a difference. Oh right, okay, it's the same end result just a different way of achieving it – in one the doctor drills holes in the side or on top of the patient's skull to get to the frontal lobes, in the other, the brain is accessed through the eye sockets."

"Ouch," was all Ruby could say to that.

"I wonder if this Gould ever came to Cromer?"

"As one of the biggest asylums in the south, he must have done."

"Yeah, you're right. His claim was that the operation had dramatic benefits for some patients," again he paused, "note the use of the word 'some', Ruby. By cutting into the brain to form new patterns, it would rid the patient of delusions, obsessions and nervous tension. Apparently they seemed 'happier' afterwards but a psychiatrist who followed up several hundred of Gould's patients found that only around a third benefited; a third it didn't affect at all, they remained as they were, and another third were actually worse off. From the mid-1950s, the operation fell out of favour, partly due to these poor results, and also because psychiatric drugs were becoming more effective. According to a psychiatric nurse in this article, Margaret Mead, who later trained as a neurosurgeon, patients who'd been lobotomised – chronic schizophrenics mostly – were apathetic and slow, rendering them completely incapable of living life outside the asylum. She said, and I quote, 'they were totally ruined as social human beings.'"

"As human beings full stop."

"Yeah," Cash's voice was grave as he agreed.

Both of them lost in thought, it took a moment to register what the Sat Nav was saying: *You have reached your destination.*

"Shit, Cash, there's the pub, The Red Lion."

"And bang on one too. Do you want me to come in with you, initially I mean?"

"I would; I'd love you to, but... this is something I have to do on my own."

Jed materialised in the back seat of the car. "You've got company," she continued, "Jed's here."

"Have I? Oh good. Well, look, if anything goes wrong, you know where I am."

"It won't go wrong though, will it?"

"I don't know, I can't see into the future."

Instead of getting out, Ruby slumped dejectedly on the seat.

"Hey," Cash reached out. "What I said, it was just a figure of speech."

"Yeah, I know, but—"

"It'll be fine, Ruby."

She turned to him. "So why'd you have to say it mightn't be? When I first told you about Peter, you were hesitant then as well. I just... Oh, I wish you hadn't said that. I'm nervous enough!" And she was, her skin was tingling with nerves.

Cash's voice was firm. "It's going to be fine. Take a few deep breaths, get out of the car, and get yourself into that pub. What I meant to say, what I *should* have said is, I'm here, okay, and so is Jed, we're waiting for you, and we wish you a ton of luck. I know this means the world to you."

She smiled somewhat ruefully at him. "Not the *entire* world, but yeah, it's important. Thank you and sorry about my outburst."

"This is a stressful time."

"Stressful but happy too, I hope."

"Go, on, Ruby. Stop prevaricating."

"Prevaricating?"

"That's right, scram."

Half opening the car door, she turned to him again.

"I feel bad leaving you out here like this."

"Will you stop worrying? I've got more than enough to keep me busy on the laptop. Actually," he said, as she finally exited the car, "I know I had a big breakfast, but… you know… if there are any leftovers from lunch, don't chuck 'em, will you?"

"You want a doggy bag?"

As Cash nodded, Jed wagged his tail too.

"You two," she replied, tension giving way to laughter. "You're priceless."

Chapter Eleven

THANKFULLY the toilets were right by the entrance to the pub. Taking advantage of them, Ruby popped in so she could check her appearance. She looked okay, if a little like a rabbit caught in the headlights, but at least her hair was behaving itself, falling neatly past her shoulders, and her clothes weren't too crumpled from the journey, although she still smoothed them down with her hands. Peter had appeared ordinary in his photo, a man who wouldn't stand out from the crowd. She considered herself ordinary too. *Like father, like daughter,* she thought, her nerves tingling even more.

Taking a deep breath, she forced herself from the sanctuary of the ladies loo and made her way into the main bar. There were quite a few people there for Wednesday lunchtime, either propping up the dark oak of the bar or sitting at a variety of tables scattered around. The atmosphere was quite dark too, not in a preternatural sense, but because the pub was so old, with hardly anything to relieve the fading grandeur of its fixtures and fittings except for a red carpet beneath her feet and red upholstery on the chairs, and that was worn in places as well.

Where was he? Where was Peter Gregory?

"Ruby?"

On a sharp intake of breath, she turned. At her side stood a man of similar height to her, perhaps a couple of inches taller, with greyish-green eyes and with more grey in his sand-coloured hair than had been in the photograph. He was dressed smart-casual, in navy trousers and a lighter blue zip-up cardigan. He looked nervous, perhaps more than she did, his eyes searching just as her eyes were searching – looking for something; a similarity perhaps, something to latch onto.

"Peter?" she enquired and he nodded. "Oh God, it *is* you. Finally we meet."

His face creased into a smile – a shy smile, tentative. He was older than her mum by quite a few years; in his late-fifties, fifty-nine to be precise. Jessica had been twenty-four when she'd had Ruby, whereas he'd already been in his thirties and was a family man; a man with two children, a son and a daughter and then… her. She was the child he hadn't wanted to know about; the child he'd left, not enquiring about her whereabouts or wellbeing until she'd had the wherewithal to enquire about *his*.

Ruby, don't let such thoughts ruin this.

It was good advice. Besides which, she wasn't bitter – just curious. And hopeful too, that it wasn't too late; that now could be the beginning of something.

"Let me buy you a drink," she said, but he wouldn't hear of it.

"It's me who should be buying the drinks, young lady. What would you like?"

Cash had offered to drive back so she plumped for her usual rum and coke, inwardly glowing from his use once again of such a sweet endearment. He gestured towards a table and she made her way to it, already impatient for him to join her. The chair felt heavy as she pulled it out, reminding her a little of the chairs at The Waterside Inn, another ancient pub with traditional décor. Sitting down, she could barely take her eyes off Peter, who looked as if he'd got himself a pint – Dutch Courage needed by both of them perhaps – committing to memory as much detail about him as she could. Was he a handsome man? She imagined he was when he was younger – certainly he was pleasant to look at now. His being in the police might well have impressed a young Jessica, his age and his experience too, and his worldliness. It was all such a contrast to her and how she'd been – *otherworldly*. Not that he had known anything about that. Having questioned Jessica on the matter, Ruby'd learnt that she'd kept her abilities hidden from him during the time they'd been together; that, rather similar to Ruby, she'd also just wanted a dose of 'normal'.

Still staring at him, all she could establish regarding how alike they were was that they were roughly the same height. He was also quite slender of build, as she was. When he was sitting beside her, she'd be able to study him better. Maybe they shared a mannerism or two. She bit her lip sometimes when she was nervous, did he have the same habit? Perhaps they might have a similar laugh, or favoured inclining their head to the same side when listening. Just as he started walking towards her, carrying two glasses, someone else caught her eye; someone sitting a couple of tables away and who was waving. Ruby frowned. Who was he waving at? Curious, she looked around to see if anyone was waving back at the man. Nobody was; they all seemed engrossed in what they were doing – talking to friends, drinking or reading the papers. When she looked at him again, the man, maybe in his sixties or so, had moved and was sitting in another chair, albeit at the same table. He was still waving, the smile on his face containing a world of excitement. Was it she who'd grabbed his attention?

"Here you go," said Peter, placing their drinks on the table. "I take it you're not driving?"

Ever the policeman, thought Ruby, but not without affection.

"No, I'm not," she replied.

"That you're boyfriend in the Ford outside, is it? The dusky fellow?"

Dusky? "Yes, that's Cash, he's… driving me back."

"Sensible thing, bringing back-up. You can't be too careful nowadays."

He was a *cynical* policeman at that, or rather *ex*-policeman. No big surprise really. It must go with the territory.

"Why didn't you invite him in?" Peter continued.

"It's fine, he's catching up with work. Besides…" her voice trailed off.

Peter shrugged. "If you're sure," he said, lifting his pint glass and swigging from it.

It wasn't quite the response she'd hoped for. She'd hoped he might want their first meeting to be just the two of them too, and perhaps he did; she mustn't jump to conclusions. He looked pleased to see her, which was something.

The 'waving man' had moved closer still; he was one table away now and not waving anymore, but staring at Ruby, avidly, his body bent forwards over the table as if he was about to leap. His eyes were a little too wide for comfort. What was his problem? Another man stopped

127

and placed a pint on the same table. A temporary gesture as it turned out, he simply needed to free his hands so he could check his phone. Once he'd done that, he retrieved his pint and carried on – seemingly not noticing the man sitting there. Realising this, Ruby felt herself go hot all over. Of course! It was a *spirit* sitting at the table next to hers. If she'd not been so preoccupied, she would have known that straightaway. He'd picked up on the fact she could see him. A slave to her job as she sometimes was, this was *not* the time.

"… I googled Psychic Surveys by the way."

"What? Oh, sorry, you said something about Psychic Surveys?"

"I did. I googled it."

She gulped, caught between the worry of what he was going to say next and what the spirit was going to do.

"So you're psychic?"

What could she say? She couldn't lie, she wouldn't. She was proud of what she did. Hopefully he might be too – one day. She kept her gaze steady. "Yes, yes I am."

His eyes held curiosity rather than shock. "You've got a good reputation by all accounts."

"We have. We work hard at what we do. We've had a lot of success and we've been lucky. An unusual business was a risk, but it's worked so far."

Was that a slight smile on his face? "Who'd you get it from? Not me, that's for sure."

"Jessica. From Mum."

His smile vanished, replaced by a frown instead. Mentally she kicked herself; she should have perhaps been more vague. Initially, anyway.

"Jessica never mentioned anything about being

psychic."

"She was, I mean she *is*; my grandmother too and my great-grandmother. In our family it seems to be passed down through the maternal line."

He supped at his pint again. "Like, I said, you certainly don't get it from me."

"Peter," she began, "is it a prob—?" Oh no, the spirit was standing now, looking hurt as well as perplexed. He didn't like the fact that Ruby was ignoring him one little bit, and he wasn't going to leave her alone, Ruby could sense that well enough. She didn't know how long he'd waited for someone who could see him, but she was guessing quite a while. His clothes weren't terribly old-fashioned but they weren't exactly modern either – was he from the 60s or 70s? Silently she addressed him. *Look, as you know, I can see you and I'll talk to you soon; properly talk to you, I mean. But right now, I'm busy. This meeting, it's important. Please, be patient.*

"Were you going to ask if it was a problem?"

It was Peter, also looking at her in a perplexed fashion, clearly noticing she was being distracted but not realising by what, or rather by whom. This was a disaster! Why had they met here, at a pub with so much history? Why hadn't she thought to suggest a café, somewhere more modern? This didn't happen every time she set foot in an ancient building, far from it, but there was a higher chance in such a place.

Shooting the spirit a beseeching look, she turned to Peter and nodded.

He didn't answer straightaway. In fact, he took what felt like an excruciatingly long time to formulate a reply. "I don't know about it being a problem, as such. In my lifetime, I've been used to dealing with cold hard facts."

"Peter, although there is guesswork in dealing with the paranormal, I can sense spirits; sometimes I can see them, they…" again she glanced at the spirit who was still staring at her, still standing, but at least he wasn't gesturing anymore, "…*talk* to me. Psychic Surveys helps those who remain grounded; we encourage them to go towards the light, which we believe is home. It may sound slightly off the wall, but surely you must know that even the police themselves use psychics. In fact, one of my colleagues, Ness, did quite a bit of work for Sussex Police."

"No cases I was involved with ever saw the need to use psychics."

"Were you involved with murder cases?"

"Murder?" He wrinkled his nose, as though the word alone disgusted him. "I wasn't in homicide, no."

"What about abductions, or lost persons?"

"Not routinely."

"Perhaps that's why."

There was a silence, an awkward silence in which Ruby reached for her drink and tried to refrain from necking it. The spirit had moved forwards, she was sure of it; a foot or two, maybe more. *Oh Christ!*

"I'm not ashamed of what I do," Ruby said at last, defiant and subdued at the same time, if such a thing were possible.

"Good, I'm glad. A person should be proud of their profession."

"What were you, Peter, in the Force I mean, a sergeant, or—?"

"I remained a constable, by choice."

A constable who'd taken early retirement? She

remembered him mentioning red tape as one of the reasons he'd left the police. She was again curious as to the others. Before she could question further, he'd started speaking again.

"Look, you know the history between me and your mum; that when I found out she was pregnant I walked. I want you to know that I wasn't a man who easily succumbed to affairs. My wife and I... we'd been going through some pretty hard times when I met Jessica. Your mother, she was so... free-spirited, so *different*." He paused. "Although if what you say is true, she never let on *how* different."

"It *is* true."

At her insistence, he simply nodded. "What Jessica and I had, it was never meant to lead anywhere. I thought she was taking precautions, you know..."

"To avoid getting pregnant?"

Peter was defiant too. "That's what she told me and I believed her, why wouldn't I? There was no reason to lie. And to be honest, we were only together for a few months. I didn't see her all that often during that time either. I couldn't, what with working hours and..." he had the good grace to falter, "...family."

"My mother said she was in love with you, surely you must have known that. Did you have feelings for her?"

"I wouldn't have been with her if I didn't have feelings for her. But no, I wasn't in love. As I said, Ruby, it wasn't meant to lead anywhere."

There was a bang on the table, a loud thump, which made Ruby jump. The spirit had shot forward; he was now right in front of her.

"What the—"

"Ruby, are you all right?"

Glaring at the spirit as he was glaring at her, Ruby had to fight to tear her gaze away. How could she explain? How the hell could she even begin to? Peter knew about her gift, although she got the impression he was sceptical; but to utilise it now, in a busy pub, in front of a man who was her father, who she was trying to get to know, it wasn't a good idea. But this spirit was determined. As well as thumping the table, he bent down, his face mere inches from Ruby's. No excitement now, just anger. *Shit!* This had to be the most awkward situation ever.

"I'm... fine, I just thought..." *Please, give me a few minutes. I can't speak to you now, but I will, soon. I promise.*

Want... speak... now!

No, I can't.

Lonely.

I'm sorry, but this meeting is important. Please, try to understand.

Now!

Look, I...

More movement caught her eye – *oh no, not more spirits.* What if like at the Shoreham pub, there was an entire gang? Almost too afraid to look, she had to force herself. It was indeed another spirit, but one she knew. *Jed! You've got to help me.*

Jed didn't even glance her way. He ran straight to the man and nudged him. The man was clearly surprised. Surprised and then delighted. His attention on the dog now rather than Ruby, he bent to touch Jed – wonder back on his face. Jed barked a couple of times, wagged his tail, truly delighted to see the man too it seemed, and then he started to back away, as if leading the man. To Ruby's relief, the man followed, a sigh escaping her as she saw it. *Jed, you're a godsend!* He'd given her a respite; time to claw back whatever she could from this meeting with Peter Gregory.

"I'm so sorry about that," she apologised, cursing her burning cheeks, "I thought I saw someone I knew; not Cash, not my boyfriend, an old friend."

"In Windsor?" Peter questioned, clearly not buying it.

"I do have friends outside of Lewes," Ruby mumbled, trying to brush the whole episode aside. Jed was drawing the spirit even further away. As soon as she was done with Peter she'd go and find them; speak to the man as she'd promised; help him. "Peter, I know it probably came as a shock, me getting in touch with you. And I realise that your relationship with my mother," she'd carefully avoided the word *affair*, "was never meant to develop into anything long-lasting, but even so there was a consequence and it was me. I've always wondered about you, you know. You were this mysterious figure in my life that I knew next to nothing about. It's wonderful to know at least something about you; to actually say I've met my dad. But here's the thing, I don't expect anything from you – truly. I realise how awkward this is – that it could upset the apple cart, with your family I mean, not so much mine. Jessica knows I'm meeting you, although my gran doesn't, not yet. She's a little frail right now so I've kept it quiet; she tends to worry, as grans do. You'll get no recriminations from me about what happened with Mum. It's all in the past. I'd just… I'd like to keep in touch a little bit, that's all."

Again there was silence, Ruby bit at her lip as she gazed not at the man in front of her – analysing his mouth, his nose, the shape of his eyes and comparing them to her own

– but at her half empty glass. Her hand encircling the tumbler, she had to remind herself to relax her grip in case it shattered.

"I've told my children about you."

Ruby could hardly believe her ears.

"You have? What about your wife?"

"Laura? I'm a widower."

"Oh." Briefly, words failed her. He hadn't said so during their former correspondence. "I'm so sorry."

"Thank you, me too."

"How did your children react?"

"It's fair to say they were surprised by the news. They knew nothing about you beforehand of course. But, on the whole, their reaction has been very... mature."

"I'm glad," replied Ruby, although really she felt somewhat bemused that she was regarded as 'news' – this illegitimate offspring; this bastard child.

"I'd like to keep in touch with you too, Ruby." As he said it, her heart leapt. "Perhaps you could even come and visit my home at some point and have dinner. Bring that poor young man who's still waiting outside, with you."

"Cash? He'd love to. He'll do anything for food."

Peter smiled. "A man after my own heart then. We love cooking in our family."

"Do you? Wow! I'm rubbish at it."

"You can't be good at everything."

"I suppose."

"Do you think Cash would mind if we had another drink and a light bite of some description?"

"He won't mind at all, especially if I order him something too – not to eat with us, I don't mean that, as I said, he's working – but I can deliver it to the car at least."

"That sounds like a plan and maybe, over lunch, you can tell me about the latest case Psychic Surveys is working on?"

She almost gasped. "Do you really want to know?"

"Actually, I'd *love* to know."

Chapter Twelve

WHEN Ruby went to give Cash his baguette, he asked her how it was going with Peter.

"Good, thanks. But would you bloody believe it? There's a grounded spirit in there and it got really awkward at one stage." Quickly she explained about Jed and how he'd bounded in and saved the day. "Look, we won't be long—"

"Be as long as you like, Ruby, I'm as comfortable here as anywhere. What are you going to do about the spirit?"

"I'll check on him after Peter's left. Oh and Cash, he wants to know more about what I do; I think he's quite accepting of it."

"Brilliant, another turn up for the books, eh?"

The second hour passed much easier than the first, especially with the spirit still waylaid. Ruby told Peter about the Brookbridge estate and the building that was due to be torn down, and that they were trying to find out the exact date from the developer. She rechristened Eclipse 'Edward' – fearing Peter's attitude to such a fey name might be similar to Cash's and would somehow belittle what they were trying to do. She also played down her experience inside the building, ensuring it came across as a serious problem, but not an outlandish one. The paranormal was real to her because she experienced its existence every day, but it wasn't real to everyone, no matter how keen they were to hear about it. And this man, he might be her father – her *father*, Ruby still couldn't get her head around it – but she didn't know him yet, not really. Although she was working on it – they both were.

"The Cromer Asylum," Peter mused, after she'd finished speaking. "There used to be a secure unit there, for the criminally insane."

"Ash Hill? It's still there." Ruby took a sip of her drink, coke without the rum this time. "But it's on the edge of the estate; pretty well hidden."

"Some pretty nasty people got sent there when I was in the Force. I didn't have anything to do with the cases, but you'd hear about it; you heard quite a bit on the grapevine. Roughly speaking, the term criminally insane refers to someone who can't understand the wrongfulness of his acts, or is unable to distinguish between right and wrong, due to a mental defect or disease. But a lot of people know how to play the system. They think a stay in a psychiatric unit will be a hell of a lot easier than a stay in prison; that they'll get treated better, although that applies more to recent times than in the past, and actually it's true to a certain extent; they *do* get treated better, they get their own room for a start. So they manipulate their defence, the defence allowing it because, hey, it's no skin off their nose. But some of these perps knew exactly what they were doing at the time of the offence and if they were ever released, they'd do it again in a heartbeat. And that's the thing – nowadays they *do* get out. When you've played the system once, it's easy to play it again."

"But that's the *criminally* insane," Ruby responded, "as opposed to those that occupied the majority of the buildings; people who weren't even actually insane, that were depressed or grief-stricken perhaps; that had fallen on hard times; some were just…" she thought again of Rebecca Nash, "*misunderstood.*"

"Sure, I get what you're saying and I agree. Have you ever been inside Ash Hill?"

Ruby shook her head. "Have you?"

"No. I wonder how many spirits are, as you say, grounded there – evil spirits as opposed to misunderstood."

"I…" She didn't know. She also didn't want to get into a debate about evil either – she had her beliefs and they were integral to her work. What others believed was up to them.

He sensed her hesitancy. "Have I said something wrong?"

"No, not at all."

"Ruby, tell me, *why* are spirits grounded?"

"Gosh, that's a question. Where do I start? It's for so many reasons. If their passing was violent or unexpected it could be shock, if they've hurt others it could be fear of retribution. It could be they can't bear to leave a loved one behind, a child perhaps, or a partner. I could go on and on. In a nutshell, they haven't accepted that they're now in spirit form and they cling to all that's human. But everyone has to let go at some stage and start the next leg of their journey. Some of them *do* let go, quite easily in fact, they just need a gentle nudge; others dig their heels in."

"In that old building, I assume it's the latter."

"Unfortunately yes."

"Because they're institutionalised."

"Exactly."

Peter's expression was one of quiet contemplation. "Look," he said, after a few moments, "if you don't have any luck regarding a demolition date via this friend of yours, Edward, perhaps I can help. Use a bit of police influence."

"You're not in the police anymore, though."

He raised an eyebrow as he smiled. "Love, once a copper, always a copper."

She smiled too. "Thanks, if we need to, that'd be great. I can let you know."

They'd finished lunch – beer-battered cod and chips, both of them with a taste for plenty of salt and vinegar – and promised to keep in touch, organising between them a date for her to go to his house near Oxford for either lunch or dinner.

Accompanying Ruby to her Ford, Peter rapped on the window. Cash, who was no longer working but had nodded off, woke with something of a start. He wound down the window and Peter bent slightly to have a word with him.

"She's all yours, son. I'll see you soon."

"Erm… yeah, thank you. And will I? Oh… good. I'll look forward to it."

Peter turned towards Ruby. "Goodbye," he said.

"Goodbye." There was an air of awkwardness between them until she decided to step forward and give him a hug. His grip was loose at first, but it soon tightened, one hand patting her back in a gesture that again Ruby found heart-warming. She had to fight against a sense of loss as they parted, reminding herself that this was a beginning, not an end. He took a step backwards, his gaze still on her, as if he too was reluctant to leave, and then finally he turned and walked away.

As he drove off, both Ruby and Cash waved. When his car was no longer in sight, Ruby gestured towards the pub. "I'd better go and see what's going on with Jed and that man. You coming?"

Together they entered The Red Lion, Ruby casing the joint, even asking Cash to stand guard whilst she inspected The Gents. There was no sign of them.

Returning to Cash's side, she was at a loss. Where was he? Where was Jed?

Heading back towards the car, she spotted Jed in the back seat.

"Oh my God," she said, hurrying towards him.

On sight of her, Jed wiggled on the seat, his tail beating furiously and woofing every now and then in an excited manner.

"What's he saying?" asked Cash, aware that something was going on.

"Saying? How would I know? I don't speak dog."

"Well… tell me what he's doing."

"He looks pretty happy, I know that much."

"So hang on, he lured this spirit away, you say, so that you could spend time with your dad uninterrupted?"

"That's right."

Cash shrugged. "Perhaps he lured him all the way into the light."

"The light?" Ruby looked at Jed in wonder. "Did you, boy?"

Jed barked again – victoriously. She turned to Cash. "You know I think you're right; he did exactly that!"

* * *

Ruby was on a high that evening, considering it a successful day and wanting nothing more than to celebrate with Cash over a takeaway and a bottle of wine. When an emergency call came in from Brookbridge, she could have cursed. Luckily, neither the takeaway had been ordered nor the bottle of wine purchased. She didn't think she could send Jed in to do the honours in place of her, despite his sterling work at The Red Lion, and as it was getting on for seven o' clock, it'd be unfair to call her other team members. Cash, however, seemed happy enough to accompany her to the house on Elm Drive, belonging to the Griffiths family. 'If it's more than we can cope with,' Ruby said to him on the drive over, 'we can always come back, but Mrs Griffiths sounded so desperate, I couldn't leave her until morning. If we do nothing else but reassure her tonight, it'll be worth it.'

When Mrs Griffiths had rung, she'd said that a commotion had started suddenly in the kitchen downstairs – pans had begun rattling; mugs and plates had been crashing against each other on the draining board; the microwave had been switching itself on and off.

"I know some of the houses on the estate have problems and I know the reason why," she explained, "but nothing's ever happened in my house before, although…" she'd paused for a moment. "The kitchen's supposed to be where everyone gathers, isn't it? Well, we don't. None of us like it in there. I cook, do what I have to do, then we head for the living room and eat in there, in front of the telly."

So activity *was* increasing on the estate, it wasn't just a coincidence. The pressure to find out that demolition date was mounting.

When they arrived at Elm Drive, full darkness had

descended. Not yet autumn, officially still summer, the evening nonetheless had a 'smoky' quality to it, reminding Ruby of bonfires and sunsets and all the good things that autumn brought. But what was happening at Brookbridge wasn't a good thing – it was like a cursed piece of land, the tears of human misery still in full flow. It was so easy to forget the existence of the secure unit, hidden as it was by trees, encircled almost – although an alarm sometimes sounded when one of the patients tried to escape. According to the residents of Brookbridge, this was quite often, but Ruby had only heard it once before. When the residents spoke about it, it was all quite matter of fact, but to Ruby it felt like living under a shadow, or even more apt, with a threat of some kind.

Entering the Griffiths' house, she found there was indeed a sense of acute distress in the kitchen. Whilst Cash sat with the family of four in the living room – mum, dad and two children – listening to what they had to say about recent events and doing his utmost to soothe them – Ruby got on with the job in hand, an impossible job as it turned out. As in the Barkers' house, the spirit was agitated but in hiding, finding it hard to let go after Cromer or to believe that peace of any kind was waiting. After an hour or so, Ruby called it a night. She joined Cash and the Griffiths family and advised them regarding holistic practices to keep the kitchen clean – *psychically* clean that is, with the use of crystals, oils and sage, *plenty* of sage, she said, suggesting they filled as many vessels as possible with the herb. She also asked them to enter the kitchen with love and compassion rather than fear and terror, and to try and project those feelings as strongly as possible. "I know it sounds odd, but that alone will have a huge impact. It'll chip away at the fear the spirit is feeling."

Mrs Griffiths immediately protested that it was far from odd. "Do you know what, I think it's bloody wonderful we've got someone like you that we can call on; that'll you come out, no matter what the time is, and help us. I'm grateful for your advice, and believe me we'll be following it to the letter. But… if things don't improve, will you try again? There's something wrong on this estate at the moment, I'm telling you, it's just… nothing feels right; everything feels… wrong."

Mr Griffiths nodded his head in enthusiastic agreement with his wife, whereas the kids, both under ten just looked dazed and upset. "At least it's okay in their bedrooms," said Mrs Griffiths, noticing, "it's only in the kitchen there's a problem."

Their house was where the men's wing had been, but whether it was the men's, the women's, or a mixed wing, the unhappiness was still simmering away.

Assuring the Griffiths family that of course they'd return if things didn't calm down, Ruby and Cash left the house and returned to her car. Although Ruby was tired from such an epic day, Cash wanted to stop briefly outside the empty remaining building, so she pulled up before it and turned off the engine. She thought they'd just sit there and look at it, but as Cash immediately got out of the car, she followed suit.

"So how'd you get in?" Cash enquired.

"We have to go round the back," Ruby replied, her breathing a little shallower she noticed as she stared at the building, at its huge windows covered with boards, remembering how dark it was inside and the smell of it; the walls that had writhed. Cash started walking to where she'd indicated. "Cash, what are you doing?"

"Having a look."

"What? No! Come back here."

He slowed his pace, but only by a fraction. "Is it really that bad in there?"

Momentarily confused, she had to remind herself how much she'd played her experience down when telling him about it. It was time to come clean.

"Yes, Cash, it really is *that* bad. If you're thinking that we might go in there again tonight, just you and me, you're wrong."

"You went in alone with Eclipse."

"Yeah, I did, to get an initial feel for the place."

"So why not go in with me?"

She frowned. Was he being serious? "I'm sorry, Cash, there's no way I'm going back in again, not unless I've got the rest of the team with me. I… can't do it alone; it's a massive task. The biggest I've ever faced, that's for sure. I need their help."

"What about *my* help?"

Her frown deepened. "Yes, of course your help, if you're able to give it. And Eclipse's too."

Cash raised an eyebrow at that.

"Cash," she asked, "have you got a problem with Eclipse?"

"No."

"It's just…"

"It's just what?"

"Oh… nothing. Look, I'm tired, really tired. I haven't got the energy to do anything more today, let alone battle an army of institutionalised spirits."

Cash sighed, his shoulders sagging slightly as he

relented. "Actually, you're right, I'm tired too. It's been a bloody long day."

She suggested they went home and got some sleep. In the morning she'd call an emergency meeting with the team – try and sort Brookbridge out before the lid blew.

Chapter Thirteen

ALL the team were able to come into Ruby's office that morning. Already, she'd texted Eclipse to let him know they were due to discuss a plan of action and he'd texted back saying he was looking forward to meeting everyone soon, and getting the job underway. Unfortunately, he'd had no luck with getting his friend to wrangle a demolition date out of Rob Lock. The boss was elusive it seemed, and, when around, far too busy to speak to a menial – a word Eclipse's friend had used to describe himself, Ruby hoped in a tongue-in-cheek manner.

To take the chill off the air, Ruby fired up the Calor gas heater. Immediately Jed appeared, making her smile. "That's all I've got to do, isn't it? Turn up the heat and you appear. I must admit though, the days are getting colder, especially up here in the attic. I thought heat was supposed to rise. Either that's not true or the solicitors below are acting all Scrooge-like and ignoring their radiators."

Curling up in a contented ball, Jed looked as if he couldn't care less about those labouring below.

"Silly mutt," Ruby said, setting the kettle to boil, "it's not as if you can feel the heat anyway." Although she didn't consider Jed grounded, he, like so many others who were, clung to what they remembered in life – the good as well as the bad. That was something to keep in mind. Some spirits remained grounded simply because they'd enjoyed their time in this realm and they wanted to stay a little longer, not rush headlong into another existence – The Waterside Inn gang being a case in point. But those at Brookbridge, who'd been forced to call Cromer their home, were in distress. As far as she could ascertain, they needed help, but there were more of them than she could deal with. She'd already told Cash that and now she needed to tell the others.

The door to her office opened and Theo bundled in, just fitting through the narrow doorframe and huffing and puffing as usual from the steep climb.

"Hello, sweetie," she said, the minute she was able to, "is the kettle on? I'm gasping."

Ness was a minute or two behind Theo, and then Corinna arrived, all of them seating themselves around the meeting table whilst Ruby made teas and coffees.

Finally sitting down too, she found only Corinna was her usual bubbly self, her green eyes bright as she sipped her tea. In contrast, Theo and Ness seemed a little tired – was that the right word? Ruby reconsidered. Strained would be more apt.

"How is everyone?" Ruby asked, hoping for enlightenment. However, it wasn't forthcoming, at least not from Theo and Ness.

"You know – managing." It was a very un-Theo-like statement; normally she was as enthusiastic as Corinna about life, and all those who filled it. Ness she expected a more subdued reply from, that was just her nature, but even Ruby was surprised when all she did was sigh in reply; a rather *ragged* sigh.

"Right... well... okay," Ruby continued. "*I* actually had rather an incredible day yesterday. I met my father, in a pub near Windsor."

"Oh wow, Ruby," Corinna exclaimed. "How did it go?"

Even Theo and Ness perked up.

"Yes, how was it?" Theo echoed.

"Good, really good. He looked how I imagined."

"Like you?" checked Corinna.

"Well... no, but I suppose I need to look at photos of him as a younger man really, I expect I'll see similarities then."

"You're meeting him again then?"

"Yes, Corinna, we've got a tentative arrangement for dinner at his house. We'll organise that soon, I should imagine."

"Brilliant, just brilliant," she enthused.

"I'm very pleased for you, Ruby," Theo said.

Ness concurred. "I wish you all the best."

"Thanks," Ruby replied. "I'll keep you up to date, of course, but so far, yeah, I'm happy with the way it's going. He even knows now what I do for a living. It's fair to say he was surprised. Jessica never told him she was psychic, you see."

Ness nodded. "I can understand that. I think its wise to choose who you tell, rather than blurt it out to just anybody."

Maybe, thought Ruby, but Peter hadn't just been *anybody*; he'd been her mother's lover, intimate with her, and still she'd held back. Then again, they hadn't seen each other an awful lot during the short period they were together, apparently. Maybe in time she would have felt comfortable enough to tell him. Who knew? There was no time to mull it over; she had Brookbridge to focus on.

"Guess where I was called out to again last night?"

When she revealed where, she thought she saw Theo's back stiffen. A brief glance at Ness also showed her lips were a thin white line.

"Is it okay to go on?" Suddenly Ruby was unsure.

"Yes," answered Ness. "Please do."

She explained about the Watkins', the Barkers' and the Griffiths' houses – the Watkins case was now for filing only, but the latter two were ongoing, Corinna having offered to visit the Barkers' house for more coaxing of the spirit. "We'll have to do a similar thing with the Griffiths' house, I think, and who knows how many other houses on the estate before the day is out." She explained too about the main building and described her experience whilst in there with Eclipse, not playing down anything this time, but revealing every lurid detail, as well as what she'd found out about various individuals, including Rebecca Nash. "I've only got snippets to go on, but regarding her, I've come to the conclusion she was psychic; that's why she was admitted to Cromer because she could see and hear spirits – something she was open about, *insistent* about in fact."

Ness inhaled at this, staring not at Ruby but at her mug.

"Is Rebecca Nash one of the spirits grounded in the main building?" enquired Theo.

"I don't know, but if not, perhaps there are others like her."

"Did you get a handle on how many spirits there were?" It was Ness asking this time.

"No. There's a lot, though. It's hard to explain, but what I experienced were the feelings of the mass rather

149

than the individuals."

"Far out!" Corinna sounded horrified rather than wowed.

Worry nagged at Ruby. "Look, this isn't a paid job. As you know I was the one who contacted Eclipse, so in effect it's a private job, Eclipse's and mine. You don't have to go in there with me, I know how busy you all are, but the upshot is, it's a job that needs doing, and soon."

Three pairs of eyes stared solemnly back at her.

"Of course we'll go in there with you," Theo finally replied. "The welfare of the spirits has always been our priority; *Brookbridge* will be our priority."

Ness agreed, as did Corinna, who was nodding avidly.

"Count me in," she said. "I can't wait to meet Eclipse, he sounds like one of us."

Ruby smiled. "Well, he's not psychic as such, or as sensitive as you, Corinna, but he is empathetic."

"Which is a wonderful trait," remarked Theo. "Any particular reason, however?"

Ruby mentioned his grandmother.

"I see." Theo exchanged a look with Ness, one that caused unease to prickle the back of Ruby's neck.

"Are you sure everything's okay?" she asked.

Her gaze on Ruby now, Theo attempted a smile. "It's this case we're working on, it's taking its toll, that's all."

"Anything I can help with?"

"No, it's just… a tad gruelling."

"A tad?" Ness snorted before collecting herself. "Yes, I suppose you could say that. Ruby, when would you like us to join you at Brookbridge?"

Before she could answer, Ness's mobile rang. "Excuse me," she said, rising. "I'll take this outside."

While she was absent, Ruby related what she'd discovered about Cromer; about asylums in general, in both the UK and the US, and twentieth century methods of treating the mentally ill.

"Better than nineteenth century methods, I can assure you," Theo declared. "And even before that. That's when it was truly barbaric."

Corinna too was incensed. "And these were people who'd done no wrong; some of them weren't even ill?"

"That's right," Theo replied, "they were *considered* ill. Those who stood in judgement were often far more warped than their patients could ever be. Treatment is better today, it really is; there's a greater attempt at understanding, plus, of course, doctors, psychiatrists, nurses and surgeons are all held so much more to account; not treated like they once were, with those ranked below them unable to question their actions and decisions. Like the church, the medical profession got away with so much." She shook her head in abject disgust. "Did you know, half a century ago, there used to be an asylum in virtually every British city? Now before you criticise that, let me say that for many, asylums were a refuge; a place where those shunned by society because of ill health could blend in. In many ways, being in the outside world was far worse for them. Their own families turned against them, mental illness being seen as something shameful. Even the royal family are guilty. The Queen had two cousins who were considered mentally defective and they were shut away in an asylum in Surrey, never to be heard of again. Brushed under the proverbial red carpet, just like that. It's a shocking story, actually; one I won't go into great detail about now, but the alternative to the asylum for those truly suffering was often worse." Theo paused. She looked sad as well as tired. "Mental illness is rife amongst us. We all know people who've suffered from depression. Heck, *I've* suffered from depression. Did you know that?" Ruby nodded, Theo had mentioned it before in passing. "Even when you have supportive people around you – and I did, my mother, my dear husband Reggie, even my children – the gift we have, it's hard to deal with sometimes. There's enough to contend with in this world, let alone the spiritual world too. It can all get a bit much. But it's a different type of suffering to those who suffer *critically*; people who are compelled to commit vile acts because their brains aren't quite wired up correctly; living people, I mean, those at Rampton, at Broadmoor— "

"And at Cromer," Ruby interrupted.

"Yes, at Cromer," Theo acknowledged, swallowing slightly. "Look, I'm babbling, getting carried away, but here's my point; I know people suffered in asylums and that there were plenty who were treated abysmally, but there were also people who *needed* to be in them. I'm as empathetic as the next person, as this Eclipse lad, but it's true to say some people can't be allowed to walk the streets."

Surprised at the direction in which Theo's speech was heading, Ruby was about to comment when Ness came back into the room.

Immediately, Theo turned to look at her. "What is it, Ness?"

"They'd like us to go back in; to talk to him some more."

Ruby looked at Corinna, both of them frowning. Who were they talking about?

A moment of silence ensued during which Theo and Ness's gaze remained locked. Were they communing with each other via thought? It still blew Ruby's mind that they could do that – their gift having developed in such a way. It seemed her hunch was right.

"Okay," Ness conceded. "We can tell them the basics."

A few minutes later, Ruby and Corinna were reclining in their chairs, completely stunned. Whilst she'd been at Cromer, so had Theo and Ness, dealing with a *live* patient unlike Ruby, who was dealing with those who had passed.

"Oh Christ, I've just remembered, I saw your car when I was there last Saturday, or rather I *thought* I saw it. You were quite a way in the distance and then you turned off the main road and I got stuck in traffic, and lost you. Was it you?"

"Last Saturday? Yes, it was."

"And you say this man, Aaron Hames, as well as being criminally insane, is psychic?"

Ness nodded.

"What crimes did he commit?" Corinna breathed.

"Darling," Theo answered, "because we've been asked by the police as well as psychiatrists for an insight into this man's nature, much of it remains confidential. Suffice to say that in terms of his psychic skill, it's really quite extraordinary. It's as though he can see deep inside a person – their past experiences, their fears, their darkest desires – every petty emotion they've ever felt."

"He can see the dark stuff?" Ruby confirmed.

"*Only* the dark stuff. It's… very draining being with him. We're only there for short bursts at a time. Sometimes its mere minutes, which is all we're able to stand. How can I explain it? It's like he holds a mirror up to you; one that just reflects your flaws."

"*For now we see through a glass darkly*," Ruby muttered. "That's the saying, isn't it?"

"Yes," confirmed Ness. "It's a Biblical phrase, the first Book of Corinthians."

"Topically, there's a film called *Through a Glass Darkly*; an old black and white," Theo said. "Ah, you all know how I love the old black and whites, you can't beat 'em! Max von Sydow's in it; such a wonderful actor. It's topical because the theme of the film is madness; a young woman descends further and further into its clutches. But yes, I agree, that expression does rather tend to sum up our experience with Hames. In his company that's exactly what you get to do, see through a glass darkly." A cough seemed to stick in her throat. "*Very* darkly."

"I know you can't say anything concerning Hames's criminal activities, but can you tell us the reason why you've been called in?"

"I'm afraid that's confidential too, Ruby," Ness replied. "I'm so sorry we can't tell you more, but it's ongoing and, as Theo says, it's draining. Bite-sized chunks mean regular chunks, and afterwards I'm afraid we haven't been fit for much else."

"But regarding the old building at Brookbridge, of course we'll go with you to that," Theo assured Ruby. "I'm glad you're not contemplating going in there alone, in fact, I'd advise against that wholeheartedly. As I've said before, living or dead, there are some people that *need or needed* to be incarcerated, and by exposing ourselves to them we expose ourselves to danger. That rule may still apply in the non-criminal section of the asylum – madness is hard to understand sometimes, and what's more, it knows no boundaries. Because of that it can push us to the very limit of ours."

Again, Ruby was surprised. They were sage words from Theo, and delivered with such solemnity.

"Theo, Ness, considering the difficulty you must be going through at the moment, I really hate to ask you regarding this, and I wouldn't if I felt I could cope alone. But, everything you say, I agree with. We're so much stronger together."

"We are," agreed Ness, Corinna and Theo nodded too.

"I just wish there was something I could do to help you with Aaron Hames."

"Believe me, Ruby," Ness replied, "I'm glad you're not involved."

"Fair enough," Ruby felt quite solemn too now, their mood rubbing off on her. "When would it be convenient for us to go to Brookbridge?" she asked. "Ideally, I'd like to go back with clearance from the developers, rather than what's tantamount to breaking in, but as Cash said, we have to tread carefully. Depending on what sort of man Rob Lock is, not to mention health and safety rules, we may never get clearance."

A hint of Theo's usual sparkle danced in her blue eyes. "Goodness, forced into being criminals too, eh?"

"Looks like it."

"I've said we can't see Hames until tomorrow," Ness informed her. "So why don't we go there tonight?"

"Tonight?" repeated Ruby, at first wondering if she needed more time to bolster herself, but then quickly deciding Ness was right – it'd be a blessing if they could make headway as soon as possible, for all concerned. "I'll see if Eclipse is available."

"So we get to meet him at last?" Corinna cooed.

"Yep." And so would Cash if he accompanied them. Something she needed to psych herself up for too, perhaps.

Chapter Fourteen

IT was a full house – the Psychic Surveys team plus Cash and Eclipse and, of course, Jed, all making their way towards an abandoned psychiatric building – the last of its kind, the medium-secure unit that housed Aaron Hames notwithstanding.

They'd already agreed to park their cars away from the building, so as not to arouse suspicion from the residents; to park them in various side roads and walk the remaining distance. Theo and Ness had parked the closest, Ruby, Corinna and Cash a ten-minute walk away, and Eclipse slightly further. Jed was by Ruby's side as she walked with Corinna and Cash; in fact he stuck to her side, rather than bounding ahead as he usually did, clearly nervous too, and little wonder. He'd seen with his canine eyes what she'd seen with her human ones, and neither of them really fancied encountering that again. *Needs must,* she thought, and Jed's ears pricked up as though he'd caught her words. Ruby frowned. *Jed, can you read minds too?* This time he glanced at her and she couldn't help but smirk. Of course he could read what was on her mind. Jed *always* knew what she was thinking.

Coming from their respective locations, the team all congregated at the back of the building, in the shadow of the woods – Ruby once again thinking how dark it was behind her and in front of her too, with the six of them sandwiched in the middle. When, a couple of minutes later, Eclipse rounded the bend, Corinna whispered, "Wow, he's a bit of a dish" and Cash muttered, "I knew it", possibly referring to his coat.

"Hey, Ruby," her newfound friend greeted, a wide smile on his face. "Hey, everyone."

Ruby greeted him warmly too and then made the introductions.

"I can see who's who from looking at your pictures on the website," Eclipse informed them, "all except you, of course," he finished, looking at Cash.

"Me? Oh, I'm just the lackey, good for carrying a bag of crystals, that's all."

"Cash!" Ruby admonished. "That's not true. You're as valued as anyone on this team."

Cash shrugged, only slightly appeased. "Good to hear it."

What was wrong with him? Why did he need reminding? Or perhaps he was just mucking about; sometimes his sense of humour erred on the wicked.

Eclipse was talking again, his excitement that he had a team of people onside, palpable. "Ruby, this is… brilliant. Organising this, taking me seriously – you're amazing, do you know that? Crap! Of course you'd take me seriously, you're psychics! But… thank you. It's good to meet you. *All* of you."

Theo smiled indulgently at him. "Lovely to meet you too, and I'm loving your name, it suits you. I believe Ruby's explained company procedure?"

"She has, yeah; to project white light, to act with good intent, to go in with love and understanding." He paused.

"To be honest, that's something I've always done."

Once again, Theo graced him with a smile. "Keep close to us when we're in there, and don't go wandering off, not under any circumstances. Ruby's told us what happened on your last visit. There's a lot of unrest, more than ever it seems; a lot of emotion. The light will protect us, but we need to protect each other too. That's why there's no splitting up; we go in, we try to connect, and if we possibly can, we help."

Eclipse nodded enthusiastically, his ponytail bobbing. He then showed them the way in, holding up the fence for all of them, including Cash. Theo complained bitterly at having to crouch so low but Jed disappeared straight through the fence, no crouching required. Theo eyed him. "I do envy that dog sometimes," she muttered.

"There's more climbing I'm afraid," Ruby warned her. "There's a low window we have to get through."

Theo looked aghast. "Seriously?"

"I'll tell you what," Cash began, "there's a door—"

Eclipse interrupted him. "Hey look, this door's pretty rotten, I'll see if I can get it open."

"Saves me a job, I suppose," Cash said, nonetheless looking slightly peeved.

Ruby hurried over to Eclipse accompanied by Theo, Ness and Corinna, all of them shining their torches on some kind of side door, which, as Eclipse had said, was by and large rotten.

A few shoves and it was open, revealing a yawning chasm behind. Ruby took a deep breath. What was waiting in there this time, hiding in the darkness? What horrors?

Ness turned to her. "Are you okay?"

"I'm fine. Are you?"

Ness nodded, but she didn't look fine; she looked as fragile as Gran.

They filed in – Eclipse first, looking back at Ruby as if inviting her to enter next. She did, followed by Cash, Theo, Corinna and lastly, Ness. Jed stood at the entrance, unsure. *Stay there if you want, Jed, stand guard.* After all, there might be living people to worry about too, either those keen on exploring, or the police.

Never one to shirk responsibility, Jed positioned himself squarely in the doorway. Facing the great outdoors, he stood there as if he meant business.

The remaining six took their first steps over the threshold. Unlike the utility room of last time, they'd stepped straight into a corridor, one of those endless corridors that the building had been designed around. At the far end of the main corridor would be the doctor's office, and the operating theatre, which Sir Ralph Gould, the eminent surgeon she and Cash had read about, could have visited in order to perform his lobotomies. If so, what effect would it have to call out his name in there? "Catastrophic," Theo answered, reading her mind. Ruby couldn't help but agree.

"As I know this building really well, shall I lead the way?" Eclipse asked.

"Ooh, he's masterful too," Corinna whispered to Ruby, giggling. Ruby knew well enough Corinna didn't mean what she was saying; she was a flirt by nature. Heck, she'd even flirted outrageously with Cash when she'd first met him, but it was all just harmless fun. Unfortunately, she, Cash and Corinna were standing together and considering Corinna was going out with Presley, Cash's brother, she wasn't sure how much he'd appreciate that remark. Not much, judging by his expression.

Theo thanked Eclipse for the offer and took him up on it. "It makes sense that you lead," she declared. "Everyone okay with that?"

There were general murmurs of consent, and, as a unit, they moved forwards, various torches doing their utmost to breach the gloom, but as before, not having much of an impact. The plan was to explore the downstairs first, cataloguing psychic experiences and trying to make a connection; to grab on to a unique experience if possible – that of an individual. Theo had called it trying to provoke the 'herd response': if they were successful with one spirit, others might be encouraged to come forward, and they'd be successful with them too.

As they walked, slowly, carefully, Ruby tried to banish the memory of writhing walls; to think of them would make her uneasy, putting her at a disadvantage. She needed only light to fill her mind – light and love – and to project that outwards with no hint of fear. At the bottom of the staircase the group stopped.

"Is everyone all right?" asked Theo.

They were, or at least they acknowledged Theo with a yes.

"The dayroom's through here," Eclipse informed them, setting off down the corridor again. Beside her, she felt for Cash's hand, registering the warmth of it as his fingers closed around hers and gave them a gentle squeeze. She squeezed back – a gesture to show him she was fine – for now. But the pressure in the atmosphere was mounting; surely they could all feel that? It was as though a thousand pairs of eyes were watching from behind a murky veil.

"Ruby and I have explored in here already," Eclipse

SHANI STRUTHERS

explained, shining a light just below Ruby's line of vision, putting her in the spotlight almost. "You didn't feel anything in this room, did you?"

"Nothing out of the ordinary," Ruby replied. "In fact, I was fine until…"

"Until what?" Ness prompted.

Eclipse answered for her. "Until we were in the doctor's office, that's when everything changed. We really need to take care of her when we go in there."

Ruby heard Cash's intake of breath. She turned her head but he was looking straight ahead, at Eclipse, as if to say something. Theo beat him to it.

"We realise that, Eclipse. As I said, we all need to take care of each other and also ourselves. If it gets too much for anyone, we retreat – *all* of us. There are no exceptions. I don't want anyone volunteering to stay behind. We haven't got one shot at this; we can come back multiple times if needs be to try and make inroads."

"The demolition date…" Eclipse reminded her.

"Is hopefully not immediate," Theo remained undeterred, "but even if it is, none of us are to put ourselves in danger. We're not superhuman, and we're not stupid."

Eclipse nodded, not chastised exactly, but certainly more aware.

Rather than a huddled mass, as they'd been up until now, they broke away from each other, but only in the confines of the dayroom, each exploring a different part of it. It was such a big room. Space hadn't been something to worry about on the Cromer site; rather it had been made the most of. Ruby tried to imagine what it had been like in the past with the patients that had been there milling

162

about. She didn't have to try too hard as an image abruptly flashed in her mind, similar to a photograph. There were three huge windows, just as there were today, but in her mind the panes were intact, with no boards across them, daylight doing its best to filter through, but like their torches, not having much success. There were chairs lining the wall by the windows, wooden benches too, and on them sat an assortment of figures in various states of repose; women, they were mainly women. Were some of them asleep? Ruby shook her head. It was more likely they were drugged. Her gaze shifted to the floor, as hard then as it was today, an unforgiving floor. On it another woman lay, her body curled in a foetus position, her arms wrapped tightly around her, the soles of her bare feet black with filth. Ruby knelt. *Who are you? What's your name?* Was the woman's rocking beginning to slow? Was she turning her head to the side, and responding? *Tell me your name,* Ruby urged, a*ll I want to do is help. Are you still here, still suffering? Look at me.*

"Is everything okay?"

It was Eclipse, kneeling too; reaching out a hand just as she was doing, but towards *her.* It came to rest on her arm. At his touch the vision faded.

She forced a smile. "Yes, I'm fine."

"Did you make a connection?" His blue eyes were so eager.

"Maybe, but it's gone now." His arrival had seen to that.

"Shame," he muttered.

"Yeah." It was, for Ruby, but more for the woman who'd lain on the ground. She was gone now; she'd flown back into the shadows to join the others.

163

"Here, let me help you."

Before Eclipse had a chance to raise her to her feet, another hand reached out – Cash's. "Ruby, what's the matter?"

'Nothing," she said, suppressing a sigh of exasperation. She had not just one man fussing over her, but two. Asking them both to leave her alone would sound rude. But she had to admit, while there were pros to being part of a team, there were also cons, the main one being that sometimes she needed to focus, to concentrate, have no other distractions. Who was that woman? What had she been admitted for? And the women that lined the seats – there was one man, or maybe two – but otherwise they were all female and of varying ages. Why had they been here?

Theo called time on their exploration of the dayroom. "We can always come back, but for now let's keep moving. We don't want our energy getting as stagnant as the energy that's in this room."

With Eclipse in the lead again, the rest of them followed. Ruby reached upwards to touch the tourmaline necklace she'd put on earlier that evening. They all had their talismans. Cash had on the obsidian necklace she'd given him when they first met and Corinna her malachite. Ness favoured obsidian too, of the snowflake variety, and Theo rose quartz – the colour of the stone an exact match for her hair.

In the corridor it was Cash who grabbed her hand now, not because he was scared, but for another reason Ruby suspected, but which she couldn't contemplate right now. She just wanted to focus. The corridor was as littered as ever with debris which all of them trudged doggedly through or around. Either side the walls were blackened, but as a result of mould rather than something preternatural, with layers and layers of paint peeling off them. Ruby wondered what colour they'd been in their heyday. *Grey,* a voice whispered, making her flinch with surprise. *Everything at Cromer was grey.*

As quickly as it had come, the voice disappeared, but it was encouraging, she decided, and made her curious as to what Theo, Ness and Corinna were experiencing – if anything, although they soon would be, the further they ventured.

"What are these other rooms leading off the corridor?" Ness asked, her voice also making Ruby jump. In such heavy silence anything above a whisper was deafening.

"There's a kitchen, more utility rooms, a gym, and this…" Eclipse said, opening a set of double doors to a room that he and Ruby had bypassed on their first visit. "It's quite a grand room," he continued, standing back so they could enter. "Cromer described it as their ballroom. It was used, you know, for dances and stuff like that; for socialising I guess. It's so odd to have a ballroom in an asylum."

The light from various torches revealed a room that did indeed seem to be at odds with the rest of the hospital. Cavernous, it had a vaulted ceiling, punctuated at regular intervals by arches that ran to a series of columns either side. Between each arch was a ceiling rose, several of them and all intact. There were also several large windows and beneath Ruby's feet, wooden floorboards rather than concrete.

"Wow!" Corinna was as amazed as the rest of them. "It can't have been that bad a place, not if they had a ballroom."

Ness gave a derisory laugh. "You'd think so, wouldn't you?"

"I've said this before," Theo replied, "not all doctors and nurses who worked in asylums were monsters. There were some very good people; people who wanted to help, to make a difference, to find a way to cure the afflicted."

"Not all of them needed a cure." Again Ness's voice held contempt.

"Some of them did," Theo insisted. "You know that as well as I do, and it's not odd to have a ballroom in an asylum. In the twentieth century dancing was regarded as a way for patients to express themselves physically in what was otherwise a restrained environment. It offered an incredible release. And if mixed dances were held, who knows, romance may have even blossomed in here! Can you imagine that? There's a song, isn't there, by Rihanna? What's the name of it? My granddaughter loves it. Oh, hang on," to everyone's surprise, Theo started singing, "'We found love in a hopeless place, we found love in a hopeless place.' Rather apt lyrics, don't you think? Being here puts a whole new slant on that record for me." Before anyone could comment, she continued, "Sound therapy was another method of treating patients from the end of the nineteenth century. Music can be very calming to some."

"Not when Theo's singing, it isn't," Cash, more like his old self, whispered.

As Theo raised an eyebrow Cash suppressed a laugh, but Corinna did no such thing; she giggled loudly and as she did, Ruby heard more laughter. As had happened the first time, the dark receded and the light from past years

166

began to filter through the windows. People other than the team filled the room, mainly women, as before, dancing with each other; *shuffling*. At the far end of the room was a band, a three-piece with someone playing the piano, someone else a violin and the third person a cello. It was a moving image Ruby was experiencing, not static; a glimpse into a different age. Far from unpleasant, the atmosphere did indeed seem calm and the room – it was beautiful. Not simply beautiful, but wholly decadent. It was a wonderful scene, and yet… if you looked closer, you could see the cracks. They came in the form of vacant eyes, slack expressions, and feet that weren't nimble but heavy. On seeing this, Ruby shook her head. Putting on a dance every now and then did NOT make up for having your liberty stolen from you. And music might have a calming effect, but so did lobotomies and drugs; they destroyed you.

The scene faded; became black again – too black.

"Brace yourselves," Theo instructed, clearly noticing the same phenomena. "And project white light – you as well, Cash and Eclipse. Imagine vast swathes of it, all-powerful, swirling around us; formidable in its brightness, completely able to protect us."

They did as instructed, Ruby didn't just imagine 'swathes' but an entire wall of light, and just as solid. Against it, black figures hurled themselves; maddened figures. And who could blame them? If you hadn't been mad before entering the asylum, you'd surely go mad whilst in here; you'd be driven to it. Those in charge may have subdued that madness in life, thanks to so-called treatments and prescription drugs, but death had pulled the recipients out of stupefaction; it had released their inner rage and brought it crashing to the fore. If ever love

167

had blossomed within these walls, as Theo had suggested, there was no sign of it now.

"There's just so many." Ness was looking repeatedly from left to right.

"*Too* many," Theo concurred. She raised both her hands and her voice. "We're sorry if we frightened you, that wasn't our intention. The only thing we have in our hearts is respect and a desire to help. This place was a prison not a home. You've somewhere else to be now – your true home, which is in the light."

Having addressed the spirits, she addressed the living. "Back out everyone, towards the corridor. I don't think they'll follow; I'm getting the impression certain spirits have attachments to certain rooms. There isn't a great tendency to wander."

They followed her instruction, keeping their footsteps deliberately slow, not wanting to arouse further alarm or show fear thus giving the blackened shapes something to feed on. Her boot connecting with something on the floor, a chunk of masonry perhaps, Ruby stumbled. Cash's hand shot out but it was Eclipse who made first contact. "Easy," he said. "I've got you."

"I'm okay," she assured him.

Cash intervened. "Take *my* hand."

"Like I said," she reiterated, to *both* of them, "I'm fine."

The words had barely left her mouth before an assault was launched. It wasn't the blackened figures, the shapes, the shadows, for they seemed to recede; rather it was more visions – the figures in them as substantial as anyone living and breathing. There were faces close to hers, an array of them; some looking straight through her, others with mouths wide open and screaming, their hands reaching up to tear at their hair; tearing bloodied clumps from their scalps. Ruby closed her eyes, but it made no difference – these pictures were in her mind's eye, and that one she didn't know how to close.

Shit! Shit! Shit!

Having not made it to the threshold, she was in the ballroom still, the walls not grey, but a serene green, making her feel as though she were in a deep, deep ocean, cut off from the world and all who resided in it – all except those who were trapped beneath the waves with her. Not an observer this time, she was in someone's arms; she was dancing. What a rare thing it was, a mixed dance! How she'd been looking forward to it. She liked men. She missed them. Well, that's why she was in here in the first place, wasn't it, because she liked them so much?

Who are you, Ruby whispered, but as quickly as her consciousness surfaced it faded, the stranger taking over again. The man that was holding her smelt nice; clean. She marvelled at that. In the asylum it never smelt clean and nor did the patients; rather there was an unholy stench, and it tainted everything and everyone, but not this man. Not tonight. Why was he at Cromer? What was wrong with his brain? Oh, what did it matter? Who cared? He was a good dancer, that's all that mattered, that and his nice smell. She giggled; couldn't help it. 'You're a flirt,' that's what her mother used to say to her, and not affectionately, but with disgust in her voice. 'It pains me to see what you're like. I didn't bring you up that way. Act proper. Act like a lady.' But being a lady like her mother – to be so repressed, so prim – was boring. Besides, she wasn't doing any harm, just having fun, so much fun. What had happened, could she really be called the devil because of it? That's what her mother had said, and worse besides. Another giggle escaped her. Was there anything worse than the devil? A whore maybe; a slut, a harlot? 'Lock her up and throw away the key,' her mother had instructed. 'I never want to see her again,' neither her nor what was in her daughter's belly – the devil's spawn. Regarding the latter, her mother needn't have worried. It was born dead. Here, in the asylum. A tiny grey thing, as grey as the walls, as dead as the rest of them, even those who walked, talked and danced.

The man's arms tightened around her. It was so long since she'd been held, since she'd felt a stirring in her groin. This was nice. This was innocent. But hadn't it been innocent before? Hadn't it been lovely before? That man had smelt nice too. He'd had the brightest of smiles. He'd liked her. Really liked her. But he hadn't stood up for her, not when it mattered. He'd abandoned her. In this place abandoned was what they all were, including this man with his arms around her; who had moved one hand lower; who was touching the small of her back. She tensed. What was he doing? His hand went lower still. There were rules about that sort of thing, strict rules. Didn't he realise? They'd be watching out for this, the doctors, the nurses, the powers-that-be, and they'd see – nothing escaped them. There'd be repercussions, a thought she couldn't bear. She'd suffered so much already. She started to struggle, to pull away. *Stop it! Stop it! We mustn't do this, not anymore. We can **never** do this.* Managing to lift one hand, she struck out. She screamed. She cried. She wailed. What if she got pregnant again? What if the baby lived? If it stayed here like she had to stay here? If it never tasted freedom, not even the once? When had she been free? It was so long ago. And she'd never leave either, she knew that; never feel the warmth of the sun on her face as she walked in the meadow, a sweet man's touch, not a mad man's; a man who'd said he'd loved her and who she loved too. Where was he now, that man? Why was she with this man instead? He wasn't nice, like she'd first thought, not at all, despite his soap and water smell. If he was nice he wouldn't be disrespecting her. Why wouldn't he let go of her? He had to let go. He had to! When you were desperate, you were strong. It lent you strength. Made you superhuman even. She giggled again. Is that what she was, superhuman? Because in here, she felt she was something else entirely – *sub*-human. And that's why she was locked away. She was something evil that crawled the earth; that slunk along these grey corridors. Pining, always pining. If she shut her eyes, she could see the scrap that had been her baby. It had died, and no one cared; no one around her had even shed a tear. The nurses, they'd reach her soon; they'd tear her from this man's arms; they'd punish them both, but before they did, she'd scream and scream as loud as she could; she'd give rise to her fury and her grief; she'd let them know that *she'd* cried for that baby, and that she always would. They'd stick needles in her arm; it's what they always did, forcing those cries back inside her, the liquid adding to her tears, but not stopping them. In that they were powerless. Her screams, they'd still be as loud as ever, despite the calmness of her demeanour. The tears wouldn't cease, despite her dry eyes. No matter what they did they could never stop the pain. She wouldn't let them. Because pain was all there was, all she had to cling to. Pain. Pain. PAIN!

"SHIT!" Ruby's scream caused Eclipse to turn to her

again, to reach out for her and hold her, and it caused Cash to glare at him, physically remove his hand and grab her back.

"Cash, stop it, leave Eclipse alone. Oh God, this place, this fucking place!"

Theo was by her side too. "Ruby, what just happened?"

"One of them got inside my head – her story, Christ! Why would your own mother have you locked up? I can't bear to think about it, Theo."

"Then let's get you out," she replied.

"No, I… Aargh!"

Corinna was gasping. "Ruby, what's happening now?"

"More… images… need to get out of ballroom, into corridor. Cash… help… now."

If she thought there might be respite in the corridor, however, she was wrong. There was none to be had anywhere in this building.

"Ness," Theo checked, "are you all right?"

"I'm… dealing with it," was her somewhat strained reply. "You?"

"Same," Theo responded. "Corinna? Cash? Eclipse?"

"I'm okay," Corinna assured her.

"Me too," Cash and Eclipse said in unison.

"But… But…" protested Ruby. "I can't leave; I have to help. They *need* help."

"Not at the expense of your wellbeing," declared Theo, her voice firm.

"But…"

Beside her Ness gave a yelp. Ruby turned and looked at her; they all did. She'd dropped her torch and had doubled over, hands clutching at her stomach.

"Ness!" Theo yelled.

In contrast, Corinna's voice was awestruck. "Jeez, look at the walls. I don't know if it's my imagination but… they look *alive*."

"Ruby," Cash said, "what's going on here?"

Jed appeared, leaving his post at the entrance, but still in combative stance, growling, whining, and hopping from foot to foot as if the ground was molten lava.

There was another noise now, not a banging or a crashing; not more screaming in the confines of her head or ill-played music. It was an alarm – loud and clear; the alarm from Ash Hill. It almost drowned out the sound of footsteps running on the floor above them; frantic footsteps that were running round and round in circles and going nowhere, because where was there to go? To what fresh hell?

"Theo's right," Ruby admitted at last. "We have to go."

As they all, Jed included, started running, three words kept going through her mind. *You. Don't. Know.* Not just a fact, it was an accusation, hissed at her. But how *could* you know – unless you were mad too – exactly what they'd endured; the torture that had turned them from victims into something vengeful.

Chapter Fifteen

BECAUSE of the alarm, Ruby expected the streets of the Brookbridge estate to be teeming with people, but nothing could be further from the truth. Instead she saw curtains being drawn. She could practically hear locks being secured on doors and windows, the residents safeguarding themselves against the possibility of a fugitive on the run. Only they, the Psychic Surveys team, were on the streets, looking at each other wild-eyed and confused, wondering if there really had been an escapee.

"Ruby, don't worry," Eclipse said, singling her out, "it's unlikely."

Immediately, Cash challenged him. "What makes you so sure?"

"Well—"

"Eclipse is right," Theo replied before he could. "Security is very tight in there."

"But how do you know for sure?" It was Corinna checking this time, still worried.

"Because..." Theo shot a brief look at Ness before continuing. "Look, darling, I think it's all about unrest – the whole estate seems to be jiggered up at the moment. God knows, *we're* jiggered up. I consider myself a tough old bird, but look at my hands and how much they're shaking! It's getting late, it's past ten already, let's just go home, grab some sleep and then we can reconvene tomorrow."

Eclipse seemed disappointed in Theo's decision. He nodded towards the main building, the alarm still ringing in everyone's ears. "We never made it as far as the theatre; we never went upstairs even. We actually didn't get very far at all."

"For a reason." Ness's voice had a slight edge to it. "We're psychics, which makes us susceptible, more so than those whose psychic abilities aren't particularly developed, who go more on instinct. We don't do that; we *know* what's there." She turned her attention to Ruby, batting her black hair out of her eyes. "I presume you made a connection in the ballroom, with an individual, I mean?"

"I did, a woman, a young woman; her boyfriend had got her pregnant and she was sent to Cromer because of it. Her mother was instrumental in that decision. Her baby was born at the asylum, born dead I gather. After that, it was back to the mass again and tuning into them as a whole. There are so many of them; *too* many."

Ness agreed. "There are *hordes*. And when you're dealing with something on this scale, it can't be rushed."

Eclipse looked stricken. "The building's being torn down soon!"

"You don't know how soon," Cash remonstrated. "You haven't got a timeframe."

Ruby was on Eclipse's side. "Whatever's happening here, it's hurtling towards climax. As much as I don't want to, we have to go in there and try again. Not tonight, I agree with Theo; we need a breather, but we have to sort this out and soon. What concerns me, as Eclipse said, is we didn't get very far. It's like those inside are doing everything they can to prevent us. But that's no good for anyone, least of all them."

The alarm ceased. "Thank God for that," muttered Theo. "You've explored everywhere, haven't you, Eclipse? The doctor's office? The theatre? Upstairs?"

"Yeah."

"And the atmosphere in those places, is it worse?"

"Oh yeah," he answered. "It's far worse."

* * *

The team eventually dispersed. When they got home, Ruby was so tired she prayed for nothing more than a dreamless sleep and was surprised when her wish was granted, waking the next morning to bright sunlight. For a few moments she stared at the ceiling and then she turned to Cash, who was also staring at the ceiling.

"Cash?"

"Uh huh?"

"What have you got against Eclipse?"

He looked at her. "I haven't got anything against him."

"You forget I'm able to sense things, especially when my boyfriend is jealous."

"Jealous!" He was incredulous. "Seriously, Ruby, have you lost your mind?"

Stunned, she could only stare at him.

As realisation dawned, he had the good grace to look sheepish. "Sorry. That was a stupid thing to say all things considered, but no, I'm not jealous. Why'd you even think that?"

"Why? Because you've barely said a civil word to him and when he tried to help me when I almost fell in the ballroom, you smacked his hand away."

"I did not!"

"You did."

"For God's sake, Ruby, he's just... he's all over you, isn't he? It's like no one else exists; his focus is entirely on you."

Ruby pushed herself upwards into a sitting position. "I barely know the guy."

"And yet you're putting yourself out for him and he's putting himself out for you."

"Cash, I'm putting myself out for the spirits that are grounded in that bloody awful building! Do you know, I wish sometimes that you could see what I could see – the *terrible* things. I know you're not psychic, but you're a bit bloody casual at times. Eclipse isn't psychic either, but he empathises so much, and his determination to help those he can't see, only sense, I admire it. I do, I think it's incredible."

Cash pushed himself upwards too, a vein in his neck pulsating. "If you think he's incredible, then good luck to you both. I hope you enjoy your little case together."

As he rose from the bed, she pulled him down again, causing him to sit with a thump. "It's not a *little* case, Cash, it's a bloody big one. And I said I think *it's* incredible, not him: how he feels so passionately about the cause. You know what? I never had you down as a jealous type. You learn something new every day, I suppose. *Why* are you jealous? Is it because you can't stand the competition?"

Rising again, this time shooting her a look that told her she'd better not try the same stunt twice, he located his clothes and began pulling them on. "You know what,

Ruby, perhaps I'm just human. Sorry if that leaves you disappointed, being as you always bang on about how perfect I am."

"Bang on…? Cash, what the hell is—?"

"Perhaps Eclipse is like you, as determined, or perhaps together you're just a little bit overkill. I guess we'll find out soon enough."

"I don't understand this! What are you doing? Where are you going?"

"Home."

"*This* is your home… technically."

"Yeah? Well right now I don't feel very welcome in it."

As he stormed from the room, Jed materialised by Ruby's side, both of them staring at the door he'd slammed behind him with open mouths.

* * *

Still breathing fire after such a stupid argument, Ruby drove to the high street as it was raining, let herself into her cramped and dusty office, and switched on her computer, intending to lose herself in a bit of research. The way Cash had acted, how he'd jumped down her throat, she couldn't believe it. Then again, maybe she should never have mentioned the possibility of his being jealous of Eclipse – perhaps it was like waving a red rag in front of a bull. Even so, to go for her like that, to storm out… *Focus, Ruby, just focus. Give both of you time to calm down.*

There'd been male wards at Cromer to the west of the building, and going by the plans she'd seen, they were equal in size to the female wards on the east side. In her visions, however, it had been mainly women she'd seen.

She opened Google. Much of what she read supported past research. In Victorian times, women who rebelled against domesticity risked being declared insane – she took a deep breath, appalled at the gravity of it – *insane*, for God's sake, because you didn't fancy being someone's slave? A woman's husband or father could get her committed and she had no right to contest or appeal. There were those that bucked the trend during that time, Elizabeth Packard for example, who won her freedom after being confined to an asylum by her husband, and then wrote a bestselling exposé about it, advocating asylum reform and women's rights. Dorothea Dix also lobbied successfully for reform in public asylums throughout the US and the UK; but overall, women were still considered more fragile and sensitive than men, more prone to breakdown and mental ill health. *Yeah right,* thought Ruby, pursing her lips. Even as late as the 1960s and 1970s, women's lives were still organised around Victorian stereotypes of the loving mother and dutiful housewife. Women deemed not to be behaving appropriately risked ending up in psychiatric care, like the woman whose eyes she'd looked through in the ballroom; who'd become pregnant out of wedlock and both she and her baby condemned because of it. What about the man who'd got her pregnant? Had he been blamed for his part in it? Or had he got off scot-free? That woman's plight was typical of so many; of thousands. Ruby shook her head, her blood beginning to boil. 'Moral infidelity' it was called by those that did the locking up; men predominantly, hypocrites that they were. Women were more vulnerable because usually they had less money and therefore less power. Bethlem, which was widely dubbed 'Bedlam', was a notorious London asylum and she discovered 'overwork' was another reason women were incarcerated in it. One example, Daisy Ladd, who was no more than twenty years old, had been in sole charge of looking after a ten-bedroomed town house in the city and its resident family. The author of the article had visited the Bethlem archives and matched Ladd's story and photograph together, describing it as an 'explosive experience': the girl's face when she was admitted to the asylum, had been covered in bruises. Had she been beaten for not being able to keep up with such a vast amount of housework created by a demanding family? An official declaration lodged by the family declared she was 'feebleminded', but to Ruby's mind exhaustion seemed more likely. At any rate, her case highlighted that it wasn't just husbands, fathers and even mothers who could have a woman committed; their employers could too. All it took was two people to persuade a doctor that a person was of unsound mind and off to the asylum they went, and clearly some doctors didn't need much persuading.

If Ruby had been pissed off before, it was nothing to the mood she was in now. Even in modern times a popular newspaper had featured the headline: *'Women are 40% more likely than men to develop mental illness'*, thus ensuring that the stigma was still alive and kicking; that women were far more emotional than men. But men, well, men could be jealous; *very* jealous.

Trying to get a handle on statistics, she read an extract by none other than Charles Dickens, who'd visited St Luke's Hospital for the Insane in 1851. He wrote: *The experience of the asylum did not differ… from that of similar establishments, in proving that insanity is more prevalent among women than among men. Of the eighteen thousand*

seven hundred and fifty-nine inmates St Luke's Hospital has
received in the century of its existence, eleven thousand one
hundred and sixty-two have been women. The article made it
clear he was writing from a 'sympathetic' viewpoint, but
his continuing sentence – Female servants are, as is well
known, more frequently afflicted with lunacy than any other
class of persons – caused Ruby to sigh heavily. It seemed odd
that such an intelligent man, whose empathy with the poor
and downtrodden was such a feature of his literature,
should be so blind as to assume that incarceration was
proof of insanity and not social injustice.

What had become of St Luke's Hospital, she wondered.
What flats or houses now stood in place of it, and, more to
the point, what spirits lingered there? She shook her head,
trying not to get carried away. There were plenty of
abandoned asylums in the UK; plenty given over to
building sites too – she couldn't save them all. But she'd
do her best by those spirits that remained at Cromer. She'd
promised Eclipse and she'd promised herself, and despite
feeling fed up to the back teeth with Cash, she mustn't get
all het up about the feminist aspect of madness and its
history either; plenty of men had been incarcerated; were
victims too.

Again, Ruby had an urge to study the photos Eclipse
had sent her. There was no photo of Rebecca Nash to
accompany her notes, but if she'd been able to match
them, she felt certain that would have been a pretty
'explosive experience' too. Clicking on photo after photo,
her screen was soon littered with them. They were as good
as anything held at the record office, although the
originals, those in the doctor's room, must be revisited. She
had to handle them; glean what she could from actual

physical contact – a practice known as psychometry.

The phone rang, was it Cash perhaps, apologising? If so, she'd remain decidedly frosty for a few minutes, not just let him get away with what had happened earlier. It wasn't him, however, it was a worried-sounding Eclipse.

"Oh, Ruby, hi. How are you? I've barely been able to sleep for thinking about you."

"Oh?" Good job she was on the phone as she could feel the blood rushing into her cheeks. "I'm fine, honestly. You needn't have concerned yourself."

"Really?" He sounded stunned that she was anything other than traumatised. "I feel so guilty about what happened."

"No, don't." Ruby's voice grew firmer. "This is what I do, it's my job."

"But I don't want to put you in any danger."

"You haven't, I'm not. Look, I really don't want you to worry."

"It's a crusade for you, isn't it?"

Her eyes grew wide – a crusade – that's exactly how she described her work.

"It is for me too," he continued without waiting for an answer. "I mean I know I'm not psychic, but my heart's in it, my heart *belongs* to it."

Cash was right – she and Eclipse *were* alike. Not just flip sides of a coin, as she and Cash were, but the same side.

"Ruby," he continued, "what are we going to do next? What's our plan of action? When should we meet? Should I head over to Lewes today?"

"Eclipse, of course we can meet again. But I need to speak to the rest of the team first; set a time and also…"

she nudged, "the demolition date?"

"Yeah, I don't know what we're going to do about that, we're getting nowhere fast, or rather my friend is."

"It's just as Ness said, this isn't a rush job."

"Is there such a thing in your profession?"

"You wouldn't believe how straightforward it can be sometimes."

"I might if we worked together a bit more in the future."

She laughed. "One step at a time, eh?"

"I'm really sorry regarding that date; I'll try again."

She pitied how morose he sounded. Perhaps she should get on the phone to Rob Lock herself and explain; take a chance regarding his beliefs and what he'd do. Or… Another idea occurred.

"Hang on, Eclipse, I think I might have hit on a way we can get that date. And once we know, that's when we can really plan. Without it we're fighting blind."

As she ended the call, her father's words were at the forefront of her mind: '*If you don't have any luck regarding a demolition date via this friend of yours, perhaps I can help. Use a bit of police influence.*' Maybe it was time to take him up on his offer, and whilst she was at it, arrange that dinner date. She dialled Peter's number and as she waited for him to answer, butterflies once again danced in her stomach.

Chapter Sixteen

PETER had been delighted to hear from her and, true to his word, had invited both her and Cash to dinner, that very day in fact, which had taken her by surprise, the immediacy of it. It was a nice surprise though, and she certainly wasn't about to turn it down. What wasn't so great was that, after speaking to Peter, she'd had to text Cash to see if he was still keen on coming.

He'd taken a while to reply, an *annoyingly* long while, but eventually a response had come through. *Okay.* That was it, one word. One stupid word! Rather than pick up the phone and yell at him, she phoned home instead to check how Gran was.

Jessica answered rather than Sarah. "Hi, Ruby, how are you? You're fine, oh good, that's great to hear. No, sorry, Gran can't come to the phone at the moment; she's still in bed. No, I know it's not like her, she's usually up bright and early, but she's developed a bit of a cough, I hope it's not the start of a cold or something. It's best not to disturb her I think. How are things at Brookbridge?"

Ruby told her the case was still at a critical level, but they were dealing with it, after which Jessica enquired about Peter. "Did your meeting go well?"

Was that a slight accusation in her voice? A case of 'why didn't you ring to tell me about it sooner?' or was she being paranoid? After all, Jessica had said she didn't want to know the details; that it was Ruby's business entirely. Perhaps she was being paranoid, recent matters making her oversensitive. She related how the meeting had gone and also told her mother that she and Cash were driving to Peter's that day for dinner.

Jessica was aghast. "All the way to Oxford?"

"It's not that far, Mum. We could do a round trip but actually he's asked us if we want to stay the night in his spare room. As it's the weekend, I've accepted."

"Oh, right." Again there was surprise in Jessica's voice. "What does he look like?"

Smiling because her mother hadn't been able to resist asking, she told her, followed by a question of her own. "How does it compare to how he looked then?"

"He was handsome, or at least I thought he was. His eyes were lovely; they used to remind me of the sea. Of course it was a long time ago, but I think I stood in awe of him; you know, young girl, older man, it's a scenario that plays out often enough. Oh, Ruby," she sighed. "As I've said, I hope it works out for you. Were you going to tell Gran about your plans for today?"

"I was going to try and explain. It's just… I'm worried she's going to be upset about it somehow. She's done so much for us, I don't want her to think that searching for my dad meant I thought there was anything lacking."

There was a brief moment of silence on the other end. "But there *was* a lot lacking, wasn't there? And not just a father figure; I wasn't there for you either, not really, for so much of your childhood. Gran was our rock, but Gran's only one person. Sometimes there needs to be another influence; a different point of view."

More silence followed. Jessica had put into words what Ruby had always felt. Ending that silence, Jessica wished her good luck for the weekend and, after promising to come home soon, Ruby had rung off. A mini-plan had been put into place over the weekend in the form of distance healing, something Theo specialised in, and Ness had a good grip of too. She knew they were going to pay another visit to Aaron Hames again, so they'd pass by the building at Brookbridge. They wouldn't go inside. What they would do was visualise it in their minds and all within it, sending love in abundance. They'd wrap the building in love, and so would Ruby. Although her weekend schedule was packed, she'd do whatever she could when she had a free moment. Courtesy of the documents Eclipse had photographed and sent, she gave Theo and Ness as many names as she could so that they could target their efforts. She'd also rung Eclipse, told him about her father and the possibility of him helping them find out the demolition date, and briefed him about the distance healing that was underway. As enthusiastic as ever, he said he'd begin doing the same and that he'd spend all weekend visualising. Corinna was also on board with the practice.

With all that in place, she felt ready to face her father again… and Cash.

* * *

They'd apologised to each other – after a fashion, although Ruby didn't really think she had anything to apologise for, and she was damned sure Cash felt the same way. Yet she let it go; she had to. She had bigger fish to fry – this meeting with her father for one, just their second time together and at his house too. *Let's hope it's not haunted.* The thought almost made her giggle. What a disaster if it was; if it was anything like when they'd met in the pub. She'd have to call on Jed again, who right now was nowhere to be seen. She wished she could laugh about the prospect with Cash, but thanks to this unease between them, she didn't feel able to. She was at the wheel again, driving to Oxford, excitement bubbling inside her despite Cash's poker face.

The radio was a godsend at least, giving them an excuse to hardly speak. Cash also kept checking his phone. When she asked him why, he muttered 'work' – which was fair enough; she couldn't argue with that.

As they were approaching Wayland Copse, a cul-de-sac leading off a main road, nerves finally got the better of her and she stopped the car, still a few metres from Peter's house.

Perhaps because of this, Cash took notice of her, *real* notice, even going so far as to reach out a hand and lay it on her arm. "It'll be okay. Peter seems like a nice bloke, even if he did call me dusky!" A wry laugh escaped him. "I have to say, that's a first."

"He *is* a nice bloke, Cash, I know that. A bloke that also happens to be my father, which is… incredible." She took a deep breath and then rapidly exhaled. "I've found him, Cash, I've actually found him! And it seems he wants to get to know me as much as I want to get to know him." She practically squealed as she said it.

"Good, I'm glad."

Was he? His voice sounded so flat. "Are *you* okay?"

"Fine." He glanced at his watch. "Come on, we were due fifteen minutes ago."

Trying to regulate her breathing so as not to descend into panic, she drove the remaining distance.

Peter Gregory's house was as wonderfully ordinary as him – she really was embracing this aspect of his character, as her mother had once done. After parking the car, they both got out, Cash grabbing their shared holdall from the boot.

"Ah, there's Jed at last," Ruby said, pointing to him as he ran up the pathway. "Seems he wants to join in the fun too."

Cash smiled but otherwise remained silent, causing a flash of annoyance in Ruby. What had happened – their argument – she wished he'd let it go, and stop sulking. She was happy; was it so hard to at least feign happiness on her behalf? Perhaps it was wrong to drag him out here, but she hadn't insisted; he could have refused.

Ruby rang the bell and, after what seemed like an age, the door to the ordinary house in the ordinary cul-de-sac opened to an ordinary man: Peter – as neatly groomed as ever. Stepping forward, he kissed Ruby on both cheeks and shook Cash's hand. Jed raced in, coming to a standstill at the entrance to the living room, his head inclined to one side. Seeing this, Ruby winced. *Oh no, please, please don't let there be a grounded spirit, not here, not today.*

Taking their holdall, Peter pointed them in the direction of the living room, which Jed was still surveying. Despite not detecting anything untoward in the house, she braced herself; Jed wouldn't just stand and stare for no reason.

When she saw what he saw, she didn't know whether to be relieved or otherwise. It was two people, thankfully two *living* people, a man and a woman standing boldly in the centre of the room. There was a look of Peter about them; his son and daughter? If so, they were her half-brother and half-sister.

"Oh!" The word fell from her mouth.

By her side now, Peter explained. "This is Kirsty and this is John, my other children. They were eager to meet you."

Jed stared, Cash stared and she was staring too – she already knew they were older than her, but Kirsty had red-hair, an inheritance from her mother perhaps, and she was also tall and willowy, whereas Ruby had brown hair and was of medium stature. John was also tall, his hair sandy like his father's. There was nothing about them physically that Ruby could identify with. As for wanting to meet her, was Peter sure about that? They were viewing her with barely disguised suspicion.

Immediately her heart sank. Peter had originally claimed via their emails that he wanted to take things slowly and in all honesty, she'd been fine with that, but this wasn't taking things slowly. This was way too fast. She'd have liked some time to prepare herself before meeting further relatives, especially those so close in blood. Peter asked them all to sit before hurrying off to make tea and she consoled herself that perhaps it'd be all right after all; in for a penny in for a pound. She was glad of Cash beside her though, even a sulking Cash, and Jed, of course – *her* family. She didn't yet fit in with the new family that awaited her; she was an outcast still; the one who'd been abandoned and was trying to make a comeback; *forcing* a comeback even.

It was John who broke the silence.

"It's nice to meet you, Ruby. Dad's told us all about

189

you. And you… Cash," he stumbled ever so slightly over his name, "good to meet you too."

"It's lovely to meet you," Ruby replied, keeping her smile firmly in place.

Beside her, Cash muttered something in reply.

"Although," it was Kirsty who spoke next, her voice refined, thought Ruby, dismissing the more uncharitable 'snooty' that sprang to mind, "as I'm sure you can understand, it was quite a shock to find out about your existence."

"My existence?" Ruby glanced at Cash, who also looked surprised that Kirsty had used such a phrase. "Well, it was only recently I found out what his name was – Peter's I mean."

"Any reason for that?" Kirsty asked.

How the hell could she answer? Yes, actually, *lots* of reasons. This wasn't the time to reveal everything – she'd prefer to do that gradually, over time, and for it to be something of a two-way street. "It was just difficult," she said, "for my mum."

A mother who just decades before would have run the risk of being sent to the asylum for her predicament, like the woman in the ballroom. Jessica had been lucky she'd had Ruby in the nineties, not the fifties or sixties, but even today if you failed to conform, by no fault of your own, there was a stigma attached. Some things changed, but not nearly enough. This woman, her half-sister, was she looking down on her? Would she have preferred it if Ruby had just stayed away, remained hidden, like those that weren't wanted; that were an embarrassment; were hidden?

Peter entered the room with a tray. "Here we are, tea and biscuits. Kirsty's been a darling and cooked our supper; I just have to warm it through. She's a dab hand in the kitchen, aren't you, my love? Very accomplished. I keep telling her she should go in for that *MasterChef*. She'd win, no doubt about it."

Peter sounded so proud of his offspring, which was a good thing, Ruby decided. It showed what a kind father he was.

As Peter set the tray down, John leant forward. "Here, Dad, let me pour."

"Good lad," Peter replied, smiling indulgently at him whilst also taking a seat.

The three of them – they were a real unit. But perhaps it could be four of them in the future. She mustn't think otherwise, not at this stage. Peter looked at her curiously; perhaps aware of the thoughts careering through her mind.

"Ruby," he said, "I know we said we wanted to take things slowly, but I tend to include my family in everything I do; my two children I mean. Following the success of our initial meeting, I thought we should start the ball rolling."

"That's fine." Politely, Ruby sipped at the tea she'd been handed, thinking how much he sounded like he was following procedure. "It's a great idea, isn't it, Cash?"

Cash had already dived into the biscuits and had his mouth full – typical behaviour that comforted her somehow; brought her back to her own familiar world. He could only nod, but it was confirmation enough; confirmation that she needed.

"Dad's also told us about what you do," John said. "Interesting."

It was the exact same word as Peter had used when he'd found out about it.

"Can't say such a talent runs in the family," Kirsty added, placing a slight emphasis on 'talent'; a mocking emphasis perhaps.

"I get it from my mother's side," Ruby explained, refusing the offer of a biscuit when Peter again tried to proffer them. There was no way she could eat; her stomach was churning. At her feet, Jed nudged her. If only they knew that there was the spirit of a Labrador in the room with them; a ghost dog. Would they believe her if she told them? She didn't think so. Not at this moment in time anyway.

"Is it a good earner?" John asked.

"I make enough to get by," Ruby replied. "Erm… what do you do?"

"I'm a solicitor."

"And I'm a doctor," Kirsty pointed out. She asked Cash's profession too.

"I'm in IT," was his answer.

"Oh," she said, not as impressed as she could be.

We're the poor relations, thought Ruby, swallowing slightly.

His children's professions established, Peter began to explain why he'd left the police. "I retired due to ill health; stress of the job, you know." His face clouded slightly. "Personal issues too. Luckily, I have a decent enough pension to live on."

Kirsty leant forward slightly as he said this, her gaze fixed firmly on Ruby. "Dad suffers from his nerves. Fighting crime day in day out for years and years, it's not easy, not for those on the frontline that work the streets as opposed to sitting all cosy behind a desk. Dealing with criminals poses a risk, a very real risk, and it takes its toll.

I'm gong to be honest with you, that's another reason why we're here; we keep an eye on Dad, and we always will."

Peter smiled. "Kirsty, love, come on, I'll be okay. You know that." To Ruby he said, "She does fret about her old man sometimes. Right, now we've got the basics done and dusted, let's just… have a nice evening. I'll put the coq au vin in the oven in an hour or so. Better not eat too many biscuits, Cash, you'll spoil your appetite."

As the conversation duly continued, over the remains of the tea and then later over dinner, no more warnings were directed Ruby's way. Inwardly, however, she was still reeling from the last one. Peter's children didn't trust her; they were here to keep an eye on her, intimating two things: that the threats she faced via her work were not real but perceived, and perhaps that Ruby herself was a criminal, setting out to con a vulnerable man. Even if she was who she said she was, they clearly thought she was an opportunist. She could easily be angered by those suggestions, but she tried to understand it instead, admitting she might feel the same in their position. Besides, it was what Peter thought that mattered at this crucial stage and every time he looked at her his eyes lit up; she wasn't imagining it, and the truth of it lit something in her too.

At the table, Kirsty and John waited on them. They wouldn't hear of Cash or Ruby getting up to help with the dishes. Afterwards more tea was served back in the living room where Ruby glanced at pictures of young children in photo frames – modern children, grandchildren clearly. *My nieces and nephews,* she thought, her sense of wonder continuing. When Kirsty and John finally left – they lived very close by, Kirsty had taken great pains to point out –

Peter showed them to the room they'd be sleeping in and bade them a good and restful night.

In bed, Cash held her, but there was still a distance between them. When she asked if he thought the evening had gone well, he just shrugged.

"It's early days, Rubes, but yeah, I think so, all things considered."

His cautious reply grated slightly, but he redeemed himself somewhat by adding, 'He really seems to like you.' She was thrilled he'd also noticed that.

In the morning, she, Cash and Peter had breakfast together in the conservatory, a far more relaxed affair with just the three of them. There were more framed photos in the conservatory, a woman in them this time, with reddish hair. It was the first time she'd seen any photos of Laura, but here she was in all her glory, two headshots rather than full views, the camera catching the loveliest of smiles. There was an innocence about her, Ruby decided, which gave rise to mixed feelings. As glad as she was to find her father, that Peter and Jessica had deceived this woman made her somehow feel culpable too. Had Laura been aware of her husband's affair? Had she even had the faintest suspicion? Ruby longed to go over to one photo in particular, depicting Laura and Peter with a young Kirsty and John; to pick it up and examine it, but perhaps now wasn't the time. The four of them seemed so happy in that photo, creating even more strange emotions – a feeling of exclusion perhaps; a realisation that she'd *never* belong to the family no matter how hard she tried. She shook her head. It was no use being negative. As Cash had said, it was early days, *really* early days, and maybe from them a wealth of possibilities could spring.

Breakfast finished, Cash took their holdall to the car, lingering there tactfully to give Ruby and Peter some space to say goodbye, which she was grateful for.

"It's been lovely having you here," Peter said, "I hope you didn't mind me inviting Kirsty and John."

"It's fine, it was a great evening."

"It was indeed. It was magical."

Ruby wasn't sure she'd have used that word but she was supremely pleased he thought so and even more chuffed when he made the first move to hug her this time. So chuffed, in fact, she had to fight back tears. *Don't cry, Ruby, just... don't cry.*

Eventually he released her. "You'd best get going, that young man of yours – a very nice young man," he added, a touch of surprise in his voice, "is waiting."

"I'm glad you like him."

"Does he come from good stock?"

For a moment she had to think what he meant. "Good stock? You mean his family? His mother's lovely."

"And his father?"

"He's estranged from his father."

"Oh?"

"He left the family when Cash was little more than a baby. They have had contact, though," she assured him. "A little bit of contact anyway."

"Shame. But it happens; we know that. I'm glad at least that *we've* found each other."

I found you, thought Ruby, but her smile was as wide as Laura's nonetheless.

As she turned to go, he called out. "Oh, Ruby, I'm sorry, I almost forgot."

She faced him again. "Forgot what?"

"That date you wanted; the hospital building that's going to be torn down?"

Her heart quickened. "Oh God, did you manage to find out?"

"I told you, police contacts can work wonders, even *ex*-police. It wasn't Rob Lock I spoke to, it was his secretary, and she was very forthcoming indeed."

"When is it?" Ruby asked, barely able to breathe.

"Well, you're going to have to move fast, young lady. By this time next week, it'll all be gone; a pile of rubble. And it's probably for the best… don't you think? It's all for the best."

Chapter Seventeen

CASH agreed to drive whilst Ruby fired out a series of texts.

"I must let Eclipse know. Theo, Ness and Corinna too." Immediately she winced. Why had she said Eclipse's name first? She should have been more tactful than that.

"Don't panic, Ruby, we'll sort it out."

"In a week? Something as large scale as this? I admire your faith, Cash, but honestly, I'm really not sure. It'll take a miracle to sort it out in a week."

Even Jed, riding shotgun and whining intermittently, seemed agitated at the prospect.

Her phone pinged.

"Who's that texting you back?" asked Cash. "Theo?"

"No, it's Eclipse."

"Oh right, trust him to be the first."

Ruby saw red. "Cash! Can we just focus on the problem at hand, which is helping to release the spirits that are trapped in that building, or as many of them as we possibly can. Personally I'm grateful for his help."

"But he's not psychic."

"Nor are you, but you tag along too sometimes, don't you!" Damn! She'd done it again, put her foot in it. 'Tag along' was so demeaning. It was also untrue. Cash had been a real boon in the past. Trying to counteract the blow, she added, "This is his quest, remember? In some ways we're all just tagging along."

"Whatever," was Cash's less than appeased reply. "What's he saying, anyway?"

"That he's on standby." It wasn't actually true. What he'd said was that he was there for her day and night; that he'd do his utmost to protect her when they went inside again, and that he'd make that his priority. They were sweet words, well meant, but words that would incense Cash further if he ever saw them. Making sure he wouldn't, she erased their conversation, a little peeved that she felt she had to.

"Why don't you phone the others rather than text?"

"Good idea, I'll do that. I worry that's all, what with it being Sunday. Everyone's entitled to a bit of time off."

"There's a time you didn't think so," Cash pointed out, referring to her somewhat workaholic ways. But she'd tried to remedy that in recent months, not get so involved. Why he was taking pains to point it out now was beyond her.

Bigger fish to fry, she reminded herself, dialling Theo's number.

"Theo, hi!" she greeted. "Did you get my text?"

"Text? No, dear. I've been, well… resting."

"Resting?" She looked at the clock on the dashboard. It was nearly one in the afternoon. "Are you okay?"

"A little tired, that's all."

She sounded worse than tired, she sounded upset. Ruby hesitated, should she tell her the not so good news?

"Theo…"

"Yes?"

She must be exhausted if she wasn't even bothering to read her mind.

"Rest up today if you're not feeling great. Are you free tomorrow at some point to talk about Brookbridge?"

"Yes, darling, of course, and I'll continue to send love and healing today."

"Perfect, thank you. I'll talk to the others; scrape a time together."

"I'll wait to hear."

Ending the call, she phoned Corinna next, who said she was heading to Brookbridge in less than an hour, to sit with the spirit at the Barkers' house, to try and befriend it some more. After that she was heading to the Griffiths', to carry out the same task. Although busy today, she was up for a meeting on Monday, especially when Ruby mentioned the impending deadline.

After they'd said their goodbyes, Ruby wondered whether to phone Ness, but decided against it. She'd text them all with a suggested meeting plan of ten o' clock Monday morning. "Cash," she asked, "what do you want to do this afternoon?"

"When we get back?"

"Well, yeah, not while we're driving!"

He shrugged rather than laughed. "It depends. We can either go to the pub, watch a movie or I can clear some work so I'm free to help in the week if you need me."

The latter sounded like a sensible idea, even though she badly wanted to just curl up with him on the sofa and heal the rift between them; a rift that would widen if he knew what she had in mind.

* * *

With Cash back at his flat, where all his computers and

displays were, enabling him to crack on with what he needed to do, Ruby was free to contact Eclipse. More headway had to be made urgently, and he was the only one she felt comfortable enough calling out during Sunday evening. The pair of them arranged to meet in the same spot as before.

On the way over, Jed appeared in the passenger seat, a puzzled expression on his face.

Ruby's shoulders sagged. "I know, I know. I said I wouldn't go to the asylum again, not without the rest of the team, but look, at least I've got Eclipse with me. The good thing is, he doesn't seem to be affected by what's in there. He's not immune, I'm not saying that, but he's not as vulnerable as I am. What I'm trying to say is he can get me out of there if it starts to get too much. He's strong enough to physically carry me if he needs to. Besides which, Theo and Ness have been sending love and healing towards the building all day." Whether this had had the desired effect or not, she'd soon discover.

Spotting her as she hurried along the streets of Brookbridge towards the building, Eclipse picked up pace too. "I'm so glad you came, Ruby," he said, hugging her. "Sometimes I think we're the only ones who take this seriously, yeah?"

"We're not," she assured him upon release. "My team do as well, but this isn't the only case they're working on. Ness and Theo are going through a particularly gruelling time at the moment." She didn't tell him that they were also involved with the estate at Ash Hill. "They need to rest and replenish their energy before coming here again. You can't go in to a building like this unless you're fully fired up."

"And what about you, you on top form?"

She thought of the weekend that had just passed and the night spent at her father's. Despite a bit of frostiness between her and Cash; despite Kirsty and John and their painfully obvious suspicions, she *was* on top form. In fact, she'd never been happier.

Rather than explain fully, she nodded in reply and turned to face the building. Against the darkening sky, it looked so forbidding. Even the moon, which was a bright shining orb in the night sky, eschewed it. As for the tension in the air, she fancied you could reach out and grab it. Although all was silent, all was still, she wasn't going to be fooled again. Remembering the din that had been in her head, how it had banged against the walls of her skull, she prayed it wouldn't start up again. How she wished they could come here in daylight and not be so sly in their endeavours, but they couldn't take any chances, not at this stage. She was glad her father had only talked to Rob Lock's secretary instead of the man himself, to identify the date of demolition. Perhaps the boss man was still oblivious. Her father had said maybe it was for the best the building got pulled down as soon as possible, and in some ways she agreed, but that didn't mean she wouldn't do what she could for the grounded in the meantime. What was the sentiment? *Save one, save the world?* If she could form a proper connection with just one of them – send them to the light – it might just prompt the 'herd response' as Theo called it, encouraging others to follow.

Spurred by that thought, she motioned to Eclipse to get moving. He fell into step beside her, his blonde hair as usual tied back, his coat of many colours buttoned up. The thought again crossed her mind, *we're the same but different*. Would he be keen to work with her on future projects too? In terms of devotion he'd get the job, but what would it be like to have someone who was as passionate as her on the team, but essentially non-psychic? When it came to it, was passion enough?

The dark woods at their back, Eclipse located the damage to the fence and held the flap of chain link up for her again. It was like a portal, a passage to another world. Straightening, she was about to take a step forward when an image filled her mind. There was a bed, surrounded by windows, but the room was dull and soulless despite them. The walls were grey – a *relentless* grey – and the curtains at the windows were as stained as the sheets. On the bed a dark and shapeless thing writhed. Was it even human?

Furiously she blinked, tried to clear the image from her mind. It was happening too soon. She hadn't even got through the doors of the asylum yet. But try as she might, the image – the vision – refused to abate. The figure, it *was* human; it had to be, but what was wrong with its limbs? Why was it so twisted?

A voice screamed in her head.

Don't call me 'it'! We're treated like vermin. But we're not! We're human.

"I'm sorry," Ruby's voice was loud too in response. "I didn't mean to."

You! You're no better than them!

"I am. I'm trying to help."

There was such cruel laughter.

You can't help. You're not qualified to help.

"Who are you? Tell me your name. I *can* help."

"Ruby, Ruby, what's happening?"

The voice, the image fled. Once again, Eclipse had

effectively broken the spell. She turned to him. "I made a connection, I don't know who with. The trouble is no one will identify themselves. The only names we have are from those documents you found, but it doesn't mean a thing, not really – there's so many in there, we couldn't remember everyone anyway. But if one person would tell me, just one, I could single them out; try to reach them further; persuade them to leave. But they won't let me – I'm not *qualified* to help, apparently."

"What does that mean?"

Ruby shook her head. "I don't know, not for sure. But in appealing to one, we appeal to the masses. That's the only way I can think of to deal with this."

To her relief, Eclipse didn't question further; he seemed to understand what she meant, even if she herself didn't, not fully. She'd dealt with troublesome spirits before, like the one in Gilmore Street, full of anger and despair; the one at Old Cross Cottage too and, of course, Highdown Hall, but in the main they were individual spirits. The building in front of her, that stood defiant in the face of its impending doom, contained hundreds. When the walls came down, where would they scatter?

Another image forced her to her knees. A child, dressed not in bright or comfortable clothing, but in some kind of dressing gown. The smell of the institution clung to him; it seeped from the image into the air around Ruby, filling her nostrils, so much she thought she might choke. The child rocked back and forth, spittle dribbling from his mouth. Ruby wiped at her mouth too as saliva had formed there. Another figure now came into view: a woman in a nurse's uniform. Ruby sensed a fondness in her for the child, a keenness to help. *At last*, she thought, *some light amidst the darkness!* A nurse, an angel, someone devoted to the cause, trying to help. She also sensed Eclipse wanting to know what was happening, but she held up a hand to stay him, not wanting this vision to be broken. *Tell me your name, please. Give me your name.* The child ignored her, ignored the nurse too, continuing to rock. He was another one declared 'feeble-minded'. A child locked within himself, whom no one could reach, not Ruby, and not the nurse. He'd constructed a silent world, the walls too high to scale. The image fading, Ruby cried out. She didn't want him to go, to be lost again. In his place, there were several children; in a nursery with cribs like cages, they were crying and reaching out, but there were no arms to pick them up; no one doting on them. No children now, there was a woman like the one in the Watkins' house, broken inside, life responsible for breaking her, and she being punished because of it. There were so many women, so many men. Image upon image flickered in her mind, like a black and white showreel gone crazy.

She felt hands on her, Eclipse was holding her shuddering body and she was grateful for it, grateful too that he remained silent. This process, this revelation, she had to endure it. So many wanted to show her how they'd suffered.

But I need a name!

There was another nurse, not kind or gentle like the first, she was a squat creature, brutish. Those on her ward were terrified of her temper, of displeasing her. There were doctors who strutted like gods and so many cowering before them. There was another dance – a song she recognised, *La Vie En Rose* – that ordinarily she loved, but not here, not in the confines of the asylum; ill-played notes serving only to capture the horror of the place rather than any sweet sentiment. A patient sang along. *Give your heart and soul to me, And life will always be, La Vie En Rose.*

I only want your name!

The singing patient opened his eyes to look at her, and in them she saw the tragedy of his lifetime; multiple losses, one after the other; all the dreams he'd had, that he'd nurtured, dashed against the rocks, to lie there broken and bloodied. Although it was hard to bear, she forced herself to keep staring.

What's your name?

The man began to recede as if invisible hands were drawing him backwards. In his place someone else materialised – another man, who, in contrast, came closer and closer until his face was immediately before Ruby's, his eyes boring into her.

They were soulless eyes, she thought, bracing herself for more horror. Although how could that be? Everybody had a soul. Still the thought persisted. *Who are you?* She asked the question, but this time she wasn't sure she wanted to know. Rather, she wanted him to fade away; disappear entirely. She was suddenly desperate for him to do just that, to leave her alone. She wanted nothing to do with him, nothing!

"Eclipse?" Her voice was small, reedy, as she groped blindly for him.

"I'm here, Ruby, I'm here."

Thank God, because she couldn't endure this alone. The man's eyes, there was such madness in them. Theo's words – *some people need to be here* – flashed neon in her mind. It was just too dangerous to allow them to roam free.

205

Don't you want to know my name?

What a bastard he was; he was teasing her. Vehemently she shook her head, causing him to laugh, to reveal blackened stumps for teeth.

Oh, you'll know it soon enough, Ruby. You'll know it soon enough.

Chapter Eighteen

"YOU did what? You went back to the asylum, with Eclipse? You told me you wouldn't go in there without the full back-up of your team; that you wouldn't *contemplate* it."

Cash was angry, and he had every right to be, but Ruby wished he would back off; be gentler with her. She was still reeling from what had happened the previous night; the fact that she hadn't even got as far as the entrance to the building before a tide of images consumed her – human stories – with a face finally appearing that didn't seem human at all; that belonged to a monster.

"It's just… Theo and Ness seem to be going through the mill lately, and you wanted to get on with your work—"

"Don't use that as an excuse! You *encouraged* me to get on with my work and I only did it so I could help you later in the week."

They were standing in the living room of his flat, surrounded by all his computers, displays and hubs, multi-coloured cables snaking everywhere. It was a world she found impossible to understand sometimes – ironically. It was late morning and she was tired, having hardly slept at all as the man in that final vision kept floating in front of her whenever she'd closed her eyes, just as vivid as he'd been outside the asylum. She must have dozed at some point, however, as the night passed quickly enough, and, knowing that Cash would be working from home today, she'd got up, and headed there, with Jed keeping as close to her as he'd done all through the night, and she drawing comfort from him. He'd disappeared now. As soon as Cash and Ruby had begun to raise their voices, he'd hightailed it back to some distant Elysium field.

"Look, Cash, I don't know what's wrong with you these past few days. You're not like the Cash I know."

"I don't like lies, that's all."

"I *wasn't* lying!"

"You weren't being honest either. And it's not the first time."

"The first time? Oh, you're not referring to Old Cross Cottage, are you?"

"You said we were going on holiday…"

"I've apologised a hundred times for that. More probably. Regarding last night, I *didn't* lie."

"Right, okay, so what would you call it, being *economical* with the truth, just like you were with the landlord at The Waterside Inn?"

"Okay, yeah. But for good reason, on both counts!"

"Ruby, if you were planning on going to that building, you should have said. *I* would have come with you, not Eclipse. He's no more bloody psychic than I am, but hey, if you prefer his company… Actually, there's no *if* about it, you clearly do."

Bewildered as well as angry, Ruby stringently denied it. "Of course I don't prefer his company. How can you even think that?"

Cash made a show at looking aghast. "Pretty damn

easily."

Unable to keep still, she started to pace the living room, kicking a few wires out of the way while she was at it. "It's like you don't trust me."

"I'm not sure I do."

She whirled round. "For God's sake, I'm not going to run everything I do by you! I know we're together, Cash, we're a couple, but we're also our own people. I have the right to make a decision about my business without consulting you. It's not as if you *ever* ask me my opinion about running your business."

"Because other than the basics you don't understand computers."

"And you clearly don't understand *my* business, despite giving a good impression that you do!"

She paced right up to him and they stood glaring at each other, barely an inch apart. It seemed like an eternity passed, although in reality it was probably moments. Her shoulders slumping, she felt deflated suddenly; opening her mouth again, not to shout, not this time, but to try and reach an understanding.

"Cash—"

"Perhaps we need a break."

She was stunned by his suggestion, temporarily rendered mute. As he continued to stare at her, his words sunk in, the meaning of them.

"You're not serious?" she said.

Breaking their locked gaze, he turned his head to one side slightly, as if unable to look at her anymore. "It's just, I'm feeling a bit… *I* need a break."

She reached out a hand and laid it on his arm. "Cash, can we stop with this Eclipse thing? I don't want him, I want *you*."

"This isn't just about Eclipse."

"So what else is it about?"

He backed away from her, an action that stung.

"Cash…" she tried again. There was no way he was being serious.

"I've got stuff on my mind at the moment, Ruby, and I need some time to think. I know you've got this case on, but I don't feel as if I'm involved in it anyway. And well… it's not as if I'm leaving you alone to deal with it; you've got your team."

And Eclipse.

The words hung in the air like lead.

A sob lodged in her throat, but she forced it back down. "Cash, tell me what's wrong, why you're saying all this. The *real* reason."

Cash shook his head. "Just leave it, Ruby. I want you to leave it."

"So, you're breaking up with me?"

"No! I want a few days, that's all!"

She was as vehement as him. "Cash, Eclipse is just a client!"

"Like I said, this isn't just about Eclipse. Give me some time and space. That's all I'm asking. *Please*, Ruby."

It was the plea in his voice that got to her more than anything – he was begging her, actually *begging* her. Taking a step back and then another, she fled the room.

* * *

Ness lived the closest to Cash, and so Ruby went there, desperate for a shoulder to cry on. Damn it, she was crying already, her head down as she hurried through the streets, barely able to see the pavement in front of her, her vision was so blurred. How was this possible? To be so happy one day, so full of hope for the future, and then to have one of those hopes wither and die? *I want a few days, that's all.* Why? Besides Eclipse, what other reason was there? And if he was the one lying, if it *was* solely about Eclipse, how come he was so quick to distrust her? She was *working* with the man for Christ's sake, not flirting with him. Not once had she flirted with him.

When Ness opened the door to her modest terraced house in the Malling area of Lewes, Ruby burst into proper tears. Alarmed, Ness stepped forward and embraced her in a hug. It felt awkward at first – she and Ness had never really hugged like this – but it also felt good. Ness was a good friend as well as a colleague; a *best* friend, despite any differences they may have had in the past. She'd done the right thing in coming here, for she knew Ness could provide the comfort she so desperately needed; could soothe the emotions which had built and built over the last week thanks to Brookbridge and the contact with her father, the anxiety and excitement of getting to meet him at last. It had been a layer cake of emotions, an onslaught at times; there was no other word for it, but all of it bearable, all of it… because she had Cash. The thought that she was in danger of losing him prompting a fresh tide of tears, Ness was quick to usher her inside. In the living room, she ordered her to sit on the sofa, offered a tissue and then asked what was wrong.

So many words came spilling out of Ruby's mouth, some of them coherent, some of them a garbled mess. Ness got the gist, though, she always did.

"Ruby, listen to what Cash said, he wants a few days that's all. Maybe it is Eclipse on his mind, or maybe there's something else. Whatever the reason, everyone needs a bit of space on occasion."

"It *is* Eclipse, Ness. He's jealous. Right from the start he's been jealous and there's no reason to be! It's all so... unfair. It feels like I'm in the dock being accused of something I'm not guilty of." Ness raised an eyebrow at this analogy and Ruby groaned. "Yeah, yeah," she continued, "it's the story of so many, I guess."

"With far worse consequences," Ness reminded her.

"I know, but the way he's behaving, it's odd."

"Ruby, Cash loves you, and you love him, it's as plain as day, but as much as we might want to, we can never know another person fully. There are aspects to everyone that remain private and rather than fear that, or rail against it, perhaps it's just easier to accept it. It's just not possible to understand someone all the time, what motivates them and their actions. The same applies to ourselves."

Ruby was so preoccupied with her own tumbling emotions that it took her a moment to register a slight hitch in Ness's voice as she uttered that last sentence; a glassiness to her eyes; a shadow that slid across her face, fleeting, but full of pain.

She reached across. "Ness, what's wrong?"

"Nothing. I'm fine."

She'd been brushed off already today and wasn't about to let it happen again. "Ness..." she said, her voice as authoritative as Theo's.

Ness seemed to fold in on herself. "It's this private case Theo and I are working on. We've told you before how gruelling it is."

"Aaron Hames? Yes, you have, although contrary to what you were saying, he *can* see inside your soul, but only the dark stuff. Because of that, you only visit him for short bursts at a time. What you didn't say is *why* you're visiting him."

"In short, it's a case study. We've been called in because it's hoped we can understand him, and in understanding, shed some light on how best to treat him." Ness leaned forward, her dark eyes earnest. "Hames is on drugs, the strongest they're able to give him, but even on those he has periods of startling lucidity. My recommendation and conclusion is that Ash Hill is not equipped to deal with him. I think he should be sent to a high security unit where treatment and observation can be continued in more rigid circumstances. After what happened recently, his team are in agreement."

"What happened recently?" Ruby asked, held spellbound by what she was saying.

Ness hesitated, but only briefly. Ruby sensed a need in her to talk; to lift the weight off her shoulders; to share the load. "A suicide. One of the staff."

"Because of Hames?"

"And what he could see; the taunting that followed; the digs, the bullying."

"Oh, Ness." Ruby exhaled. "That's terrible."

"It is. There's a great reluctance to work with him and you can understand why. It's hard… to be exposed like that." Tears sprang to Ness's eyes and Ruby was stunned, her own troubles temporarily shelved. She'd never seen Ness cry. "Theo's a good person; there isn't much he can grab on to, but with me… there's plenty."

"Ness, don't do it anymore, don't put yourself through

this."

"But there are people at risk," Ness replied, reaching for a tissue. "If I can help in any way to disarm Hames, I have to do it. Theo feels the same. They don't treat patients how they used to, you know. You can't just lock them up and throw away the key. The medical team are accountable for his wellbeing, for the measures they use. What I'm trying to say is, *someone* has to work with him."

"But not necessarily you. Not if it's too much."

"What you've faced at the asylum, the visions that fill your head, the *insights*, are they too much for *you*?"

Ruby's smile was a pained one. "You could say that. Last night, I didn't even get as far as the doorway. Pretty soon, I won't be able to set foot on the estate!"

"What?" Ness was as shocked as Cash had been. "You went last night?"

After explaining why she'd gone and what had happened, an overwhelming feeling of tiredness descended on Ruby, a tiredness reflected in Ness's eyes. "I'll have to go back though, and soon. All other cases and enquiries are on hold at the moment. I sorted that out this morning, before I went to see Cash. This has to take priority. I'm going to give it my best shot, Ness. If I fail, I fail. At least I'll know I've tried."

"That's all we can do, our best."

"It's what I've promised myself, promised Eclipse, and in my mind, it's what I've promised them, the lost souls."

"And it'll stand you in good stead, Ruby, that you're with them; that you're on their side; that you'll stand by them when so many didn't; that you have their best interests at heart, when others didn't care at all."

We're treated like vermin. But we're not! We're human.

That's what one spirit had declared – such anger, such *astonishment* accompanying those words, that anyone could treat another human that way.

"Hopefully one of them will realise it," Ruby replied, "even just one."

"*Save one, save the world*," Ness said, perhaps reading Ruby's mind, that sentiment being very much at the forefront of it – or perhaps it was a sign of how in tune they were with each other, especially in this moment. Ruby wasn't like Hames; she didn't know Ness's deepest darkest secrets – the woman was still an enigma in so many ways – but whatever those dark secrets were, there was enough good to balance, if not outweigh them. And that was enough for Ruby, more than enough.

She glanced at her watch. "Christ, look at the time, the day's slipping away. I need to crack on."

"Ruby," Ness's voice was firm, her gaze too, "you're going nowhere, not today. You can't go back to Cromer depleted; none of us can. You need to rest."

"Rest?" she queried, contemplating it. Rest meant returning home, to her flat, alone. As she bit down on her lip, Ness squeezed her hand.

"Stay here, in the spare room. Believe me, I could use the company too."

Chapter Nineteen

MUCH to Ruby's surprise, a very pleasant evening passed at Ness's house, with the older woman proving to be something of an accomplished cook. She rustled up not one course but three, Italian in theme, opened a bottle of red, and then another, both of them clearly in need of dulling the edges. They chatted and they laughed, many times. The conversation wasn't particularly deep; they'd done the deep stuff. It was more light-hearted than that, again something they both needed.

Ruby couldn't resist talking about Peter, mentioning both his son and daughter, and how she wasn't sure she was going to be able to take to them; that she got the impression they looked down on her and her profession. She was even able to laugh a little about it although at the time, it had actually irked her considerably.

"They sound like a pair of stuck-up arseholes."

Ness's remark caused Ruby to almost splutter her wine everywhere – 'arseholes' not a word she'd ever envisaged leaving Ness's mouth. After being so distraught, she went to bed feeling upbeat. Not just that, surprisingly hopeful. When she checked her phone, however, there was no message from Cash declaring that he'd been an arsehole too. Before she could well up again, she climbed into bed in the somewhat sparsely furnished bedroom and practically forced herself into a deep sleep, not waking until eight the next morning to the smell of sizzling bacon in the air.

When she entered the kitchen, Ness was starting to dish up. She had coffee on the go as well, and several rounds of toast that were dripping butter. Beside the table, Jed stared eagerly upwards, his tail wagging. Ness didn't acknowledge him when she brought the plates to the table, but she did neatly swerve sideways, suggesting she knew he was there all right. Of them all, only Ruby could see him clearly; her mother could too, and on a few occasions, Theo.

"I'd better not stay here too often," remarked Ruby, sitting on the chair she'd occupied the previous night. "I'd be the size of a house the way you feed me."

Ness groaned. "Oh, Ruby, my head! It's been a long time since I've drunk that much, I can tell you. A good fry-up should put us right, though. We need to eat well and sleep well this week if we're going to be dealing with Cromer and its residents."

"I couldn't agree more," Ruby said, picking up her knife and fork. She'd stopped herself from checking her phone this morning, although she was itching to, because somehow she didn't want anything to burst this bubble she was in with Ness, it would pop soon enough, when both of them started tackling the outside world again and all who occupied it; but right now, being here, it was like being in hiding; protected almost. Actually, there was no *almost* about it. She felt safe with Ness, loved.

"You would have made a good mum," Ruby said, in between mouthfuls. At once her hand flew to her mouth. What on earth had possessed her to say that?

Rather than take offence, Ness smiled – albeit

tentatively. "Thank you, Ruby, that's very kind. And before you ask why I didn't have children, it's because I've never met the right person." She paused. "Don't get me wrong, I'm not a nun. I'm a normal woman with needs. I have a male friend I see on occasion, but there's an understanding between us to only take things so far. I'm just... happier on my own."

"Happier," Ruby questioned, "or is it easier?"

Ness swallowed, averting her gaze slightly, looking at the spot where Jed was still sitting, ever hopeful of a crumb. "Perhaps it's easier. I answer to no one."

Her latter point resonated.

"Ruby, Cash is good for you. You're good for him. You'll work this out."

"It's not easy on partners, is it, what we do?"

"Cash is enthusiastic about your profession."

Not as much as Eclipse, thought Ruby.

Ness frowned. "Are you sure you don't have feelings for Eclipse?"

"No, Ness, I don't."

"It's just—"

"I know, you read what's on my mind," finished Ruby. "I admire Eclipse's passion, that's all. He feels the same way I do. If there was no Cash then perhaps it might be different. But," she had to pause and take a deep breath before continuing, "I'm a one man woman. It's Cash I want. I hope you're right, I hope we can work this out."

With breakfast over, it was time to make plans. Ness and Theo had another session with Hames this afternoon, something they couldn't cancel, as other professional bodies would be present observing whilst they interviewed him, and so the arrangement had to be honoured. Ruby understood that and wouldn't dream of objecting. "We've got tomorrow and Thursday, although Thursday's cutting it fine."

"Unless you can get a stay of execution?"

Ruby frowned. "How would I do that?"

"Peter again, if he's willing to phone Rob Lock and plead our case. I could try my police contact, Lee, but I know how stretched he is at the moment; he's got a lot on his plate. I don't want to keep asking favours, putting him under more pressure."

"Fair enough, Ness. Something to keep in mind though is what Cash said. We might blow it if Lock knew our intended purpose. He might forbid us to go anywhere near the site, not least because of Health and Safety reasons."

"Heath and Safety?" Ness queried, one eyebrow raised. "Those dilapidated warning boards really show how much he cares about that."

"Yeah, but rules are rules. I'll tell you what, I'll go back to the office, sort out a bit more admin – there's always loads to be done; get my house in order so to speak, then I'll phone Dad and see what he thinks." She smiled as she said this, couldn't help herself. What a novelty it was to be even talking about her father. It went some way to softening the confusion and distress she felt regarding Cash. "I'll phone Theo, Corinna and Eclipse too, set a date to go to Brookbridge tomorrow at dusk. Is that okay?"

Ness nodded. "Rest in between, though. Conserve your energy. If we can't get an extension, than we need to make the most of the time we've got. Those names you got from the patient notes, have you memorised them?"

"Most of them, erm… there's Agnes Jones, Doreen Hughes, Mary Wilson, Ronald Brown, Stephen Evans,

Annie Gibb. Oh, and Rebecca Nash, of course."

"She's the psychic?"

"Uh huh."

"That's good. If we can go in there, if we can *personalise* our approach, we may get a result. You never know, one of them might still be in residence."

"I'll also access the online archives for the asylum, gather as many as possible."

"A whole litany of them."

"A whole litany," Ruby repeated.

"Take care, Ruby."

"You too, Ness. I hope today's not too taxing for you."

Even as she said it, she knew it would be nothing less than that.

* * *

Without Ness to bolster her, Ruby could feel the misery of yesterday kicking in again. Alone in her office – even Jed was busy elsewhere – she did as she said she would and kept herself busy. Having phoned Theo and Corinna, both of them more than willing to join her on Wednesday evening, she also phoned Eclipse, who offered to come and help collate names of Cromer's former patients. Although it'd be nice to have some help, she turned him down, just on the off chance that Cash might have a change of heart and come bursting into her office, a bunch of red roses in hand. She swallowed. Chance would be a fine thing. It wasn't until later in the day that she called Peter, her nerves still jangling at the prospect – when would that begin to ease?

"Hi, Peter," she said. They hadn't discussed properly

the use of 'Dad' and she didn't dare push her luck. "How are you?"

"Ruby?" He sounded surprised to hear from her – surprised and a little… nervous. "I was going to call you."

"You were? Wow, that's great, it's always lovely to hear from you. Was it about something in particular?"

"Erm… y…you go first. I insist."

Why was he stammering? He didn't normally stammer. Not as far as she knew.

"Oh it's something and nothing. Well, I hope it errs on the 'something' actually, and it's only if you've got time of course, if you're willing. If you're not…" She stopped, took a deep breath, mentally admonishing herself for babbling. "As well as to say hello, Brookbridge was the reason I was phoning again, just on the off chance really, and whether you could use your influence again. We might be able to do what we have to in the time we've got, but it's tight. If you could get us a few more days, a week perhaps…" Even as the words left her mouth, she was embarrassed. This was too much. How could she possibly expect him to phone a land developer, tell him one of his buildings was severely haunted and that demolishing it would cause the spirits grounded there further distress? But, hey, not to worry. He knew a team of psychics who were sneaking around, doing their utmost to move them into the light where they'd find peace and comfort at last. But in order to do this, or at least to enable them to give it their best shot, could they possibly interrupt their building schedule and delay razing it to the ground? Yep, it sounded mad, wholly mad. What must her father think of her? "Peter?" she said hesitantly, meaning to apologise for such a cheeky request. They had to work with what time they had left and that was all there was to it. An extension due to spiritual unrest was not on the cards.

There was a brief moment of silence, in which Ruby hung her head. Could her life in this moment get any worse? She'd alienated Cash, although unwittingly, and now she risked doing the same with her newly found father. "Look, sorry, forget I asked," she continued. "Honestly, it's fine. You've done enough for us already and I'm grateful. We're supposed to be getting to know each other, father and daughter, and here I am setting you to work. It's really wrong of me."

"Ruby…" His voice was barely above a whisper.

Ruby frowned. Had she really pissed him off? "Yes?"

"I said I was going to call you, didn't I?"

"That's right. Is everything okay?"

"Okay?" Again, his voice was barely audible. "Ruby, where are you, at work?"

"I'm in my office."

"Is Cash with you?"

"Cash? No, he's… erm… at work too."

"You're on your own?"

To the side of her, Jed appeared, not occupying his usual spot in front of the heater but standing and looking at her, his head to one side, his dark eyes sad for some reason; something else in them too. Concern? Fear crawled up her spine, a many-legged spider.

"Peter, is there something wrong?"

There was another brief moment of silence and then he started to speak, slowly, deliberately, as if he wanted each word to sink in, to compute. "Kirsty and John were understandably concerned when I told them you'd got in touch; that you claimed to be my daughter."

Claimed? Ruby couldn't help it, she baulked at the word.

"When you came to visit, they wanted to be here." He laughed but Ruby detected no humour in it. "They really are terrible those two. They seem to think I need looking after now I'm on my own. I don't. I'm perfectly capable of looking after myself, but that's kids for you. I've told you, we're very close."

Yes he had, but this time it felt like rubbing salt into a wound.

"Ruby, I like you. I meant that when I said it. You're a nice kid, a fascinating kid. What you do, I'm genuinely impressed. I never used to believe so much in all that spooky stuff, but talking to you, you made it seem so real. I like you. I hoped…"

Ruby gulped. "You hoped? Hoped what?"

She heard him exhale. When he spoke again, there was a tremor in his voice. "As you know, Kirsty's a doctor. From the cutlery you used, the cups you drank out of, she took a sample – a DNA sample. We fast-tracked the result and it came back a couple of hours ago."

Ruby felt as though she'd gone into free fall. "A sample?"

"Yes. I'm sorry."

"You mean asking me over; your children being there and them being so helpful during dinner; not allowing Cash and I to even leave the table – it was all a set-up?"

"No," he denied, "not originally. It was a genuine offer and I did want to get to know you more, but Kirsty—"

"Kirsty had other ideas?"

"As I said, she was looking out for me. You have to understand that."

Understand? "What was the result?"

There was silence again, a maddening silence. Jed had come closer, laid his ethereal head on her knee, his whole body tense. Glancing at the dog, she knew what Peter was about to say, but still she had to hear it.

"Peter?" She screwed her eyes shut, held her breath.

"I truly am sorry, Ruby, but we're not a match. I'm not your father."

Chapter Twenty

RUBY threw the receiver from her. Quickly locating her keys, she grabbed them and ran out of the office, flying down three flights of stairs and out on to the street. Her Ford was parked a few metres away and she ran to it and climbed in, finding Jed already in the passenger seat. For a minute she could do nothing but sit and catch her breath, her hands shaking too much for her to insert the key into the ignition.

A set-up, I walked blindly into a set-up!
He's not my father.
Who *is my father?*
He said he was sorry, truly sorry.
Why *isn't he my father?*

So many thoughts tumbled into her mind, each one vying for attention as much as the visions she'd experienced at the asylum ever had. Finally managing to fire the engine, she pulled out of the parking space when a horn blast startled her – she'd driven straight into the path of an oncoming car. Accompanying the blast with a rude gesture, the other driver finally manoeuvred round her, whilst Ruby gripped the steering wheel, choking back a flood of tears. Beside her, Jed was agitated, shifting his weight from side to side, but she couldn't take his emotions on board as well as her own, not at the moment, although she did whisper 'sorry' as she advanced further into the road.

Hastings – that was her destination – and the house in the Old Town where she'd grown up with her mother and grandmother, but no father. Not then and not now. Not ever it seemed. Why had her mother lied to her? Or had she? Did her mother really not know who the father of her child was? Ruby knew about Jessica's history – that she was wild in her youth and had had a succession of lovers, but how many for God's sake? That DNA test, what if it was wrong? Was a saliva sample really that conclusive? Didn't you need a blood sample or a cheek swab to be one hundred per cent sure? What if Kirsty had tampered with the results, not wanting the competition of another daughter? It was possible. *Anything* was possible. Her life was crumbling, just as the asylum would soon crumble, and she, like the spirits, thrown into utter turmoil.

The journey passed in a blur, Ruby keeping her foot on the accelerator, eating up the miles. Entering the Old Town, she abandoned her car as soon as she was able to. As she and Jed hurried through the streets to Lazuli Cottage, seagulls circled overhead, people milled about, oblivious to the world collapsing around one person. Many were smiling, at each other, and at her, people were so friendly in the Old Town. For residents and visitors alike, the place had such a happy atmosphere, but today all happiness and colour had been sucked from the world.

The cottage in sight, she picked up pace, and hastened along the pathway with its flagstones and weeds, then banged on the door, demanding entrance.

It was Jessica who answered. "Oh, Ruby, it's you. Haven't you got your key?"

She stood aside as Ruby pushed past her and headed straight into the kitchen. Sarah was sitting at the table, no such look of confusion in her eyes; there was resignation instead, and weariness. Seeing this, Ruby tried to rein herself in, but when Jessica followed her into the supposed 'heart of the home', words came tumbling out of her mouth in what seemed like the fiercest of accusations.

"Mum, Peter is *not* my father. Why did you tell me he was?"

For a moment, Jessica just stared at her – her mouth slightly open. It took her a moment to gather the wherewithal to speak. "I don't know what you're talking about, Ruby. He *is* your father."

"Ruby, why don't you sit down?" Sarah suggested, even though she'd begun to rise from the table, both hands holding onto it for support.

"No, I... Mum, what's going on? Was it all just a lie?"

Still Jessica denied it, shaking her head vehemently. "*He's* the liar if he's saying otherwise."

"His daughter's a doctor," Ruby explained. "She was there when I went to visit at the weekend. She took a sample of my DNA from a cup or cutlery or something, I don't know how she did it, she's the doctor not me, and with Peter's contacts, well, the upshot is we're not a match."

"Why would she do that?" Jessica asked, her eyes huge with disbelief.

"Because she was concerned obviously," Ruby's voice had started to rise, "suspicious of this girl who'd come calling, insisting Peter was her father too." Her eyes started to sting and she had to turn away slightly, take a deep breath before carrying on. "When I met Peter, I expected to see some sort of likeness between us, but there was nothing. And then I thought, it doesn't matter; a child can take after only one parent, and, Mum, you and I look quite alike. I've even known people who don't look like their parents at all, so who cared if there was no resemblance? I know… I know he left you, Mum, but he seems like a nice enough guy now; someone I could build a relationship with. I liked him and he said he liked me. And then I met his children, Kirsty and John, and they were nothing like me either; they're much taller, Kirsty's got red hair and they've both got blue eyes. They're nothing like me at all!" As she said it, she realised again that none of this had anything to do with looks; it was something more intrinsic that had been missing. She hadn't belonged in that family, and on a deeper level, Kirsty knew it every bit as much as Ruby did. Swinging round to face Jessica again, tears having broken rank and pouring down her face, Ruby couldn't help but ask. "Just how many lovers *did* you have at any one time?"

The years had fallen away from Jessica; she looked like a young kid, startled, as her past was being dragged up and put on trial when really it should have been left. But this was *her* past too, Ruby's. "Mum!" she cried. "Tell me!"

"I… erm… It was him, I'm sure it was." Her mother had tears in her eyes too, but more than that, worse than that, there was panic. "It *had* to be him!"

Ruby's skin grew cold. "What do you mean, it had to be? Who else was on the scene? Who didn't you want it to be?"

Jessica's hand came up to her brow. "It was all such a long time ago."

"That's as maybe," Ruby protested. "But some things,

surely, you don't forget."

"I've told you, I was a different person back then!"

"Even so, what you did, it affected me. If you didn't know for sure, you should never have said anything. I've made such a fool of myself."

Jessica extended her arm but Ruby avoided her touch. Retracting her hand, she hugged herself instead in a nervous gesture. "No, darling, you haven't. I've always said that the three of us were enough for each other, haven't I? But you were so determined, Ruby. Sometimes you're like a force of nature, you won't be stopped."

"But we *weren't* enough for each other!" Ruby retaliated. "You need to make your mind up, because you've said that as well. From when I was seven years old, you weren't there for me; you were locked inside yourself, unreachable. If it weren't for Gran..." She stopped herself just in time, but the intimation was clear. *If it weren't for Gran, you'd have been locked up.* "Maybe it's because I couldn't have *you* that I wanted him so much; one of my parents at least. But you fobbed me off; plucked a name out of nowhere."

Jessica shook her head. "At that time, Peter was my boyfriend, I adored him!"

"Okay, okay, so he was your boyfriend, but he wasn't your only lover, was he? There was someone else, someone you don't want to remember. Why don't you? What was wrong with him? I need to know, who the hell is my father?"

"Ruby!" It was Sarah, her voice little more than a hiss. "Will you sit down!"

As her gaze shifted towards Sarah, Ruby noticed she wasn't just holding on to the table, she was gripping it, her fingers having turned white with the pressure. Her face too was contorted. No longer the gentle, soft-skinned grandmother she remembered, she looked like a stranger. "Gran?" she whispered.

"Just sit, and you too, Jessica. I knew this day would come. I've waited for it. So many years I've waited. God knows all I ever wanted was to keep you safe, both of you. You were in danger, you especially, Ruby, and I wanted to protect you – it's a mother's instinct and it's a grandmother's instinct too."

Feeling her knees buckle, Ruby sank on to a chair. So did Jessica, a tremor in her as Sarah's words sank in. "Mum," she said, "what do you mean? What did you do?"

Back in her seat too, Sarah turned to Jessica. "Tell Ruby," she instructed.

"Tell her what?"

"*The truth!*" Sarah yelled, startling Jessica further. "And tell me too while you're at it, because I've never asked for the full story. Before now, I didn't dare."

Jessica swallowed. "I... Mum, you know what I was like when I was younger – my beliefs."

"I know *full well* what you were like." There was so much disdain in Sarah's voice. "You thought yourself superior to everything and everyone; not bound by society or convention. You could do whatever you liked, when you liked. Arrogant. So damned arrogant! You talk of Ruby being a force of nature, but, Jessica, there was none more so than you."

A silence ensued – *the calm before the storm,* thought Ruby, fearing what she was going to hear and yet knowing she had no choice but to sit and listen. She'd travelled too far down this road of discovery to turn back now. As her heart thumped in her chest, Jed materialised in the doorway of the kitchen, staring at her with such a solemn expression but keeping his distance. This was between the three of them, daughter, mother and grandmother – a family affair. Ruby wished she could turn back the hands of time; revert to an age of innocence and blissful ignorance. She'd been like that once, but so long ago it seemed practically another lifetime. But whatever her abilities were, rolling back the years wasn't one of them.

Jessica took a deep breath, then without glancing at Ruby or Sarah, but at the wall behind them, she began to speak. "I didn't buy into commitment, it's as simple as that." To Ruby she said, "I didn't know my father either, but despite that, Mum brought me up to be a strong and confident person, just as she did with you, and I *was* confident, in my looks and in my personality. The gift I'd inherited fascinated me rather than making me afraid." She hung her head to stare at her clenched hands. "Mum did a good job, a really good job. She was always so positive, but in me that confidence turned into something else, maybe arrogance, as she's already pointed out. Maybe it's a trait I inherited from my absent father, or maybe it's peculiar to me."

"*Your father was a good man!*" Sarah spat the words at her. "I've told you that, over and over, and at least *I* was telling the truth. He was an older man, quite a bit older, but he wasn't married; he was single, an academic in the city. He loved me, but I didn't love him, and therein lay the problem. He would have married me, but it would never have worked out between us. What little he knew of my gift horrified him and so I always kept quiet about it. You can only do that for so long. I ended our relationship, left London and came to Hastings, and that's when I discovered I was pregnant. Despite the difficulties of being a single mother in those days, I was thrilled. I also had money, Rosamund's money. The world's a different place when you're not destitute, I could buy this cottage and support us both. I did write and tell him about you, but the letter was returned. He'd moved away without leaving a forwarding address, why, I don't know. I tried to trace him, but it was no use and soon I was preoccupied with a tiny baby to look after. You knew his name, Jessica – Edward Middleton – but you never wanted to know more." She looked at Ruby then, such a depth of sadness in her faded eyes. "It was only you who wanted to know more. You didn't want to discuss finding your father with me for fear of upsetting me, but in so many ways Jessica is like an open book, so I knew something of it anyway. Believe me, I hoped and I prayed that Peter Gregory would accept you as his daughter. He's a policeman though, so I should have known better. Any policeman worth his salt wouldn't accept a situation at face value, he'd dig deeper."

Although Sarah had asked Jessica to confess, she was the one who seemed hell bent on revelation. Edward Middleton – Ruby had the name of her grandfather at least, but still no clue as to the man who'd spawned her.

"Ruby, I'm so sorry." Whatever fire had been in Sarah had snuffed itself out. She looked... Ruby tried to find the right word to describe it... *defeated*.

Immediately, Ruby reached out. "Gran, I didn't mean to upset you. You did a fantastic job of raising me too. You're our rock. We always say that. Without you... we'd be lost."

Sarah shook her head, her expression deeply troubled.

"Ruby, you can't afford to lose yourself, nor you, Jessica, you must not succumb again."

Jessica grabbed Sarah's hand. "I won't. I promise."

"You must stand by Ruby, as I've stood by you."

"Of course, Mum. We all stand together." Letting Sarah go, Jessica turned to Ruby. "I *liked* men, that's not a crime, although so many thought it was back then. It's normal and it's natural. Gran is right, I did buck convention and because of it, I met… *unconventional* men. Your fath… Peter Gregory was the exception rather than the norm." At this she paused and laughed briefly, a far from happy sound. "It fascinated me how down-to-earth he was; how preoccupied with material matters. There was nothing in the least bit spiritual about him. At first, being with him was a bit of an experiment – I told him nothing about what I could see or sense. We were just a normal couple, or as much as we could be considering he was already married. But you see, here's the thing; his wife was ill, she had multiple sclerosis and was declining fast. He was a good husband to her, but he was also human; he needed a break from being a carer as well as working in a job that demanded such a lot from him, and that's what I offered – something light, something frivolous. But things changed. For me, anyway. Yes our relationship was illicit, but he loved his wife. It was so obvious. It was in his eyes, in his voice, and in the way he talked about her. He loved her so much, despite being with me, and yet he *was* with me – for a short while anyway. And I wanted what she had – for someone to love me that much. With him I *craved* commitment. But, of course, it wasn't to be."

"His wife had MS?" Ruby gasped. "He never said." But then why should he? To Peter Gregory, Laura wasn't an illness; she was his wife, his *beloved* wife. Remembering the photos she'd seen of her in the conservatory, they were all headshots. If Laura had been in a wheelchair, he hadn't focused on that, just on her face; her lovely face. It was little wonder his children were so protective of him. It also explained why he'd remained at the rank of constable and took early retirement. He'd given up his integrity with Jessica, but for Laura, he'd sacrificed his career.

"Mum, did you get pregnant deliberately?"

"No. But when I found out, I hoped, I prayed he'd leave his wife for me. That's how selfish I was. I *begged* him to leave her."

"You begged him because you were desperate," there was anger in Sarah's voice again. "Because you didn't want to consider the alternative."

"Mum," Jessica implored, "*how* do you even know about the alternative?"

Sarah refused to answer that question. "Just tell us, Jessica, about the other one."

There was silence again. Was Jessica going to refuse?

"Mum," Ruby said, a desperation in her too. "Who was he?"

"A one-night stand," she confessed at last, "that's all he was, nothing more. Because Peter was married, because his wife was ill, I couldn't see him as much as I wanted to. Some nights I'd be fine with that, but other nights, well... I'd get angry. One of those times, I went out, not here, not in Hastings, I caught a train to Brighton, where no one knew who Jessica Davis was; where I could find someone to take my mind off the man I couldn't be with." She paused. "The trouble is, when you're on the hunt, you find others that are hunting too." Tears burst from her eyes and raced down her cheeks. "I honestly didn't think about any repercussions, I just wanted to… take my mind off Peter. I was so young and… I loved him, I really did love him."

Sarah was quietly weeping too, but Ruby was seized by shock – half of her thinking this was a terrible dream, borne of anxiety; that'd she'd wake up and it'd all be fine, just as it was a couple of days ago. Cash would be lying beside her and he'd chase away her fears, laugh at them even. "What was wrong with this man, Mum?"

Jessica sniffed, wiped her nose roughly with the back of her hand, managing after a while to continue. "As we started to talk, it became obvious he was interested in occult matters, as was I, *deeply* interested. I told him about me, that I could see spirits and he was fascinated. He kept questioning me about it, asking the strangest questions. He was also plying me with drink. Despite my growing unease, I was flattered by his interest, stupid, stupid girl that I was. He wasn't a bad looking man, Ruby. He had an air about him, a charisma. Pretty soon I was drunk. We left the bar and ended up at his place, a tiny little flat in a back street that reeked of cigarettes. I'm not going to go into details, you wouldn't want me to, but suffice to say as soon as I was sure he was asleep, I grabbed my clothes and fled, then waited at Brighton train station until the trains began running again to Hastings. It was just one night, whereas I'd had so many nights with Peter. I wasn't lying when I said Peter Gregory was your father, I honestly thought it likely that he was, I hoped, I prayed…"

"But he's not," Ruby said, not needing the proof of any scientific results to know that, feeling it in her bones. "This other man is… this *weirdo*."

There was a pause, then Ruby had to ask; she had to

know. "What was his name? Did you even bother to ask?"

"Ruby, of course I did!"

"And?"

"It was Aaron."

"Aaron?" Ruby quizzed.

"That's right, Aaron Hames."

Chapter Twenty-One

AT first Ruby thought she was dreaming again, getting everything terribly mixed up, so, so confused. And then the dream slipped away and in its place was a light, but not the light she was used to – warm and comforting, with the promise of peace in it. This was a harsh light, glaring; the light of truth, she supposed – *unwanted* truth.

She jumped to her feet and as she did, the chair behind her went crashing to the floor, causing Jed to bark furiously, desperate for her attention. But his efforts were in vain. She had one thing on her mind and one thing only.

"But Aaron Hames is insane!"

Jessica scrambled to her feet too. "Ruby, what are you talking about? How do you know he's insane? How do you even know who he is?"

"Because Theo and Ness are working with him at Cromer, that's why. There's still a building there, not as high profile as Rampton or Broadmoor, but it's a secure unit for those who suffer from extreme mental illness; who've committed criminal acts, who've harmed people." The suicide, oh shit, the suicide, the one Ness had told her about, the staff member that he'd *driven* to suicide. There must have been others prior to that. How many?

"It can't be the same man!" Jessica continued to stare,

disbelief written all over her face. "He… he was odd, granted; he made me feel uneasy, but he wasn't insane! Do you think I'd have gone anywhere near him if he was? It can't be him. It can't be!"

"Aaron Hames *is* insane."

Sarah's words stopped Jessica in her tracks and caused Ruby's heart to plummet further. Both turned to look at her. She'd remained sitting, her shoulders sagging, defeat once again overriding anger. Her words came to mind; words uttered just a few minutes before. *'God knows all I ever wanted was to keep you safe, both of you. You were in danger, you especially, Ruby, and I wanted to protect you.'*

Sarah caught Ruby's gaze. "I did what I had to do. Always remember that."

Jessica darted forwards, pulling out the chair beside Sarah and throwing herself on to it. "What did you do to him?" Once more she grabbed her mother's hands, but this time with a strength that made Sarah wince. "*When* did you do it? How? I never told him where I lived, I let him think I was on a day trip down from London." Her voice rose to a crescendo. "Mum, what did you do?"

"Just let her speak." Although able to move her mouth, Ruby couldn't move her feet; they'd become rooted to the spot. No longer in the doorway, Jed had moved forwards to stand by her, whining occasionally and yelping, as if he didn't want to listen, as if advising her not to. But it was too late for that. "Gran?"

"Jessica, Hames found out where you lived after that incident with Saul. When you conjured whatever that thing was, Saul fled, remember? He ran through the streets of St Leonards and Hastings near naked, howling, crying, and hurling rocks at windows and cars, smashing everything in sight. Finally, the police apprehended him. They came, and got him and took him to the cells. It was your name he kept saying, over and over again – Jessica Davis. Your reaction was a little different to his. When you first came home you were wild, you were screaming at me, trying to tell me what you'd done, terrified that what you'd conjured had followed you; marked you." Sarah glanced at Ruby but didn't point out what had happened instead; that it *had* followed her home, but had marked seven-year old Ruby rather than Jessica herself. "You screamed and you shouted but then suddenly you calmed down, and that was even more frightening somehow. You slumped in that chair in the living room, and you just stared and stared, your eyes glazing over. I tried to talk to you, tried to reason with you, but you wouldn't say a word; wouldn't even look at me. You'd begun to retreat, deep inside yourself, hiding from what you'd seen. I couldn't reach you; your *child* couldn't reach you. You'd locked yourself in a prison of your own making. Of course the newspapers reported Saul's story. They had a field day with it, part horrified, part amused, exploiting the whole *Satanist* aspect of it. There was nothing I could do to keep your name from being printed too; it was as much as I could do to persuade doctors I was able to nurse you at home, that I was more than capable; but that's how Hames found you, because he read the papers; that's how he tracked you down." She paused, closing her eyes briefly in anguish. "Whatever happened between you that night, Jessica, clearly he never forgot you, or rather what you discussed, what you told him, about you, and about the occult. And those articles in the paper, they just whetted his appetite further. The first time he knocked on our door, I was busy tending to you. It was Ruby who opened it. He saw her and he *knew*. After that, he kept calling, wouldn't leave us alone. He wanted access to his child. I denied it, I said Ruby wasn't his, but he wouldn't be deterred."

"*I* opened the door to him?" Ruby was further amazed. "I don't remember."

"It was only the once, and of course you don't remember, why would you?"

"I…" She'd opened the door to her father, of all she was hearing, that fact stood out. He'd found her – the hunter. She steeled herself further. "Do I look like him?"

Sarah held her gaze. "A little, but what's inside you is *nothing* like him."

What was inside her? How could she be so sure? As Ness had pointed out, no one ever knew what was truly inside someone. People could surprise you – even those you trusted implicitly – Cash for example. With him she'd never have thought… She shook her head. How could this be happening? How?

"Mum said he wasn't insane when she met him, but you're so *sure* that he is. What did you do to him, Gran, this persistent caller; how did you keep us safe?"

"Ruby," Sarah's voice was shaking slightly as she pulled her hands back from Jessica and lifted one towards her throat to rub at the skin there. "I couldn't let him anywhere near you. It wasn't Jessica he was interested in, not when he realised you existed. He did the maths, put two and two together; if Jessica was psychic, if she'd told him in her drunkenness that it was a matriarchal gift, then it followed you were psychic too." She hung her head. "What an unexpected prize you were! An innocent he could manipulate, that he could corrupt." Lifting her head and looking at Ruby, she continued. "I know when a soul is twisted; when a man revels in being that way; when he doesn't want to turn back on the road to redemption; when all he wants is to venture further. Hames was an ambitious man, he wasn't going to go away. I had to shadow you everywhere you went – be at the school gates at least fifteen minutes early; inform the teachers that there were ' father issues' and to never let you go home with anyone but me. I couldn't even let you go to your friends' houses for tea in case he was watching and tried to get to you that way. The last time he came to the house you were in bed and your mother was asleep too. The threats were getting worse. He meant to snatch you; it was just a matter of time. I had to pit my wits against his. I tried to slam the door on him, but his foot was in the way. He pushed his way into my house, defiled it with his presence. He went upstairs to where you lay sleeping; despite my begging and my pleading, he pushed open the door and once again you were marked, Ruby. He stood there and he marked you. And then he laughed, a sound that still haunts me, and in my mind's eye I saw it: what he planned to do. You're psychic, although I told him so many times you weren't, and I think he had abilities too – primitive and underdeveloped abilities, to his eternal frustration. He would use your gift to blacken his soul further; he'd disappear with you and once gone, we'd never be able to find you, not alive anyway. Like a leech, he'd suck you dry. After he left, I was panic-stricken. Bolting the door, I formed a plan of my own. Upstairs, in my bureau, I retrieved my mother's work, her darkest work."

Again she paused while Ruby, Jessica and even Jed gazed at her open-mouthed.

"I've destroyed those papers since, so don't think you'll ever be able to find them. But I was grateful for them then. Even now, I'm *grateful*. I don't regret what I did. I'm not going to go into details either, but considering what you've both experienced in the past, I think you'll get the gist well enough. I pictured him walking away, and in his wake I sent as many negative entities as I could muster – those that languish in the 'dumping grounds' as Rosamund called them, but which are always there, just beyond the veil, waiting for someone to summon them; to make sense of them; to set them to work. And that's the thing – they're not hard to conjure, these demons for want of a better word; they're always alert; always so eager to wreak havoc. I sent them after him and I ordered them to addle his mind – to confuse and bewilder him; basically to consume him. I *fed* Aaron Hames to them. I never knew what damage they'd wrought, but he didn't come calling again. If the man Theo and Ness are dealing with is indeed him, then clearly it was considerable."

"I can't believe…" It was Jessica, her hand also at her throat.

In contrast, Ruby *could* believe it. It was all making such terrible sense.

"I'm sorry," Sarah continued, looking at Ruby rather than Jessica. "Everything I've done, everything I've said to you, about embracing the light and rejecting the darkness – encouraging the good wolf within you, starving the bad wolf – it wasn't because I ever feared you were anything like Hames; I didn't. You come from a long line of female psychics; you carry the strength of all of us in your soul. You shine, Ruby, brighter than anyone I've ever known. All this man ever did was plant a seed, but your heritage, your *true* heritage is what counts; the Davis bloodline."

Jessica was still aghast. "You conjured demons too? You did exactly what *I* did."

Sarah denied it. "Not exactly, there was good intent at the root of my conjuring."

"Good intent and demons don't belong in the same sentence!" Jessica's shrill voice made both Sarah and Ruby flinch. "I felt so guilty because of what I did and how it ruined us as a family; for so long it ruined us, and sometimes, when you thought I was looking beyond you, I wasn't, I was looking *at* you, I could see what a disappointment I was, your wayward child. And yet you were capable of the same thing. Rosamund too if she wrote about it. We've all played with fire!"

Ruby didn't know if it was shock making her mother say these things, but it wasn't fair. Sarah had explained why she'd done it; why she'd sent a man insane. It was because she believed he was a danger to her grandchild, a very real danger.

"Mum…" she began, but Jessica had shot to her feet and was towering over Sarah. Beside her, Jed had started to growl, his head lowered.

"You're no better than me, you and Rosamund, but I suffered because of what I did, whereas you perhaps didn't. You think it's easy to conjure demons? It isn't. It takes time, it takes effort, and it takes dedication. And it should never, ever, be done. You could have gone to the police, got their help; but no, you used evil to fight evil. It's the *worst* thing you can do, tear back the veil and let demons come flooding through. Once opened, it'll never shut again. Not fully. And what you've unleashed, one day, when it's fed enough, it'll return to sender. Then what?

243

How are we going to handle it? Oh God, Mum, why didn't you just do what normal people do and call the police!"

Sarah tried to stand, to reach out to a distraught Jessica. "Darling, I was just so scared. You said he had a certain something about him; that he was charismatic. I agree. He was. What if he sweet-talked the police; made me look as though *I* was the one that was a danger to you. As her father, he'd have had rights."

"*If* he was her father!" Jessica screamed.

At last Sarah was on her feet. "He was! But more than that, he *believed* he was."

"But you still shouldn't have done it! All that preaching about the light – that there's no such thing as evil, that demons don't exist – you drummed it into us, into Ruby especially, day in day out, and then you went and did *this*? You bloody hypocrite!"

Ruby had heard enough. Able to move at last, she too darted forwards, intent on drawing her mother back; of putting some space between the two women, but as she did her attention shifted. Sarah's hand was raised, not clutching at her throat this time, but at her chest, all colour steadily draining from her face. *No,* thought Ruby, staring at her, *no, no, no.* Gran suffered with her heart, having collapsed nearly two years ago; surely she wasn't going to collapse again.

Jessica must have noticed too. Instead of continuing to berate Sarah, she was calling out to her, asking what was happening and whether she was all right. As Sarah tumbled forwards, she hit the table; a table that seemed to be made of rubber rather than wood as she bounced off it and fell sideways on to the floor.

"Mum!"

"Gran!"

Jed rushed to the old woman's side too and started to sniff around her.

Her knees buckling once again, Ruby sank down beside Sarah, lifted her head and began to cradle it. Dragging her eyes away from Sarah's supine form, she beseeched Jessica. "Mum, get a blanket from the front room. Quickly. Go."

"A blanket? But Ruby—"

"GO!"

"There… there's no point."

"You have to get one, please; you know the one I mean, the wool blanket, the warm one, that's on the arm of her chair. It has to be warm because she's growing cold. So cold. *Why* is she? I don't understand. Mum, she needs that blanket."

Instead of obeying, Jessica knelt too. "Ruby, look at Gran, just look at her."

Ruby began to shake her head. "No, Mum, no. I… I can't."

"Look." Tears had drenched Jessica's cheeks. "Oh God, Ruby, you have to look."

At last Ruby did as she asked. This was not a night to hide from truths, although she wanted to; she wanted to so desperately. "Gran?" Her voice broke as she said it.

So pale she looked, so still; the silver of her eyes no longer bright but dull. Sightless eyes, Ruby gradually came to realise. With no life behind them at all.

Chapter Twenty-Two

HOW they got to hospital, Ruby couldn't recall. Part of her was forever stuck in the kitchen at Lazuli Cottage, watching as Gran bounced off the kitchen table – the one they'd dined at so many times over the years, she and Gran in particular, the two of them – listening to the thud as she hit the floor. Such a sickening sound.

Gran had gone, truly gone. There was no sense of her spirit remaining; her essence. She was in the light, where she belonged. She'd crossed over. But to leave *that* way, Jessica arguing with her, calling her a hypocrite and while Ruby just sat there, not intervening sooner. If she had, would Gran still be alive? Guilt seized her. It had seized them both. As they knelt by Sarah's body in the kitchen, her mother had eventually begun to wail and to tear at her hair in a maddened gesture, until Ruby had stopped her. But she couldn't console her. Jed had done that. Instead, Ruby had become numb inside, her heart like a lake that had frozen over.

In the cold glare of the waiting room, Ruby and Jessica were sitting side by side on cheap plastic seats, staring at the wall in front of them, waiting for a doctor to make an official declaration regarding Sarah's cause of death.

"Hames can't be your father; he can't be," Jessica was muttering.

"Why are we talking about this now?" Ruby's voice was just as low.

"I… I… I just… That test they did, it could be wrong, or his daughter could have tampered with it. You said she was suspicious of you, perhaps she was jealous too."

"I don't think so."

"But it can't be Hames."

Ruby turned to her mother. Her body was shaking, just as Ruby's was shaking. "Was there anyone else during that time, besides Hames?"

Jessica shook her head. "No… not during that time."

"There you go then. It's him." *The monster.*

Saul entered the waiting room and walked straight to Jessica, who'd stood up at the sight of him, and hugged her fiercely to his chest. "Oh Jessica, I'm so sorry. But don't worry, please don't worry, I'm here. I'll look after you from now on. You can move in with me and Dad; the house is big enough. Both of us will look after you."

Breaking down yet again, Jessica sobbed loudly against Saul's chest, whilst Ruby, who had also got to her feet, looked on, her eyes curiously dry. When at last Jessica had calmed, Saul broke away, moved towards Ruby and hugged her too, albeit tentatively. "I'm so sorry," he said again.

After he had let Ruby go, Jessica mentioned she'd also contacted Cash.

Ruby glared at her. "You've done what?"

"Surely you'd want me to?"

"But…" Of course! Jessica didn't know about their argument, Ruby hadn't told her yet. "What did he say?"

"He's on his way."

No sooner had she said it than the doors burst open

again and Cash entered, Jed barking happily to see him. As Saul had done with Jessica, he enfolded Ruby in a fierce hug, whispering words that were much the same. *I'm sorry. Don't worry. I'm here now. I'll look after you.* She should be glad to hear them, hug him back and cling to him, her last remaining rock; but she couldn't seem to summon the energy. Instead she remained mute and stiff, eventually causing him to pull away.

His eyes, they were like deep wells, emotion pooling in them – love, concern, and warmth too – all the things she was terrified she might not see again, but had desperately wanted to. Strangely, it didn't seem to matter now.

At last, the official declaration was made – myocardial infarction was the likely cause of Sarah's death. A heart attack in other words, and now the work of dealing with her corpse would begin. Gran didn't want any fuss, she'd made that clear enough in the past. She wanted her body to be cremated and her ashes scattered on water. She'd loved living in a seaside town and would walk by the sea when she was able to; listening to the sound of the seagulls overhead and watching as the fishermen sailed their bright little boats back to shore to unload the day's catch. For Ruby, registering her demise and organising the funeral would take priority, over and above everything else.

As the four of them eventually returned to Lazuli Cottage, Ruby was aware Cash kept glancing at her, she able to meet his gaze only every now and again. He looked nervous and upset, seeking reassurance perhaps when she had none to give.

Later, as they sat nursing cups of tea in the living room – Ruby had refused to drink hers in the kitchen – she reached for her phone and began texting.

"Is that Theo you're texting, or Ness?" Cash enquired.

"It's Eclipse," she answered. If Cash was going to take umbrage, then let him; she had nothing to hide. "I'm letting him know that I may not be around for a few days, I'm saying sorry... about the asylum. I know how much it meant to him."

"It can't be helped," was Cash's solemn reply.

Jessica intervened. "Darling, I can deal with matters here, you know, until..." she swallowed, unable to continue.

Ruby shook her head. "I need to be here too, at least for a couple of days."

They were days that passed in a blur, taken up with completing paperwork and organising a date for the funeral – the earliest they could get – which was a week away. Cash had phoned Theo, Ness and Corinna and told them about Sarah, but so far they knew nothing about Ruby's supposed connection with Aaron Hames, and nor did Cash. Jessica hadn't said anything either, understanding Ruby's need to come to terms with it first. At night, she'd lie in her childhood bed with Cash beside her. He wanted to hold her close but she turned on her side. During those quiet hours she took the time to think. Jed would also lie at the bottom of the bed, not settling, not really, none of them did; they'd all remain awake, even Cash, staring at walls or the ceiling.

"I was an idiot," he'd whispered on the first night. "A total idiot. Can I explain why?"

"Okay," she whispered back, despite no real urge to know.

"It wasn't just about Eclipse, although yeah, I discovered I've got quite a jealous streak. I never really knew that before, it came as a surprise to me as much as anyone. I'm not making excuses here, but maybe it's because I've never cared about someone so much." There was a brief moment of silence; perhaps he was expecting her to comment. When she didn't, he continued. "It was this whole dad issue too. It stirred something up inside me, something that had its roots in jealousy as well, I think. You were just so excited you'd found him, and he seemed like a nice guy; interested in you. My dad, well, you know about my dad. He's got his new family. He's not interested in Presley or me. Whatever. None of it's your fault, but I took it out on you. Like I said, I'm a prick. Can you ever forgive me?"

"We've all got our flaws, Cash, even you."

He'd laughed but it was humourless. "You used to call me 'the ideal boyfriend'."

"Yeah, well, now I tend to think idealism's overrated."

She'd wanted to tell him at that point, but in the end she couldn't. *He's not my dad, Cash. Peter Gregory's not my dad.*

* * *

On Friday morning, she came to a decision. At a few minutes past six, Ruby rose from bed, leaving Cash to stare after her, puzzled. She padded across the landing to Jessica's room, where she knocked on the door, poking her head round when Jessica called her in.

It was strange to see her mother in bed with a man, but Saul was good for her; she was committed to him and vice versa. Time really could change so much. As most of the funeral arrangements had been taken care of, Ruby asked

Jessica if it would be okay if she and Cash returned to Lewes for a day or so.

"Of course, if you think you're going to be okay."

Ruby simply nodded.

"Are you going back to work? I know that building on the Brookbridge estate was due to be torn down. Actually it's today, isn't it?"

"Yes, it's today."

Jessica exhaled and made to get out of bed. "I'll make some breakfast before you go."

"Mum, don't get up, it's still really early. Besides, I'm not hungry."

"Cash will be."

Ruby attempted a smile. "Probably, but he can grab something later. Please, there's no need to fuss. Just… let us leave."

Jessica looked upset but tried to smile too. "Okay, Ruby, if that's what you want. Let Cash take care of you though, don't keeping pushing him away."

"I'm not."

If she thought Jessica might argue with her, she was wrong. "I'll see you very soon," was all she said.

Instead of returning to her own bedroom, Ruby crossed over to Sarah's and slipped inside. She'd been in here after Sarah had passed to look for her birth certificate and will, kept in a bedside drawer, but she hadn't been alone; Cash had been with her. This was the first time in a long while she'd been in here alone. Hoping that she wouldn't be disturbed and that her mother hadn't heard the door squeaking as it opened, she sat down on the bed. In her mind she imagined a scene from long ago: Sarah sitting in the exact same spot after Hames' most recent visit, her insides turning to jelly because she was so terrified of what he might do and the threats he was making.

Jessica was right: she could have gone to the police, but Gran was right too. The police might not have taken her seriously. Would they have provided round-the-clock protection, intent on preventing a serious crime being committed, or an abduction? Or, as happened so often nowadays, would they only pull out all the stops *after* the event? She stared at the bureau, as Gran must have stared at the bureau; a repository that had harboured such terrible knowledge. Again Jessica was right when she'd said that what Sarah had done had been too much. Her father had descended into madness because of it – *extreme* madness – and at least one death had resulted from it that Ruby knew of. There were consequences to actions, always. And, as Jessica had also pointed out, whatever had been sent after him would eventually return. But Sarah was dead, so who would be sought out instead? Who knew? She didn't. She and Jessica would have to be on their guard, probably for the rest of their lives. That was Gran's legacy. But despite that, she wouldn't blame Sarah; she refused to. That bureau, she couldn't tear her eyes from it. Would she have done the same in Gran's shoes? Given in to desperation? Would she have made the trade? Perhaps. And that's why she didn't blame her, and perhaps Jessica didn't either, not deep down – because when it came to it they would *all* have made the trade.

It took a moment to realise that she had her hands clasped together; that she was wringing them in anguish, just as Sarah might have done. Taking a deep breath, she inhaled for a count of four then exhaled for a count of four, a method of keeping herself calm in the face of adversity. It worked. After a while she was able to place her hands on her knees and breathe evenly. Slowly rising, she glanced around her, at all of Sarah's belongings. *I'm glad you didn't stay, Gran, I'm glad you're in the light. And I'm sorry if it was a hard life, that there was so much adversity in it. But there was a lot of love too, wasn't there? I loved you, Gran, and I always will. Whatever happens from hereon in, I'll deal with it. Thanks to you, I have that chance.*

Taking a final look around, she left Sarah's room and returned to her own. On seeing her, Cash sat up.

"You okay?" he asked.

"As much as I'll ever be. I need to go back to Lewes."

"To see the team?"

She nodded. "I need to arrange with Theo and Ness to see my father."

Chapter Twenty-Three

IT was barely nine o' clock and yet the Psychic Surveys team had gathered in their entirety, Cash and Jed included, not in Ruby's office, but in Ness's house.

As Ruby spoke, her tone calm and measured, there were various gasps of surprise, Cash and Ness in particular staring at her in stunned surprise.

"So Peter's not your dad?" Cash had to check and double-check. "Hames is?"

Ness echoed what Jessica had said. "He can't be."

"Why not?" Ruby asked, looking directly at her. "Why can't he be?"

"He's so… unlike you."

"In looks?"

"Of course in looks! Although…"

"Although now I've mentioned it, there is a similarity, isn't there?" Ruby finished when Ness faltered. "Where is it? Around the eyes? The shape of the mouth? The nose perhaps. In what way do I look like him?"

Theo rose from the seat she'd been occupying in order to sit closer to Ruby. "Sweetheart, to confirm parentage, we'd need to do a test."

"More tests?" Ruby raised an eyebrow. "I'm a bit sick of tests to be honest."

"Fucking bastards!" The vehemence in Cash's voice

could not be mistaken. "They invite you into their house only to set you up. If I'd known…" He clenched his fists making Ruby very glad that, like her, he hadn't suspected a thing.

Corinna reached across and patted his arm, consoling him even if Ruby couldn't.

"Ruby, this must all be such a shock," Ness continued. "The death of your grandmother is terrible enough without finding out about Peter as well as Hames, *if* Hames is your father. He might not be, he can't be the only Aaron Hames."

Ruby shook her head. "I've already run an online check. There are a handful in the north, and three down here. One of those is two years old and the other has just celebrated his eightieth. *This* Hames fits the profile. He fits it to a tee."

Ness remained adamant. "Ruby, I don't advise seeing him."

"I *have* to."

"Darling," Theo tried to cajole, "I'm in agreement with Ness. It's not a good idea. We've told you a little of what he's capable of. He's… dangerous, very dangerous. Besides, you're in the midst of grieving for your grandmother."

"Are you suggesting I can't think straight?"

Understandably, Theo was hurt. "No!"

"Good, because in some ways my mind has never been clearer. Ness, is Hames responsible for any other deaths besides the one you've mentioned?"

It was Corinna who gasped now. "He's a murderer?"

Ness sighed, did her best to explain. "He has insights into people, Corinna, negative insights. His speciality is exposing dark secrets and then taunting people mercilessly with them. He's driven people to kill themselves; that's the theory, although he's done nothing so obvious as plunging a knife into them or strangling them with his bare hands. The way he works is a lot more insidious than that."

"Christ!" Corinna and Cash said in unison.

"So now you know," there was only the slightest hint of a crack in Ruby's voice, one that she rushed to disguise. "My father is as good as a murderer and insane to boot. Be careful what you wish for, eh?"

"He may *not* be your father," Ness continued to stress.

Cash agreed. "Having the same name could just be a coincidence."

"What are you trying to do? Explain one coincidence by introducing yet another?"

"Ruby—"

"This is fate, Cash. I not only wanted to meet my father, I was *meant* to meet him." She turned to Ness. "You got Theo in, so you can get me in too. Please, try and understand I can't just brush what I've learnt under the carpet. Make a few phone calls, bend a few ears, do whatever it is you have to do; just get me into Ash Hill."

* * *

Ness had done it. She'd managed to secure herself, Ruby and Theo an afternoon visit, but only on condition that Ruby didn't meet Hames, the link between them being at present too tenuous to hold much sway. However, she'd be allowed to observe him via camera from a separate room. There was no arguing with the decision, not at this juncture; it seemed to be set in stone. Ruby either accepted it or it was a no go. Unable to wait for the wheels of bureaucracy to grind faster, Ruby accepted.

They piled into Ness's car, Cash and Corinna insisting on accompanying them, even though they wouldn't be allowed access to the unit; they'd have to wait behind. Ruby had shrugged at their dogged insistence. It was up to them. In Ness's Rover, she, Cash and Corinna squeezed into the back, while Theo occupied the passenger seat. As they drove, Theo and Ness gave some background information.

"Despite being issued with a 'requires improvement' notice in 2016, it's a pretty decent place," Ness said. "The staff there are great, they really want to help their patients, and they go out of their way to do just that, exhausting every avenue."

"Of which we're one," Theo agreed, "although in my case it's more a boulevard."

She laughed at her own joke but the others, it seemed, weren't in a laughing mood. In the back, Cash kept squeezing Ruby's hand in what she presumed to be a show of support. In the end, she smiled at him but removed her hand and leant forward slightly so she could hear her colleagues better.

"Patients sent to Ash Hill are regarded as medium risk," continued Theo, "therefore a danger to themselves and others. Some patients are criminally referred."

Corinna baulked at that. "A man who drives people to commit suicide is considered medium risk? I'd call it a lot more than that."

"As I said," Theo answered, "his crimes are at best unsubstantiated. His isn't the hand that ends people's lives. His victims do that all by themselves."

"Once he's exposed the darkness in them," Cash

pointed out.

"That's right," Theo replied. "And, as no one's whiter than white, everyone's at risk. His medical team are at their wits' end with him and this ability he has. He knows so much that he shouldn't know. A lot of those who've been dealing with him are very much alive, they haven't committed suicide, but some have gone on sick leave indefinitely. Ruby's already told us that Sarah suspected he had a crude type of psychic ability, although Jessica hadn't picked up on it – just his avid interest in the occult. But whatever he was then, he's certainly psychic now, and in his case I wouldn't call it a 'gift', far from it. Whatever Sarah did, it opened something in him."

"A door which can never be shut again," Ruby quoted her mother. "Not fully."

"No," Ness concurred. "Not fully. I've mentioned this to you before, Ruby; moving Hames to a high-risk facility is currently being considered. He's been locked up for several years now, but not always at Brookbridge. He's been in several facilities. And he goes through prolonged subdued periods, but every now and then he seems to 'flare up', as they call it. This latest bout started around two weeks ago."

Ruby frowned. "Two weeks? That's roughly around the same time I started to get a regular series of phone calls from the Brookbridge estate – from the Watkins family, the Stems, the Barkers and the Griffiths too."

"Actually, we've had a couple more," Corinna informed her. "Ever since… you know, your Gran. But I've told them work's on hold. For… several reasons."

Ruby looked at her. "Hames flares up and then the estate does too. I thought it was because of the imminent destruction of the hospital building, and perhaps in part it is; but it could also be due to *him* and the negativity he's emitting; it's bringing everyone out of the woodwork." Remembering the writhing walls in the first corridor, the *only* corridor she'd ventured down, she took a deep breath. "That's actually kind of apt. When I initially visited the rear ward block, it was as though people *were* coming out of the walls, if not the woodwork, with their hands flailing and reaching out. How long has Hames been at Brookbridge, Ness?"

"Around a year now. He was transferred from a place called Mill View in Essex, but for much of that time he's been in a subdued state."

"A year?" Ruby questioned. Her father had been within reach all that time and she hadn't known; hadn't sensed a thing. But she was sensing it now: the closer they drew to Brookbridge the harder her heart thumped, the sound in her ears, deafening.

Cash placed his arm around her. Ten out of ten for persistence, she thought. She let it linger there, unsure what else to do, but still there was no comfort in it.

Turning onto the estate, they kept to the outer edge. On the far side, demolition was most likely in progress. Would what Eclipse feared actually happen, she wondered. Would the grounded retreat further into their terror, some of them to surface in their new surroundings much later, to the shock of future residents, while others remained in limbo? She'd failed them; she'd failed Eclipse too – had reneged on her promise; but even if the two of them had tried again, they might not have got anywhere. If some did resurface, once new walls had shot up, she'd be on hand to help. All the names she'd learnt, all the patients she'd encountered in visions, she wouldn't forget them; she'd send love and light when – *if* – she was able to once again feel love for anything.

Ness slowed the car down. They were in a small car park, packed with vehicles, but she managed to find a space. Trees encircled them, as much a barrier as the green fencing, which was higher than the fence that surrounded the abandoned building, and decidedly more sturdy with no gaps in it at all.

For a while all of them sat in silence, just staring at what was in front of them. It was low-rise, redbrick, and modern, built in the 90s according to Ness, replacing what had once been there – a much larger secure wing, packed to the hilt with cells. Nowadays, Ash Hill was one of sixty units in England. In it was a 16-bed female ward and a 16-bed male ward, as well as an 8-bed for elderly males. During 'episodes', patients were kept under observation in padded seclusion rooms with communication via intercom.

Finally Ness started to move and soon they were all on the pavement staring at the building as opposed to being in the car and staring at it. The day was pleasant, blue sky evident between clouds. Lashing rain would have been more fitting.

"You don't have to do this," Cash muttered beside her.

Ness's pale complexion looked even more drained. "He's right, Ruby."

"I do," was her simple reply.

Corinna stepped forward and hugged her, afterwards so did Cash, both awkward gestures.

"Where will you go while we're in there?" Ruby asked.

"We'll take a walk to the other side of the estate," Corinna answered. A sad smile made her seem older than

DESCENSION

her years. "I'll send as much love and light to the inhabitants of that building, Ruby, don't you worry. Even if we had been able to get there this week, it was a massive task to tackle in such a short time, but you tried; three times you tried. Maybe it had an impact we don't even know about yet. Perhaps a few of those inside did take notice and moved onwards."

"Perhaps."

"Come on." Ness gently took Ruby by the arm. "Let's get this over and done with. Corinna, Cash, we'll call you when we're done."

Again Cash reached out; again he squeezed Ruby's hand. "Good luck."

"Thanks," she replied, but as far as luck was concerned, she felt hers had run out.

Chapter Twenty-Four

ONCE their identities had been confirmed, the gate slid back and Theo, Ness and Ruby were allowed inside the fenced perimeter. They stood at the entrance to the building as a woman on the other side of the door busily unlocked it and greeted them. She was wearing trousers, a blouse and a jacket – her own clothes as opposed to a uniform. There was a warm smile on her freckled face as she ushered them in. The reception area was very pleasant, spacious and airy, with lots of light, but there was that unmistakable smell; the smell of an institution. Some things you couldn't mask.

Ness introduced Ruby to Grace Ellis, who was around the same age as Ness, but didn't share her occasionally haunted expression. On the contrary, her whole persona was as bright as their surroundings. Oozing enthusiasm and compassion, she was an example of someone as passionate about her job as Ruby and the team were about theirs – their ultimate goal the same; to help people. Could there be any help for Hames? Ruby guessed she was about to find out.

Grace tackled more doors, opening and unlocking a series of them, just yards apart, her impressive bunch of keys jangling all the while. "The unit is divided into blocks," she informed them as they walked. "On the far side is the women's block. All the doors there are electronic, making life so much easier." She pulled a face. "I work in this block, however, and although it's due to follow suit, I'm still waiting… and waiting. You wouldn't believe how bad electronic card-pass envy can get!"

Her laughter suited such a cheerful environment – *relentlessly* cheerful, but that was better than how it used to be, surely. In the Victorian buildings, in those all-grey interiors, what laughter there'd been had had a very different quality. From the corridor they were walking along now, there were views into areas of garden where some patients were either strolling or sitting on benches, several staff members close by, monitoring, but also interacting. It was a pleasant enough scene, harmonious even. It was also surreal, Ruby decided, as was this entire situation.

After opening another door to a side room, Grace beckoned them in. It was little more than a square box, bright, with almost child-like pictures adorning the walls.

Noticing Ruby studying them, Grace explained they were by the patients. "Art therapy is a very important part of what we do here; it allows the patients to express themselves." She coloured a little and coughed. "Obviously, not *all* paintings can go on the wall, but some are really quite lovely, as you can see."

Ruby raised an eyebrow and turned to Theo and Ness whose smiles were as relentless as Grace's, plastered onto their faces and masking any unease.

"I'm sure Ness and Theo have told you," Grace continued, "that we only talk with Aaron in short bursts. Anything more runs the risk of being upsetting for all concerned. That's what we'll do today – five minutes if it's not going well; ten if it is." She pointed to a desk on which stood a computer. "You'll be able to view him via that. He knows we record sessions. We're as open as we can be with patients here."

It was all worlds away from how it used to be. Grace clearly cared, and she was probably one of many staff members who did; who were attracted to the job for the right reasons. Yes, the unit had had an improvement notice slapped on it, but from what Ruby could see, it wasn't a terrible place to be. Although the atmosphere contained a certain frisson, whether that existed all the time or was something she was generating, she couldn't tell. Surreal and skewed, that's how everything was at the moment – her personal involvement distorting everything.

"He has no idea I'm in this room?" Ruby checked.

"None," Grace confirmed. "It's advisable that we take the *softly softly* approach with Aaron when he's lucid. Besides which, we'd need firm evidence of a blood bond between you before we even consider broaching the subject with him. Is that something you might be open to in the future?"

"Let me see him first," replied Ruby.

Grace didn't push for a more positive answer, she simply nodded; a gentle gesture that told Ruby she understood.

"Theo, Ness," Grace continued, "shall we? Ruby, would you like someone in the room with you? Just in case…"

"I'd prefer to be on my own, thanks."

"Okay, but a member of staff will be outside. Call her if you need her."

Ruby agreed that she would and Theo and Ness trudged off, looking as if they were heading to the guillotine. Once they'd left, Ruby took a deep breath, pulled the chair out in front of the desk, its legs scraping against the blue-tiled floor, and stared at the empty room on screen. It was another square box but one with a window, a sofa and armchairs. Its magnolia walls were meant to create a homely impression, to soothe, but it was all just another set-up.

At last there was movement. A man entered the room – Hames, followed by Grace, Theo and Ness, as well as a guard who stood by the door with his arms folded. Aaron shuffled rather than walked, his head down so that Ruby couldn't get a clear impression of him. He wasn't especially tall – she'd say around five foot eleven – and he was thin, almost fragile-looking. She hadn't expected that; she'd expected a more terrifying figure to appear, someone thickset and burly with his head shaved. But Aaron had plenty of hair. It was golden brown, like Ruby's, and damn it, it obscured his face as he sat down, selecting a seat that would put him with his back to the camera despite Grace indicating the chair opposite. It wasn't her first sighting of him, it was her second, but she knew this time it would never fade from memory.

Grace started the conversation. "Good afternoon, Aaron. Thank you for agreeing to meet with us at such short notice today."

"But of course! It's always lovely to meet with you." His voice was smooth enough – some might even say pleasant.

"How have you spent your day up until now?" Grace continued.

"Sleeping and eating," he replied, his manner amicable. "Oh, and shitting."

The three women and the guard stiffened, albeit

fractionally. Ruby's back straightened too. This was it – this man, this stranger, someone she didn't feel any affinity with, not yet – was going to waste no more time being nice; not if his was just a five- or ten-minute slot. He was going to have as much fun as possible.

Before Grace could say anything further or calm him in any way, Aaron continued.

"Hey, Vanessa, you're a bit quiet today, what's the matter? Twin got your tongue? What did she do, run off with it when you banished her? When you left her alone in the dark?" His voice rose, became thin and reedy. "*I don't like the dark.* That's what she used to say. You didn't give a damn though, did you? You didn't give a flying fuck. Oh no, it was all about *you* all the time." He pulled a sad face. "No room for poor little twinny. And that's where she's languishing still, in the dark; curled up in a tight ball and scared." Again his voice rose. "*I hate the dark, Ness, I hate the dark!*"

Ruby frowned – what was he talking about? Ness didn't have a twin.

"And looky, looky," he said, his head turning towards Theo, "I swear you've put on a few pounds since our last visit. Have you been comfort-binging again? Trying to fill the gap dear Reggie left when that cancer ate him from the inside out? God, it was awful, wasn't it, watching him writhe and scream? But all you could think of was your own pain, not his. It's guilt you're trying to suffocate, stuffing food down on top of it. Never mind as big as a house, you'll be the size of an entire continent soon, because you wanna know the truth? Guilt never goes away! It eats away at you too; it swallows you whole with a gob that's as big as you are."

'Aaron," Theo's voice was impressively even as she answered him, "why is it you cling to the darkness in people? How long has it been like this?"

Aaron's head began to twitch and Ruby leant forward, rapt by what was unfolding.

"Because, you stupid heifer, the darkness is the only thing about any of us that's remotely exciting."

"Aaron," Ness continued, also determinedly calm. "We know you're in agony. That deep inside you is the real Aaron. Someone who's much better than this."

Aaron threw his head back and laughed, a bitter sound that made you want to clap your hands to your ears. "Oh please, no! Don't start with all that love and light shit again! Seriously, if you're trying to understand me, you're wasting your time. If you wanna help me, you can't. I don't *want* to be helped. Why can't you pathetic witches get that into your heads? Witch Bitches! Witch Bitches! That's what you are."

"We're not going to rise to your insults," Ness declared. "Besides, we know we're flawed as human beings, we freely admit it. And we won't give up on you either, because you *do* need help. Aaron. What's inside you can't stay if you refuse to give it a home. You have the power to evict it."

"Crazy! Crazy! Crazy! You're all fucking crazy. Crazier than me."

Ruby flinched as Aaron jumped to his feet. What was he going to do, turn around? Was she going to see his face? The guard stepped forward as Aaron continued to stand with his back to her, his body swaying from side to side. The three women, however, remained seated. Clearly this wasn't an uncommon occurrence.

Again he targeted Ness. "How'd you sleep at night,

knowing what you did? She was your fucking twin, you bitch!"

Again Ruby frowned, what did she do to this supposed twin? What was so terrible about it?

"And Theodora, you used to squawk on about how much you loved Reggie; kept calling him your soul mate, but what about Tony, eh? You had eyes for him too, didn't you? You had the proper hots. He made you laugh, when Reggie was going through a rough patch at work and had lost his sense of humour. He made you do more than that; he made you squeal with delight. You sounded just like a pig!"

"It was just the once!" Theo said, causing Ruby's jaw to drop. She'd had an *affair*?

Quickly, the old woman took a deep breath and composed herself, clearly angry with herself for having bitten back.

Aaron laughed again, "Hey, at least you managed to find yourself a fuck buddy, that's quite impressive actually. Had a thing about fat-bottomed girls, did he? Jeez, whatever! I admire his bravery." Pointing at Ness, he added, "You're so different to little Miss Frigid, though. She ain't got a fucking clue what to do with that hole between her legs. I wouldn't be surprised if the damned thing's gone and closed up."

Grace rose. "That's enough for today I think." Her smile was like a rictus grin. "Thank you, Aaron. George and I will accompany you back to your room."

"But we haven't finished yet," he protested. "We can't *possibly* have finished."

"We have, Aaron," she assured him. "George, can you help—"

"I haven't said hello to the young lady spying on me."

Again, Ruby flinched, so did Theo and Ness, visibly this time. *Young lady*, it's what Peter had called her – was it just a coincidence, or did he know?

"Young lady," he continued, "young lady." That confirmed it. He knew and he was using it as a weapon. "Lost one daddy and wants another. Even if it's me."

Ruby gasped. *Turn around. Let me see you. Turn around.*

"Bit of advice, darlin', desperate ain't never a good look. But hey, that's what you are, and flawed too, just like the rest of us. God, I'm sensing a darkness in you. Woah! It's even scaring *me*. Actually, I'm a liar. I love it. It's my gift to you."

Ness jumped to her feet too. "Grace, you said this session was over."

"Aaron," Grace's voice had grown stern. "Do you really want us to use force?"

Aaron held up a hand in what was a mockery of a placating gesture. "Hold your horses, will you? Just take a chill pill. This is why you called the fucking meeting, so this *young lady*," he spat the words this time, "could see me. She *wants* to check if there's a connection between us. What did she call it when I came in? An affinity."

Before Ruby could react, he swung round at last, to stare straight into the camera.

"I don't need no test to know you're my daughter, *of course* you are. Oh and let me tell you, your grandmother's a hideous witch too; a dead witch the voices are telling me, thank the Devil. I'll see her in hell for what she did, I'll make her suffer, but who wants to talk about a dead old woman? Not me, not when we can talk about your mum. What a game girl she was; what a cheap and easy fuck. She was up for anything after a few vodkas, stuff that'd make your eyes water. Mine certainly did! I encouraged her." He gave a short laugh. "Of course I fucking encouraged her. She'd give any whore a run for their money, that one. It's lovely to think something came of our union, something *solid*. Hello, Ruby, *Spooky Ruby*. That's what your best friend used to call you, eh? What was her name?" He cocked his head as if listening. "Ah, Lisa. Her name was Lisa. If I'd been around then, like I was *supposed* to, I'd have sewn her fucking mouth up. Father and daughter, eh? A blood bond. A *lasting* bond."

Ice-cold water poured through Ruby's veins as she continued to stare at Hames, at his face, seen not just as a child but that night at the asylum too. He was the one who'd shoved his face into hers; who'd warned her she'd know his name soon enough. And he was right. She knew something else too, just as Gran had known and as he had known on first sight of her. There would be no further tests. This man, she resembled him so much, even his eyes – his green-flecked *maddened* eyes.

For now we see through a glass darkly.

Those words would always haunt her.

Chapter Twenty-Five

THEO and Ness tried to comfort her, but as politely as she could, Ruby put a halt to it.

"Look, it's fine. I know who my father is now; no one said I had to like it."

"*If* he's your father." Still Ness persisted with that line of thought.

Ruby stared at her. "You know as well as I do, he is."

Ness lowered her head. "I'm sorry," she murmured.

A twin, Ness had a twin. Ruby considered mentioning it and then decided not to. She didn't want to repeat any of the bile that man had spewed out. And neither did she want to see him again. Not even if a way was found to banish what festered inside him. He was her father but only in a biological sense and that's the way it was going to stay. She wasn't a pawn in this situation, nor was she a victim. As her Gran had always said, she was not power*less*, she was power*ful*; she'd hold on to that and to another thing someone had said to her almost two years back – the spirit of a young girl who'd been haunting Emily's Bridge, not its namesake, she'd been called Susan. '*Never forget how good you are, how bright you shine.*' Hames had claimed he'd seen the darkness within her, had likened it to the darkness in him. But others had seen something else.

A more sombre Grace than the one who'd let them into

the building, now showed them out, all the while glancing
at Ruby as they retraced their footsteps, as if worried she
might crumble; have a meltdown right there and then in
front of them; need treatment even – oh the irony! Perhaps
it was with relief that Grace locked the door behind them.
Certainly it felt wonderful to be in the fresh air again.
Ruby closed her eyes and breathed deeply and Ness and
Theo did the same – all of them trying to cleanse
themselves of the something rotten that had tainted them.
How could Hames see so much? Once again she wondered
what Gran had done; what Rosamund had written all
those years before – instructions, or something tantamount
to that? And *why* had they done it, when the light was so
strong in them too? That's what you fought darkness with:
the light. That's what Gran had always taught her. She'd
claimed there were no winners when it was darkness pitted
against darkness. But what of darkness borne of good
intent – was that different somehow? A desire to protect
had been at the root of Gran's actions, but was that
justification enough? How sweet and gentle Gran had
been, but at heart perhaps as reckless as Rosamund – the
one who'd put pen to paper – and as Jessica, who'd
conjured a demon to impress a lover. And perhaps that
same trait was in Ruby, hidden deep and biding its time,
waiting to surface, *truly* surface. God knows what other
traits she'd inherited from his side, a man who courted evil
even before evil had found him. If Theo and Ness failed in
their endeavour with Hames, if his abuse became too much
and they had to walk away, she only hoped there were
enough drugs in the world to keep him subdued on a
permanent basis. She also hoped Gran had spoken the
truth when she said she'd destroyed Rosamund's papers;

DESCENSION

that no one else would discover them; be tempted by them. She didn't blame Gran, she'd already made her mind up on that, but it was a revelation that love could lead to death and destruction every bit as much as hate.

As they approached the car, they spotted Cash and Corinna hurrying towards them, concern vying with excitement on their faces. Ruby frowned. What on earth did they have to be excited about? Cash was the first to reach them.

"Are you okay?" he asked Ruby.

Unsure what to say, she nodded. "Where've you been?"

"To the other side of the estate, like we said."

Ruby sighed as she looked at Corinna. "How is it there? Has demolition begun?"

"No, Ruby, the building's still standing!"

"But it's late afternoon," declared Theo. "I'd have thought it'd be well under way."

"We did too," Cash answered. "We were expecting to see piles of rubble and dust in the air, builders and JCBs everywhere. We were stunned when that wasn't the case. There were just two men, walking round the perimeter of the building, taking notes, and surveying it. We went up to them, asked what was going on and they told us. Rob Lock himself told us, the boss man. He's really sound, Ruby, a good bloke. He said someone had got in touch with the council saying they suspected a sett of badgers were living in the building and that it needed to be inspected before demolition. This had delayed things until the following Friday. Lock said they'd already got clearance on bats, but as a legally protected wild animal, badgers needed ruling out too. He didn't seem annoyed or bothered, just concerned. If he knew about the spirits, *definitely* knew, I

273

reckon he'd be concerned about them too."

"Badgers?" Ruby shrugged. "I never saw any evidence of badgers."

There was a moment of silence and then Theo slapped her thigh. "Badgers!" Her booming voice startled them all. "Badgers and bats!"

"Theo, what *are* you talking about?" Ness asked her, bewildered.

"Well of course the council would get involved if there's a reported sighting! I could kick my own backside for not thinking of that. Thank God someone did, though."

"Yeah, but who?" quizzed Corinna.

Whilst they were pondering, Ruby dug out her mobile phone and downloaded her emails. Plenty came through but it was one in particular she was interested in. The one from Peter Gregory, telling her how sorry he was that she wasn't his daughter, apologising again for the 'set-up' as Ruby had called it, and reiterating how much he had liked her; that he wished it could have turned out differently. He wanted to do one last thing for her, what she'd asked of him. It was he who'd rung the council, not using police influence as such, just a bit of savvy, thereby getting the building that much craved-for stay of execution.

"It was Peter." Her voice was a whisper as she informed them. "That's who."

Cash looked at her. "He's a good bloke as well."

He was. He'd turned out to be, not that it was her concern any longer.

"Ruby," Cash continued, "no one expects you to go in there, not with everything that's happened, but the rest of us will go. We'll try and finish the job."

There were murmurs of hearty agreement from all

around: 'Of course we will' and 'Ruby, don't worry about a thing, just leave it to us.' She heard what her friends and colleagues were saying, acknowledged it, and then, ultimately, she rejected it.

"I'm going back too. I'm going to fulfil my promise."

"But your gran…" Corinna began.

"Would want me to do the right thing. She was proud of me and I was proud of her. I'm *still* proud of her, and grateful for what she tried to do. She moved heaven and earth to keep Mum and me safe. She went to hell and back. I wouldn't be worthy of calling myself her granddaughter if I didn't do something similar to save others."

"Ruby…" There was a frown on Ness's face just as there was on Theo's.

"I'm going back," Ruby reiterated.

"Sarah's funeral's on Thursday," Cash pointed out. "*When* are you going back? You're going to be pretty busy beforehand with all the arrangements."

"Thursday evening," Ruby answered. "As soon as the funeral's over."

"But, darling, you'll be in no fit state." There was a plea in Theo's voice.

Ruby looked at her, looked at them all.

"On the contrary," she said. "I'll be in the perfect frame of mind to do the job."

* * *

Time went back to being a blur. Cash was right, there was indeed a lot to do prior to the funeral, with Ruby carrying out tasks both big and small in what could only be described as a mechanical fashion. Immediately after the visit to Ash Hill, she'd been dropped at her flat with Cash. They'd spent the night there but Ruby honestly couldn't remember much about it. Cash had been very attentive, that she did remember, Jed had also been very sweet, but it was as though she was removed from the situation, somewhere else entirely. Deciding that might as well be the case, the next morning she informed Cash she'd be going back to Hastings until Thursday.

Straightaway, he offered to go with her. "I can easily work from your gra... mum's. Oh to hell with it, work can wait. There are more important things in life."

"Like me?" she replied, her aim to appear tongue in cheek but falling short.

"Of course like you! Ruby, how many times do I have to say it? I was an idiot. Being jealous of Eclipse was just plain stupid, although I have to say, there's still something really annoying about those bloody puppy-dog eyes of his every time he looks at you. As for all this father stuff," he paused, his head turning to the side slightly, although she still caught his look of utter sadness, "I guess I didn't really realise how much my dad leaving us when me and Presley were so young, affected me." His smile was a wry one. "You know how close me, Mum and Presley are. Even with him gone we never wanted for anything. Mum made sure of that. She worked so hard for us, Ruby, and that makes me sad too; that she had to. And then finding Dad again: realising he'd started another family; had two girls this time; that he was glad to see me, but not so glad that he wanted to keep in touch. His wife found the situation difficult – that was his excuse; he had to put her first, telling me I understood rather than actually asking me. I said I did, even though I didn't and I walked away. There's hardly been any correspondence between us since. I didn't even get a birthday card this year. When you found Peter it brought it all back to the surface, and instead of being happy for you, I envied you. And then…"

"And then look how it turned out, there was nothing to envy after all."

"Well, yeah. Although I wish it had been otherwise, Ruby, honestly I do. I feel so fucking crap about how I was."

She reached out, laid a hand on him and said it was okay, that there was no need to feel that way. "Like I've said before, it's our flaws that make us human."

He held her gaze, but made no reply.

"Cash," she continued, "I'm going back to Hastings by myself, and Jed too, if he wants. I'll see you on Thursday though for the funeral and afterwards at Cromer."

"You're going back without me? Are you serious?"

"Yes, I am, but it's not because I'm angry." She paused. "It's not because I'm anything." Inside her chest it just felt hollow – numbness a protection mechanism she guessed, ensuring she was able to eat, drink and sleep; do all the things she had to do until she could say goodbye to Sarah properly.

He shook his head. "You shouldn't be on your own."

"I won't be on my own, I'll have Jed as I said, but also Mum, and Saul will probably be there for much of the time as well. They've become quite inseparable those two, haven't they? But that's a good thing. Mum needs someone."

"So do *you*, Ruby, hopefully me. What happened between us, it won't—"

"This has nothing to do with what happened between us, okay? You needed a bit of space, some time to think, and now so do I. I was upset when you said that but I respected it, I gave you what you asked for, so do the same for me."

"Ruby…"

"This is not tit for tat, far from it. It'll be different after Thursday. I hope."

With not much more to say, she packed a few things, climbed in her car and drove away, Jed indeed accompanying her, sitting on the passenger seat, his manner forlorn rather than excited. Clearly, he was going to miss Cash too.

* * *

Thursday morning arrived all too soon, and the day was a cold but bright one – exactly the kind of day Sarah had loved. As Ruby lay in her old bedroom at Lazuli Cottage, so many memories crowded her mind: she and Gran taking a walk along the beach; shopping in the Old Town; having tea there after school in a favourite café, or buying fish and chips, a Hastings speciality, from opposite the fisherman's huts, with the seagulls so like Jed, always hovering whenever there was food around. They were such normal times, reminiscent of so many people's childhoods, with not much to distinguish them at all. Because that's what Gran had tried to do – keep their lives normal, even though seeing the dead was considered by most to be *ab*normal. Gran had taught Ruby how to cope with her gift and be ordinary with her friends, but had told her all about the light too; to focus on it as well as on love, compassion and understanding; to never give the darkness a chance. With her mother caught in the grip of depression, it was always Gran who'd guided her; who was there for her; who baked cookies with her; who dropped her off and picked her up from school, and sat and read to her by the fireside. Without Gran life would have been very different, her fate unimaginable. Gran was her hero, and her hero she'd remain. The strongest woman Ruby had ever known. Today was all about Gran; they'd give her a good send-off, the best they could. In the evening, it'd be about something else entirely.

I know you're in the light, Gran, but you're also in my heart. I also know that somehow, somewhere, you know what I'm planning to do. Watch over me if you can.

Cash arrived at Lazuli Cottage just after nine. There was so much hesitancy in his eyes; as if he was afraid Ruby was going to reject him. She wasn't, but neither was she going to rush into his arms. She couldn't afford to, not yet.

Later that morning, Saul drove the pair of them and Jessica to the crematorium, where the rest of the team were waiting, dressed not in black – Sarah wouldn't have wanted that – but bright colours. Corinna, who normally only wore black, had on a slim-fitting green dress and a tapestry overcoat that looked brand new, and beside her stood Presley, very handsome in a white shirt and tan chinos. Theo, always flamboyant, with her hair as pink as ever, had a turquoise scarf draped around her neck. Ness was in grey, but a lighter shade than usual. Eclipse had asked if he could come to the funeral and Ruby had agreed. He was standing with the team, his puppy-dog eyes, as Cash had described them, trained on her. She smiled at him as she followed her mother into the church;

smiled at them all: the team, Eclipse and some of Gran's closest friends, enough of them to fill the small chapel and to hear a few words said in memorium.

Jessica had written a piece about her mother, but at the last minute was unable to read it out, she was crying so much. Saul took the eulogy from her and spoke instead, his clear, melodious voice a perfect vehicle for the warmth of her words.

Ruby addressed them next, Jed accompanying her to the stand, sitting by her side as she spoke about the Gran who'd filled each day of her childhood with sunshine; who'd wrapped her and Jessica in cotton wool; whose love knew no bounds.

Everyone was crying, not just Jessica; there wasn't a dry eye in the house, except for Ruby's. Maybe that surprised some; it might even have seemed callous, but again, she couldn't afford to give her emotions free rein.

The service over, the curtains closed on Sarah's coffin. At this final gesture, Jessica started to sob again, Saul had to practically support her weight as they trudged outside to congregate on the tarmac, where not just he but several of Sarah's friends who'd known Jessica since she was a little girl, tried to soothe her. Not one of the team, not even Cash and Eclipse, asked Ruby if she was all right, even though their concern was evident, Cash's particularly. He was doing what Ruby usually did when worried; chewing at his lip. There was just the wake to go now. It was held at *The Jenny Lind* in the Old Town, close to Lazuli Cottage. Food and drink had been laid on and some laughter punctuated such a sad day, as happy memories of Sarah Davis were exchanged. Even Ruby smiled at several of the stories being told, testimony of how her grandmother had touched so many during her time in this world.

Eventually, after the last of the guests had wandered away, and Saul took Jessica back to his home rather than Lazuli Cottage, there was just the team and Eclipse left. As Ruby watched her mother's departure, she wondered what would become of the family home. It'd be sold most likely, since Jessica did indeed plan to spend the majority of her time at Saul's. That was fine with Ruby; it wasn't a home without Gran in it; it had reverted back to being a mere house, the memories created within its four walls stored in the mind rather than in anything physical.

All of them checked their watches. It was after five already. By the time they reached the Brookbridge Estate it'd be dark.

Finally Cash asked the question they all had on their lips. "Are you sure you're up for this, Ruby?"

"It's our last chance," Ruby replied, looking at each of them in turn. "But more than that, it's *their* last chance. I think we'd better get a move on, don't you?"

Chapter Twenty-Six

INCLUDING Eclipse, the team numbered six and so they divided between two cars, with Cash driving Ruby and Eclipse and Theo and Corinna riding in Ness's car. It was only a half hour journey during which Cash did his best to pass the time with some light-hearted chatter, but both his passengers responded only as and when required. At one point Ruby looked behind her and Eclipse graced her with a smile that was both eager and sad. Ruby smiled too, but more at Jed who was sitting beside Eclipse, as eager for his attention as Eclipse was for hers. They probably wouldn't work together after this job, she decided, thinking that perhaps Cash was right when he sensed over-keenness for her as well as the job. But she was glad she'd got to know Eclipse, glad that he'd brought the destruction of the last hospital building to her attention, and for the opportunity he'd given her to put right what had once been so wrong.

Ness was just behind them when they turned into the estate. It hadn't been discussed where to park, there being an assumption they'd leave the cars where they had before. Ruby quashed that assumption when she directed Cash to the Watkins' house. He was confused, as was Ness probably, but she followed them nonetheless.

"Ruby, there are roads much closer than this," Cash protested.

"I know that, but we're going to the Watkins' house."

"Who are the Watkins?" Eclipse asked, leaning forward.

Ruby told him theirs had been the house that had marked the beginning of a recent spate of investigations on the estate, paranormal activity there intensifying at around the same time as Hames had emerged from his stupor. "It could just be coincidence," she said, "or something much more. He's radiating a lot of negative energy. It's filling the atmosphere and the grounded are reacting to it perhaps."

"In what way?" Eclipse was clearly enthralled.

"Either identifying with it or in fear of it." Just before they parked, before she had to explain something else to the rest of them, she turned to face Eclipse fully. "You've spent time in the hospital building, you've sensed the pain of those who are still trapped there. Tell me, has it been worse in the past fortnight?"

He shook his head. "To me it's always been bad, I don't understand how people can run around that building, the living I mean – mucking about, scrawling graffiti all over the walls; vandalising furniture that's already been kicked in. I've seen people loads of times. I've heard them from wherever I've been in the building at the time, usually hiding behind a door or a cupboard or something, because I don't want to see the idiots or be seen by them; have them waste my time. To be honest, when *we* went in, one of the problems I was expecting to deal with was dickheads like that, but there was no one there; no ghost-hunters, no drunk kids. There wasn't anyone anywhere close to the building. That's, like, the biggest change I can think of."

Ruby nodded – it was as she suspected. Even thrill-seekers were sensitive enough to realise when something was beyond a laughing matter.

"Ruby," Cash interjected, "out with it. Why are we at the Watkins', specifically?"

In the wing mirror, she could see that Ness had pulled up behind them and that she also looked puzzled, as did Theo and Corinna.

"Come on," she said to Cash, "we mustn't keep Kelly waiting."

"You mean she's actually *waiting* for us?" An incredulous Cash turned to Eclipse. "Do you know anything about this?"

Ruby answered before Eclipse had a chance to. "Cash, there's no reason why Eclipse should know anything more than you do."

Cash's nostrils flared, a possible retort on his lips.

"Seriously," she continued. "You have to trust me. If we don't have that, we have nothing."

Briefly, he shut his eyes as if realising he'd screwed up. "I do trust you, Rubes."

"Good, and I hope that in roughly ten minutes time when I answer your question, you'll be prepared to trust me a little bit more."

Cash and Eclipse exchanged another glance, this time one of shared trepidation.

Finally opening the car door, Ruby signalled to her colleagues to follow her.

* * *

"Come in, come," Kelly Watkins greeted them. "Go straight through to the kitchen. I've boiled the kettle, but I've also got a range of cold drinks and even some wine for those who fancy it. Oh, and some nibbles too, to keep your spirits up." Her hand flew to her mouth. "Oh my days, I can't believe I just said that! I didn't mean to, I meant nothing by it. It just slipped out, honest. By the way, there's no need for formalities: my name's Kelly, my husband's Dave and my little girl is Carly, although I'm sure Ruby's already told you about her and the ghost that was in her bedroom."

As she babbled on, the team filed past one by one, entering the kitchen where at least Jed's eyes lit up at the nibbles on offer, that word completely underestimating what Kelly had provided, it was more akin to a gourmet spread.

Still in a state of bewilderment, the team looked to Ruby for an explanation while Kelly took up position by the kettle, ready to take orders.

"Ruby!" The command in Theo's voice was unmistakable.

Ruby took a deep breath. "Kelly here has been a diamond. She's offered to feed you and provide refreshments in between visits to other houses, like the Griffiths' and the Barkers', where spiritual rescue is still very much needed. Actually, they're not the only houses, as Corinna said; more calls have come in since, but I just want to point out that as far as I've been able to glean, none seem to be about troublesome spirits; they sound more distressed than troublesome. There's a lot of work to be done tonight and well… in between, if you want to take time out, or need some food to sustain you, this is your base. Kelly's also made the front room available, which is also very kind of her."

Kelly was having none of it. "Kind? Do you know what, I'm just so grateful to you, Ruby. You came out on a

Saturday, with no quibble at all, and you helped us. And now I want to help too, in any way I can. I know the Griffiths, I know the Barkers, and the other families too, and this problem we've got, it unites us." She laughed suddenly. "Never mind a book club on the estate, we've got a ghost club!"

"Not if we remove all the ghosts, you don't," Cash pointed out.

Kelly sighed. "Oh, yeah! Silly me, I never thought about that. Seriously though, like I said, we're grateful, all of us, and to think you're going to waive all charges too."

"Oh?" Ness raised an eyebrow.

"You won't be out of pocket," Ruby quickly explained, "I'll make sure you all get paid for your time, but no, there'll be no charge for the clients this evening, and I've returned Kelly's money too, what with everything she's doing for us."

"Never mind about money," Theo replied, shaking her head slightly, "none of us are worried about that. What I think we're worried about is why you keep talking about us as a separate entity from you. Going into that building, it's a major job, an *all-hands-on-deck* type of job. You're not making it sound that way."

It was never possible to get anything past Theo. "Look, over these last few days, I've had a lot of time to think, not just about Gran, but about other things too." Pausing, Ruby looked at those staring back at her, each face running the gamut of so many emotions. "Because of that, I came to a decision, about the building and how best to tackle the spirits grounded there." She turned briefly to Kelly, "It was the spirit in your house that gave me the idea. When I told her I understood her anguish, she came close to me, her mouth forming words. *You. Don't. Know.* That's what she said, what she *stressed*. And she's right, I didn't know the depth of her suffering, not then, but I've got a clearer idea now. All the more minor cases on the estate need seeing to as well and it needs to be tonight, as it's now clear they're all connected. But I'm going to tackle the main building by myself. I have a plan in mind and I don't want any of you to be there when I put it into practice. I won't be *able* to put it into practice if you are. It needs to boil down to just me and them."

Cash was shaking his head. So was Eclipse. "You can't," they chorused. They looked at each other and Eclipse signalled that Cash should speak.

"Ruby," he said, "let me come with you at least."

"No, I've told you, it won't work unless I'm on my own."

"*What* won't work?" He touched his temple in a puzzled gesture. "You haven't said! Actually, I don't care what it is. I'm not letting you go back there alone."

Ness interjected. "Ruby, I think I know what you're planning. And actually, I think you're right." Her gaze steady, she added, "We all need to go a little mad sometimes."

Of all of them, it didn't surprise her that Ness agreed.

"I'll be okay," Ruby assured her. "In the end."

"I know. I have every faith you will be."

Ruby nodded, their bond, she realised, that of kindred spirits. "I'm not saying I've suffered more than any of you," she wanted to make that clear, "or any of *them*. But my suffering is current." She swallowed. "It's also relevant."

"Okay," was Ness's sole response.

During their exchange, Theo's look of horror had faded as understanding dawned. "It's a plan," she conceded. "A definite plan. After all, what's the saying; *how do we get ahead of crazy, if we don't know how crazy thinks?* But, Ruby, appease a silly old woman and let one of us come with you, even if it's just to wait in the wings."

Eclipse's hand shot up. "I'll do it."

Before Cash could react, Ruby refused. "Eclipse, I'd like you to work with the others tonight, to see how they go about sending spirits to the light; the type of language they use, that sort of thing. It's very different to your experience with me in the asylum. It's… calmer. I want you to see that side of it, to understand that often there are no fireworks. This job can be just like any other job, although I can't say it's ever boring. It's very real and it's very human, despite the fact we deal with spirits. If it piques your interest further, that's great. It might be something you'll want to carry on with."

"With you, you mean? With Psychic Surveys?"

Resolute, she shook her head. "There are no vacancies at the moment with Psychic Surveys." She glanced at Cash – was that relief on his face? Yes, she thought so. Inwardly, she shrugged. So he had a jealous streak. She wouldn't stand for any nonsense from him in the future regarding it, but as flaws went, it could be worse.

Capturing her gaze, Cash asked for a quiet word.

"Sure," she replied and they left the kitchen, leaving the orders for teas and coffees to be taken at last and the others to discuss what had just been said.

Outside, in the fresh air, he grabbed her by the shoulders. "Humour me here, because I'm really having trouble getting to grips with this. You're going in alone to that building, and, whilst you're in there, you're planning to go a little bit mad?"

"Not just a little bit."

Her words only served to increase his horror. "Ruby, that's so…"

"Insane?" she ventured.

"I was going to say dangerous!"

"But it's the only way; it's what's going to qualify me to do the job – in their eyes, I mean. First, I join them in madness; I empathise with everything they've endured, *identify* with it, and then I show them there's a way back."

"But what if…"

"I don't come back?"

"You *can't* come back."

"You need to take a leaf out of Ness's book and trust me."

He kept his gaze steady. "Do you trust yourself though, Ruby?"

"Cash, I know what you're doing, but it's no use. I won't be dissuaded."

"I just want an answer."

"I trust that I'm doing the right thing, okay? That's the best answer I can give you."

"I'm going in there too."

"No, you're not. Look, Cash, trust me and in turn I'll trust that you'll curb that jealous streak in you; that you won't leave me again when the going gets rough."

"I won't leave you, I swear!"

"And I won't leave you, if you let me go."

His hands still on her shoulders, he was silent for a moment. "Is Jed going with you?"

"That's up to Jed."

"But is it likely?"

"Yes, it's likely."

She smiled at the concern that was still so evident on his face and did what he tried to do so often for her – tried to lighten what was an increasingly tense situation. "What's that song, Cash, an old song, by Fun Boy Three?"

"Fun Boy Three? *The Lunatics Have Taken Over the Asylum.* Do you mean that?"

"That's it. That sort of describes what I'm doing, in the singular, though."

There was no smile on his face. "You're no lunatic. What you are is brave beyond belief." After a brief pause, he continued. "There's a more apt saying actually, although I'm gonna have to bastardise that one a bit too."

"Oh? Come on then, spill, what is it?"

"*Cometh the hour, cometh the woman.* Do it, Ruby, go and shine a light in hell."

"I will, Cash, but first that light's going to have to go out."

Chapter Twenty-Seven

CASH insisted on accompanying her to the building, which Ruby agreed to only after extracting a promise from him that he'd leave her there without further argument and re-join the others. As they walked, Jed materialised, trotting by Cash's side.

The closer they drew, the heavier the atmosphere became, akin to wading through treacle. She tried to resist turning her head in the direction of the secure unit, but gave in. Aaron Hames was there, on the edge of the estate, and not only there, he was everywhere, his energy, and the dark attachments that clung to it like a stain continually spreading. Her sigh was heavy. They all had their work cut out for them tonight, not just her.

Just as Eclipse had lifted the fencing for her, so did Cash. Once inside, she turned to him, noticed him crouching. "Don't, Cash. Stay there."

His eyes grew darker as reluctantly he straightened. "It's not that I don't trust you, I just hate you going in there alone. It's not safe, not for someone with your ability."

"I have to." Behind her the building loomed, although she didn't turn to look at it, not yet. "I need them as much as they need me." God, it was obvious how much he was fighting with himself to do as she'd asked. "Cash," she continued, "if these bricks and mortar are being attacked tomorrow, then the walls in their minds have to come down *tonight*. To encourage that, the walls in my mind need to come down too."

"Really, Ruby? Is that the only way?"

"It is. Me and them, we're in this together."

He took a deep breath and then gently exhaled, the shine in his eyes nothing to do with the moon above. "Have you got your torch?"

"Yeah."

"Have you got your phone?"

"Uh huh."

"If anything goes wrong…"

"I'll call you."

"Promise."

"I promise."

"Jed's with you?"

"Jed's just left your side, he's by my side now."

"Good, that's good. Is there really no way I can change your mind?"

"I'm afraid not."

He stood perfectly still. "I'm on the end of the phone, remember?"

"I won't forget."

"Don't lose the phone."

"That's the one thing I don't plan on losing."

"Not funny, Ruby."

"Sorry."

Cash held his hand up to the fence. "I wanted to kiss you before you went in there, but I guess this'll have to do."

She lifted her hand too, and pressed it against the wire mesh, matching her fingers to his, one by one.

Again there was silence, as if the world had caught its breath.

"I love you, Ruby. I didn't stand by you in your happiest hour, and in your darkest you won't let me. But somehow, some way, we'll rectify that; we'll make us work."

"Cash, please…"

He had to go, leave her to it.

Slowly he started to back away. Finally, after what seemed like an age, he turned, his hands in his pockets and his shoulders slumped, a somewhat dejected posture. If he looked back, Ruby didn't notice, as she'd turned too, to face the building in front of her – a blackened shape, a husk, a monolith, abandoned but not forgotten, not by those who'd endured being inside it. Jed whined and she inhaled. Could she do this? Could she really do this? It was madness. And then a slow smile crept across her face. Of course it was. She knew it, Cash knew it and the team knew it.

"Best get on with it then," she muttered, as she and Jed pressed forwards.

The door that Eclipse had shoved open was still hanging off its hinges. It was a calm night, a pleasant night even. There was no wind soughing through the trees and in the woods behind her no animals stirred. Tomorrow evening, this building probably wouldn't be here – there'd be a vast emptiness instead. But, as she'd said to Cash, if she gave up on her plan, the walls *would* still be standing in the minds of those who couldn't believe that peace existed in any other realm; in the minds of the beaten and the abused, the meek and the misunderstood, all of whom were in there, so many of them, more than she knew.

293

Ordinarily, it would take years for the team to connect with each of them, even with all their time devoted to the task. But now it was her alone, and she didn't have years. She had hours. And so the *extra*ordinary was needed.

"Jed, stay here and stand guard. You don't need to see this either."

Jed whined and refused to settle.

She bent down, so that her face was level with his. Those eyes, in a way they were so like Cash's, deep and soulful. They were her protectors, but some things nobody could shield you from.

"I need my freedom. Just tonight. Only tonight."

Still Jed fussed, but at last he sat. Before rising, she reached up and removed the tourmaline necklace she always wore – her charm, her talisman, and her inheritance. Bringing it to her lips to kiss the precious stones, she then placed it on the ground beside Jed. "I can't take this in there, I'm afraid. It wouldn't be fair. I need to level the playing field. Look after it for me, will you?"

Smiling at him one last time, she straightened up, then, forcing one foot in front of the other she entered the building and stood just on the threshold. It seemed those inside had taken a deep breath, curious about the woman who'd returned, alone this time and with something different about her, with such a look of determination on her face. She knew they could see her and soon she'd be able to see them, even without a torch. But first it was time to allow the emotions of all that had happened in the past two weeks, numerous extreme emotions, to rise. No longer could she wallow in the comfort of numbness. What had there been in the beginning? Excitement, that's what: making contact with Peter Gregory, the man she thought was her father and meeting him, actually *meeting* him. She'd liked him and he'd liked her, and another meeting had been quickly forged. The future had seemed so bright! But then came bewilderment, and it had tarnished that happiness. Cash had split up with her – temporarily as it turned out, but she didn't know that, not at the time. On top of that was the 'set-up' by Kirsty and the subsequent crushing disappointment that Peter wasn't her father after all. Hot on its heels came the awful truth of who really *was*. She'd rushed home to Jessica and Sarah for answers, only to find the past unravelling in ways that had shocked both her and her mother when they learnt about her grandmother's actions and all that she'd done in the name of protection; the fury that she'd unleashed and the deaths it had led to, Sarah's included. She was dead – Gran was dead. Her heart had simply given out, her spirit fleeing. Where to, home? Ruby hoped so. She *prayed* so. And finally the meeting with Hames, still in the grip of madness, his eyes as he'd turned them towards the camera to stare at Ruby, penetrating her soul. And, damn it, something in her had responded; had squirmed; had known *exactly* who he was.

Of all the emotions that engulfed her, despair was the chief one, although, like spoilt children, grief, confusion, bewilderment and shock wanted their fair share of attention too. And anger, there was plenty of that. It was the latter she coaxed forwards from such encrusted layers; boiling, blood red anger, an energy in it that made her want to run, lash out, scream and yell and threaten anyone who'd ever threatened her. With Gran gone, there were no barriers anymore. With Cash, Jed and the team giving her free rein, she could be who she needed to be in this dark and terrible moment; her father's daughter. On her tongue she tasted his madness – it was bitter, acrid, the foulest poison – and in her soul, the light that so many insisted burned so bright was ready to be extinguished.

At one with the darkness and with those that resided in it, she burst into action, her feet carrying her down that long, long corridor that had so many rooms and corridors feeding off it. Her mouth twisted, her eyes wide, her fingertips trailed the walls on either side, walls that writhed and shuddered at her touch. The spirits were terrified, she sensed that, but it was no big deal. They were used to terror. They understood it.

On she ran, a shrieking in her ears, in the confines of her skull, pushing past the tide of human misery, withstanding it this time. She'd no longer let it bring her to her knees. The misery, the suffering, the indignity, she'd let it soak her soul instead.

Above the shrieking – not just hers she realised, the cacophony came from many others too – there was a hint of music. *La Vie En Rose* – such a haunting melody.

Her feet skidding to a halt, her head whipped to the right.

Where's it coming from? The music?

It was the ballroom. Of course! Such a grand room, so ornate, not what you'd expect to find in a place of the damned such as this. From her standpoint, she could see shadows again, scores of them; some clutching at each other in a mockery of dancing, others slumped on chairs against the walls, just as they'd been in the dayroom. There were numerous straight-backed figures too, nurses perhaps, doctors even. Some of whom were well meaning, but not all of them, oh no, not all of them. There were those who *fed* off madness, who perpetuated it.

Give your heart and soul to me
And life will always be
La Vie En Rose

Her lip curled as she remembered the words.

"Heart, soul, mind and body, that's what you took – to use and abuse!"

On a big intake of breath, she flung herself through the double doors and into the ballroom, heading straight towards the shuffling figures, as the tune played on, a note missed here, or too high there. Reaching the centre of the room, she threw her arms out and started dancing too, twirling round and around, her movements far from smooth, but wild and jagged, her brown hair flying.

"I want to know all your stories, every last one. Your pain is my pain. I want to suffer like you do, I **am** suffering, but still I want more. I'm begging for more. Tell me!"

The shadows scattered and became misty figures, fading as the music died. Then they grew more solid again and crept closer. As they did, Ruby welcomed them, a grin on her face that threatened to split it. Their stories, their lives, filled her mind to bursting. A vision of that: her head exploding, made her laugh; a sound she didn't recognise as it was far from usual. Those around her, however, had heard the like many times and didn't flinch at all. The bombardment continued. There were so many emotions, and even those that were new to her, she embraced. It was so easy to go with it now she was willing; surprisingly comfortable.

Look at her, one voice whispered above the rest, *she's wrong, all wrong. They said that about me. They stood over my cot and pointed. 'We can't keep something that's wrong.'* That same voice became a snarl. *My body was twisted, not my mind! But at Cromer they twisted that too. I hate this place! I hate them! I hate everyone!*

"Me too," Ruby whispered in reply and it was true: in this moment, hate besieged her. She *wanted* to hate, *loved* to hate, it was a *relief* to hate – the bad wolf inside her attacking the good wolf, and tearing him limb from bloodied limb.

Another voice broke free from the mass. *We're mad, we're mad, we're all fucking mad!* It was a singsong voice, high-pitched.

"We are!" Ruby declared. "We're all mad in the madhouse! Stay with me, all of you. Follow me."

Laughter in the room rivalled hers, so many voices babbled at once.

Where are we going?

What are we doing?

Follow! Follow! Follow!

To the theatre?

Is that where we're going?

"Not yet," answered Ruby, laughing so much she'd started to hiccup. "We'll save that 'til last, just like *they* saved it 'til last. We're going upstairs."

To the nursery?

To the wards?

To the cells?

Ruby nodded her head vigorously. "We're going everywhere!"

Like the Pied Piper, in charge of her raggle taggle band of misfits, Ruby started to run again. Leaving the ballroom behind, she retraced her route back to the stairwell.

Joyfully booting debris out of the way, she flew up the stairs, often two at a time, she was so eager. Graffiti on the top landing gave her more cause to giggle: '*It was more fun in hell!*'

There were giggles too from those behind her, guffaws, whoops and snorts – everyone finding it so funny, having a party, the best night ever.

She turned her head from left to right, left to right, left to right.

"Where to?" she said. "Where to?"

Before anyone could answer, she darted to the left. Like downstairs, there were so many rooms and corridors feeding off the main corridor, the walls covered in yet more drawings, some intricate, but others only half finished.

At the far end, a door swung open.

The nursery! It's the nursery!

She knew what it was, she didn't need the voices to tell her. Rather than the screams of the mass, it was the cries of the innocent that filled her head as she approached it; the young of Cromer, who'd been born into this life. Entering the room, the high-pitched wails surged to a crescendo. There were no cots in the room, it was empty, so those around did her the courtesy of showing what it was once like: the beds that had been like cages with babies imprisoned as their mothers were, and crying at first, railing against how unnatural it was to be torn from their mother's arms; those cries quieting to mere whimpers as they became more and more listless – resigned, even at that age. The grounded spirits showed her more graffiti on the wall: *You're here because the outside world rejects you.* But now no one was laughing. Not anymore. Anger filled the air again and it was as black as any demon she'd ever had the misfortune to encounter; a fury so intense it couldn't be restrained. She opened her mouth again but not to laugh this time; to howl alongside the spirits of the children who'd grown in height but not in mind, who'd been baptised with unholy water and christened imbecile.

Ruby whirled around, both words and spittle firing from her mouth.

"It was in here you taught madness, you *bred* it into these children's bones. You took what was bright and new and destroyed it. And all this you did in the name of duty. You refused to question. You just obeyed the rules. You're here too, aren't you, the nurses? And do you know why? Because you're *mad* with guilt!"

Her fury still rising, Ruby raced back into the corridor. The shadows around her, those that followed, had multiplied. They filled the space in front of her, crept out of the recesses behind her. There were swarms of them; hordes as Ness had called them, individuals that had formed a mass, an army, held entirely in Ruby's thrall.

"Show me the cells," she demanded.

The mass parted as she walked down the corridor, some leading, some skipping, some still shuffling – *the Largactyl Shuffle*; some with arms reaching out but not daring to touch her. None of them wanted to touch the maddest of them all.

More doors were flung open. In front of one she crouched and ran her fingers close to the handle. Scratches. Gouges. She knew this to be typical of so many doors in the asylum, after patients had tried to claw their way to a freedom they wouldn't know what to do with.

Her fingers becoming claw-like too, she moved her

hands upwards and made fresh grooves, digging her fingers into the hard wood, over and over again; not caring about her bloodied nails, about ripping them as the skin on her fingertips became wet and sticky. She scratched and scratched, and beside her a man appeared who was scratching too. She looked at him and he looked at her, neither of them faltering. Eventually, she rose, as did he, his shadow joining the throng. From the cells more shadows emerged, following her to the wards, where people lay on narrow beds, their eyes open but not seeing, their mouths slack. And in the corner, someone was sitting, her hands hugging her knees. She was sobbing, a sound similar to that which escaped Ruby as she sank to the floor to sit beside her.

My boy, my boy.

Losing her son had hit her hard. So what had the doctors done about it? How had they treated her? By hitting her again, with the liquid cosh; by incarcerating her.

"How long?"

Years.

"Your name, tell me your name."

There were no more answers. The woman shook her head, continued to cry and to rock herself, and Ruby had no choice but to do the same.

Her nose ran as well as her eyes, soaking her lips and her chin, dripping in elastic threads onto the thin jumper she wore and drenching that too; the well from which each tear was drawn seemingly endless. *Gran, oh Gran! Peter!* Regarding the latter, how could you cry over someone who never *was*, who was just an idea, a hope? Very easily she discovered, because to her, that hope had been real.

Ruby fell to the floor and curled up in a ball. So many in the asylum had lain that way, for days that ran into weeks, months and years, alone, yet surrounded by others exactly like them. All like the boy she'd seen with the kindly nurse, in a world within a world.

The swiftness with which her sobs turned to howls surprised even her. But quickly those that surrounded her started to howl too; more than that, they were beating their chests, bouncing off the walls, crawling along ceilings to drop beside her – shadows, all shadows, that's what they were and that's what they had been, even in life. It was a sound to crack your brain in half but there was still comfort in it; the comfort of the masses setting sail on an ocean of grief, all of them journeying together.

Setting sail, Ruby, not sinking.

To whoever had said that, she denied it. To her it felt like sinking.

You can't afford to lose yourself.

Was that the same voice, quoting words that were familiar to her, that she'd heard not so long ago? But it was so easy to go under. And so many would help her: there'd be hands, but not belonging to those around her. *Other* hands. They'd claw and they'd scratch, and they'd pull her down, down, down, all the way down, to lie with them in the dumping grounds. *The dumping grounds?*

A choke lodged in her throat. She pushed herself up, forced herself into a siting position, able to breath at last, her chest heaving. *This*, Cromer, was a dumping ground, but even so, there were worse places to be, far worse. If she did succumb, if she sank much further to lie with the others, she'd never be able to rise. She'd be like him then, Aaron Hames, the one who'd gone so willingly. *Two peas in a pod.*

"NO!"

Her cry was primal as she climbed to her feet and stood there. Pushing sweat-soaked strands of hair out of her eyes and holding her hands out for balance, she staggered from the room to enter others; laughing one minute, crying the next, but beckoning; always beckoning. *Follow me! Follow me! Follow me!*

On one door was emblazoned *Keep Out.*

For a brief moment she just stared at it, and then, as a rabid dog might, she threw herself at the door, smashing at it again and again, refusing to stop until it gave way. It was a bathroom – no, not that, it was nothing as innocuous. It was a *treatment room*, one which contained several baths, all of them rusted, all of them filled with litter and dirt, and a washstand that had been kicked over, that some were kicking at still – the shadows. She started kicking too, knocking tiles from the wall, and relishing the sound as they smashed to the floor. Her attention back on the door, she also kicked at that, dredging up strength as she'd dredged up emotions, the mass working with her, lending her their strength to finally unhinge it. As it crashed to the floor, there was an almighty scream of triumph. Good! There was no more 'keeping out'. She'd exposed it, what patients had been subjected to, and the further madness that had ensued as a result. They'd been immersed for hours, for *days*, not always in pleasant temperatures; in water as cold as the souls of those who'd administered it.

Back in the corridor, she was running again, the crowds parting as they'd done before to allow their friend access to wherever she wanted to go. Her foot slipped on some debris and she went crashing to the floor, not noticing the pain as her ankle twisted; hardly registering those that helped her to rise. Half-limping, half-running, she continued the rampage, lashing out at whatever objects there were to lash out at: still screaming, still yelling, every feeling that had ever engulfed her, that had engulfed *them*, manifesting, just as the shadows were manifesting. As in the ballroom, they were becoming more solid, none of them dazed, not now. All of them were staring at her, their expressions awestruck. In the last room, at the opposite end of the corridor to the nursery, was yet another ward, with yet more beds, and more rags hanging at the windows. She raced over, tore down the rags, upturned the beds, then finding a piece of piping lying on the floor, she picked it up and smashed whatever panes of glass were still intact, until every single one in the room was shattered, just as lives had been shattered, over and over again – before they were incarcerated, *whilst* they were incarcerated and even afterwards, for the thirty to fifty percent spat back out of the system.

At last she stopped and stared back at the faces around her, able to witness their terrible wonder more fully. "I know there are those who need to be locked away," she said, in between gasps for breath, "but that was for those who didn't."

Bringing her hand up to wipe at her nose, dragging it across her spittle-encrusted mouth, she continued to stare at them.

"Don't think this is over," she warned. "We've still got the theatre to go."

Chapter Twenty-Eight

WHERE there had been wailing, crying and screaming, there was now silence as she made her way back down the corridor to the top of the stairs; as she descended them one by one, her hand touching every now and again the cold hard steel of the banister. At the bottom, she turned to the right, again half-walking, half-limping, as she passed the ballroom, now also silent. The dayroom was long behind her, the kitchens too, and the dining room where so often plates had been hurled against walls, those that had dared to show such frustration, chained to their beds as punishment. To remain subdued was the only way to survive in a place like this. And if you failed, if you refused to comply, then compliance was forced upon you.

The doctor's office was just ahead. She'd been there before, the first time she'd visited with Eclipse, but had never managed to get as far on the second and third visit. On this the fourth, she would go there, and further still, into the very heart of darkness.

As she drew closer, the horde at her back faltered.

"Don't fall back. Stay with me. We face this together."

It was the final stronghold; the place all patients feared, even the maddest amongst them. In the theatre, every experience that had ever shaped them, that had made them who and what they were, was rendered inaccessible, and despite what had been suffered, each knew that to feel nothing was somehow the worst of all.

It was only Ruby who entered the doctor's office, a room left largely alone in the wake of Cromer's abandonment; a room in which no cheap thrills could be obtained by the building's voyeurs, just a terrible and growing sense of unease; where stark reality stared you unblinking in the face. *There but for the grace of God…*

Going straight to the filing cabinet that had housed the patient notes Eclipse had found scattered over the floor, she grabbed at them. In reality, it was a pitiful bundle, so many having disintegrated, although she thought there'd be a record at East Sussex Record Office of everyone who'd ever stayed here, a note of their condition, their life span, their fate. And sometimes there'd be photos, like the ones she held in her hand, the prison mug shots. Resting the notes on the desk, she started to call out the names.

"Ronald Brown, are you here? Stephen Evans, what about you? Sarah Carstairs, Annie Gibb, Doreen Hughes, come on, come forward if you're here. Melissa Bates, Mary Wilson, Agnes Jones and, Rebecca – Rebecca Nash. Are you still here?"

A ripple ran through the crowd waiting in the corridor, but no one stepped forward.

"Are you here? Tell me your names!"

Gradually, the ripple became a roar. Was this it? Where they doing what she'd asked so many times before – identifying themselves, breaking away from the mass to become what they had been: individuals?

Ben Fuhrman, Alan Stirling, Marion Bradley, Jane Clark, Susan Ainsworth, Helen Moore, Lisa James, Thomas Mallon. It was a cacophony once more, as so many names were thrown at her, but this time it didn't hurt. On the contrary, it was like music – a litany, as Ness had called it; a holy revelation. It was all she'd hoped for.

As the names continued to come, she began to tear the documents in her hands, her slippery bloodied fingers working to rip each and every sheet of paper to shreds.

"What I'm doing," she told them, "is freeing you. I'm destroying what you were labelled as; what husbands, mothers, fathers, employers and, of course, the medical profession, insisted you were." Letting the remaining torn papers fall like confetti to the floor, she brought her fist up to thump against the wall of her chest. "What you truly are is in here; it's complex and it's simple, it's good and it's bad, it's ugly and it's beautiful. No two people are ever alike." She shook her head as if she too had just realised this. "And that's a miracle, don't you think? *You're* a miracle. No pills, no treatments, and no fucking operation can touch your spirit. That's yours to keep and it always has been – the very essence of you. None of you were criminals, not one." She swallowed, had to force herself to carry on. "There's a place for those who are criminally insane, who deliberately hurt others, who thrive on torture and pain, who've wandered so far from source that they may never return; but they're not my concern, not tonight. *You're* my concern. If any of you are still hiding in this building, come out and join us, because soon there'll be nowhere left to hide."

Before any could respond further, she left the doctor's office, slamming the door behind her – any lingering fragments of glass falling to the floor. The theatre was just a little further, down a side corridor; another dirty secret that had been hidden away.

Like the door upstairs, the door to the theatre was

stuck, resisting entry.

"Oh no, you don't," Ruby muttered, pushing against it.

Still it refused to open; it seemed fused to the doorframe.

Her voice rose. "No one's getting away with anything, not tonight. If you are one of the guilty ones, own it. The time has come."

Again she pushed. Her ankle was twisted, her fingers bruised and bloodied, her face dirty with snot and tear tracks, and now her shoulder was screaming, as she had screamed, threatening to fracture under the pressure.

"LET US IN!"

Once again, the mass rushed to assist her, breaking down the final barrier.

As the door crashed inwards, Ruby went flying, straight into the centre of the room, where a steel gurney stood. As soon as she touched it, the visions began, of those who'd lain here; those who'd been secured by leather straps, sedated whilst their brains were tampered with and connections cut. The pleading of past patients now became a universal plea. *I'm not sick, I'm not ill. Please, Doctor, give me another chance, I'll be good. Doctor, please, I beg you. I DON'T WANT THIS!*

Their pain was Ruby's pain, transparent, vivid, and tangible. Climbing on to the gurney, she lay on her back. Above her was a giant lamp, its metal arm attached to the tiled wall behind. There were no bulbs in it and yet still the light scorched her eyes as she stared upwards, as so many had stared upwards. Such a pertinent memory, was it any wonder they'd hidden from the light ever since?

The name of the doctor, what was it? The world-famous lobotomist who'd travelled the south, performing such operations? So little time they took, no more than five or ten minutes, but long enough to wipe out a lifetime.

Her fingers gripping the steel either side of her, she sat up. "Ralph Gould." That was it! "This was one of the biggest mental hospitals in the south, you must have come here, many times. Are you still here? Do you know what you've done? Did you grow fat on the money they paid you? Did you revel in being held in such regard? Did you ever give a fuck about the truth of your actions? The *uselessness* of them?"

There was a small voice. It could have belonged to Gould. It was a protest, and a defence. It echoed what Theo had said, what Ruby had said upstairs.

Some people needed to be here.

"NO!" Ruby roared. "NOT HERE, NOT IN THIS BUILDING."

There were none she'd encountered who couldn't have been helped by validation and understanding; by treatments that were gentle and sympathetic rather than harsh; by listening, by coaxing, by simple acts of kindness. "THESE WERE NOT VERMIN, THEY WERE PEOPLE! INFIRM AND VULNERABLE, BUT NOT RATS TO EXPERIMENT ON. YOU WEREN'T A MIRACLE WORKER, AND YOU WERE CERTAINLY NO GOD, WHAT YOU WERE, WAS BLIND, WILFULLY BLIND."

Jumping off the gurney, she pushed it from her, hearing the clatter as it smashed against the tiled wall; grey tiles, a grey room, a grey building, with no place for the glorious colours of the outside world. She sank down where the gurney had been, wrapped her hands around her knees and resumed rocking herself.

His face, his eyes – Aaron Hames – they were in front of her now. He was looking at her, scrutinising her, such excitement in his gaze. What she'd given free rein to in the asylum, he obviously revelled in – this girl, this woman that was the fruit of his loins.

"So, what am I?" she said when she was able to. "A chip off the old block?"

His wretched face broke into a lunatic grin, and yes, there was something akin to pride in his eyes. "I've turned out just like you hoped I would, haven't I? Soiled. A thing of darkness, the blood that runs through my veins your blood, blood that taints me. But here's the thing, *Dad*," she spat the word out, worse to her than any profanity. As she struggled to her feet, those around her cowered, including Gould, she assumed; all of them – the innocent and the not so innocent, the misguided and the guilty. What was she going to do or say next, they wondered. In here, at the epicentre, would madness hold her as it held them – its grip as tight as the iron that was once used to shackle them?

She shook her head as she continued addressing Hames. "There's madness in me, I don't deny it, but there's madness in everyone. We all have our share of it, and that's what terrifies so many, how tenuous our grasp on sanity can be; how quickly we can slide, and continue to slide. And when we're at the bottom, there are those who would drag us deeper still. Even if we have the strength to resist, that strength is taken away, quickly destroyed. Gould, if you *are* here, I spit on your reputation. But not on you, I don't spit on you. Because I believe that you believed you were doing the right thing, and something my gran always said was *'belief is everything'*. You were wrong though,

310

which you're probably all too aware of now; emotions can be subdued, but they can never be erased. They're all powerful, they're what define us; they set us apart. Rewiring someone doesn't mean you've cured them. What lies beneath is still trapped there. All you ever did was bury it alive."

Swinging round, staring at the figures that had sidled in and now filled the theatre; at the many more that crowded the doorway and the corridor beyond, she took a deep breath and continued speaking. "Mistakes are made, by everyone. And there are repercussions, always. *I* was a mistake – the product of a one-night stand. Some may consider my mother mad, certainly she's done some mad things in the past. My father is mad too – he lost his mind many, many years ago."

There was a hissing sound, Hames' eyes firing sparks. *She sent me mad!*

Ruby pushed her face straight into his. "That's right, she did, Sarah sent the darkness racing after you, but what she did, what she never realised perhaps because guilt wouldn't let her, but what I realise, is that it would never have worked unless you *allowed* it to. You turned to greet those she'd unleashed and you welcomed them in. And you did that because you believed the darkness could make you bigger than you were; that it would empower you to rule over others, their fear nourishing you. You opened your arms and you consumed it just as it consumed you. What Gran thought she'd done, in the end, was too much to bear, it killed her – *you* killed her. And you want me to hate you for that, don't you? You want me to hate you *so much*."

His eagerness made her skin crawl.

"Tough, because I'm done with hating, with blaming, with anger, with sorrow, and misery, and pain. Upstairs, I hated everyone and everything. I extinguished one fire and raised another, and it burned inside me so badly. But fires like that, they burn themselves out. Eventually. That hatred is spent. And now that it is, I realise what I hated most was the injustice of it all; how precious lives were cut short and wasted. I hated that an ordinary, decent man couldn't be my dad, that it had to be you." Ruby hadn't wanted to cry, not again, but cry she did. "I hated what my mum did all those years ago, and what my gran did. I hated Gould and the doctors and nurses amongst you who knew better deep down, but ignored that knowledge. I hated myself too, and the darkness that I know is in me; that led me to madness; that took me over the edge. But there are many ways to get there, as all of your stories prove. Hatred is only one vehicle. And standing here, in front of you all, I have a choice, just as every one of you has a choice." She wiped away her streaming tears with a harsh brush of her sleeve as wracked sobs escaped her. "I could give in again and relight that cold, cold fire. I could let disappointment rise back up and wash over me, wave after wave of it, and each one more bitter than the last. Hames, you killed Gran – not with your hands, you never kill anyone with your hands – but by being what you are, which is a willing conduit. But I don't hate you. I won't. That cold fire, it takes too much effort to keep alight. I'll reignite the one that's warmer, that takes no effort at all. After descension comes ascension, for some of us anyway – for most of us I hope. I'm not just going to step away from the precipice, I'm going to take a giant leap; let go of all the hurt that causes my heart to ache so much. I'm going to let it go and then… well, then I'm going to see what happens."

Another roar is what happened, accompanied by an alarm ringing in the distance as well as barking, not just from Jed, but several dogs. It was a commotion, a panic. She could well imagine it, people emerging from their houses and on to the streets, repelled yet drawn at the same time, by the magnitude of what was happening, another shift in the atmosphere. Hames – it was Hames – spitting, hissing, and flailing, bouncing off every wall in the hospital and banging his head against brick like the woman who'd lost her baby had banged her head against brick. Restrained by several staff members, he was injected, obscenities and buried truths spilling from his mouth all the while, targeting those who were trying to help him; inflicting as much mental damage as he could before his body submitted. Despite becoming glazed, his eyes fixed on Ruby. Oh, the hatred in them, the darkness! She stared back. "You've made your choice, Hames, and I've made mine. You will never see me again and I'll never see you. Your progeny I may be, but your likeness I am not."

Knowing those words had hit home; seeing finally the despair at the heart of him, for a fraction of a second, little more than that, she thought her tears would continue, but every well, it seems, is capable of running dry.

With the shadowy patients now cowering in terror around her, she raised her hands in supplication. "It's okay, it's okay. He's mad, but I'm not. I'm on my way back from madness." Daring to draw closer to them, she reached out. "I still can't imagine the full extent of what some of you went through. In comparison, I'm the lucky one. But I'm closer to understanding than I've ever been before. It's so easy to lose faith in the light, to lose faith in each other too; in any goodness that there might be. Upstairs, I discovered how easy that was and in here, in this theatre, it's easier still. And so, just before I came back, I went on anther journey. I talked to those who'd survived Cromer: people who had good things to say about it, because even here, there was a light in the darkness, it didn't go out, not completely. There were acts of kindness, patience and understanding, and you had each other for God's sake – you *always* had each other. I want you to dig deep, every last one of you; find something good that happened to you within these walls; don't think of it as insignificant because it wasn't. Perhaps it was a smile that was unexpected, or a touch that was gentler than all the rest. Let it be the thing you latch onto – the good, only the good. Like a seed that's been planted, feed it and watch it as it grows."

There might have been all kinds of commotion going on outside, but in the theatre there was only silence. She closed her eyes.

"Please, it's not me that needs to shine a light in this hell, it's *you*."

A garden. Could she see a garden? She could: a patch of land, as green as the downs that surrounded them. And in it, a man who'd endured such horrors – wartime horrors – was bending to tease flowers from the ground. Was he happy? Was that too strong a word? Perhaps. But he'd found a degree of contentment in this garden, in something as simple, as beautiful, and as pure as a flower.

Another vision, this time there was a woman smiling shyly at a man: was it in the dayroom or at one of the dances? She couldn't see where exactly, just the smile that took place, and the hope of possibility in it, no matter how

314

fleeting.

Beyond them was the nurse, the one she'd seen with the child that had been labelled 'feeble-minded'. How kind she'd been, how hard she'd tried with him. Yet another nurse came into view, sitting with an elderly patient, one who was dying, holding his hand. All night she'd done that, refusing to let him pass alone.

The visions, whilst not as prolific as those in which pain and suffering had featured, were nonetheless there: gems that sparkled in the mire.

Ruby smiled to see them, relief filtering through her as strong as sunshine. She threw her head back as if to bathe in the strength of the sun's rays, imagining such warmth on her skin, penetrating deep layers; sinking into blood and bone and reaching her heart – *lifting* her heart, her soul too. It was a healing light, and it filled her – as if there were no blood and bones and she was but an empty vessel. Eventually the darkness would creep back – it always crept back – it was part of being human, but she felt more cleansed than ever before, more whole; something she suspected could only happen when you'd laid yourself bare; when you'd taken yourself apart.

How long Ruby remained motionless she had no idea, but when she opened her eyes she had to blink several times to believe it. There were no shadows, no mass. They'd all gone. She was standing in an empty room, in an empty building, one that would soon cease to exist. Empty apart from herself, of course, and one other; a woman wearing a dirty white shift who crouched in the corner. Slowly, the woman rose, her body unfurling, until she stood upright. Ruby had no need to beg for a name. Despite having never gazed on her face, she knew her well enough.

"You're the psychic."

The woman nodded. She had long dark hair, divided into two plaits and eyes that could have been blue or green.

"You're Rebecca Nash."

Again, the woman nodded. She also stepped closer and held out her hand.

Ruby raised her hand too and touched her; she was neither warm nor cold.

"What happened to you could have happened to me."

Rebecca agreed.

"I'm not sure anyone's ever apologised for your fate," Ruby continued, "so *I* will. I'm sorry, truly sorry. I share your gift and it's not a secret; it's nothing to be ashamed of, not anymore. Times change, and they'll continue to change. People are more accepting of us nowadays. I'm doing my best to dispel any lingering fear and ignorance that surrounds the likes of you and me. I'm making what we are, normal."

Rebecca started at the use of that word, but Ruby insisted.

"You *are* normal. Everyone in this building was." She paused briefly, having to swallow. "There are just different types of normal, that's all."

Her gaze lingering on Ruby, the colour of her eyes still unclear, Rebecca finally took a step back, turned and walked to the gurney that Ruby had sent thundering into the wall earlier, bending her head as she gazed down at it, her fists clenching and unclenching.

Watching her, Ruby found it difficult to breathe. This girl who'd been so much like her, who'd been denied her gift, could she do it? Could she forgive?

"Rebecca, you know where the light is, you've always known. Go towards it."

At last the spirit's hands relaxed. With her back still to Ruby, her head still bowed, she began to fade, slowly, inch by inch; letting go after all.

Now Ruby was alone.

Turning to face the door that had been torn off its hinges, Ruby returned to the corridor. Shafts of light pierced the gloom. Morning had broken; the alarm had stopped and the dogs had stopped barking too. There was no panic anymore, not even the sense of panic in the air – just peace, perfect peace. At Ash Hill there'd be peace too. A kind of peace anyway, which was better than nothing, better than the alternative.

Her hands trailed against the walls as she walked along the corridor, they were just that: the walls of a semi-derelict building, painted grey with the render crumbling. She passed the dayroom, the ballroom, and the stairs that led upwards, retracing her footsteps all the way back to Jed, who hadn't deserted his post; who'd held firm.

As she'd done before, she knelt beside him. "Thanks for waiting."

He nudged at the necklace that was still where she'd left it. Reaching down, she grasped it, feeling a power in the stones; an energy that coursed through her. Re-fastening it around her neck, she rose and the pair of them made their way towards the fencing. As she reached it, Cash rounded the corner, breaking into a run when he saw her. Eclipse and her fellow team members were close behind. Theo was huffing and puffing and Corinna was craning her neck, but Ness was as calm as Jed, and every bit as trusting. She was a woman who'd faced madness too, her own madness perhaps, but who'd also come back – a kindred spirit, but then they all were at this moment, even Eclipse, although they'd part company soon; even him.

Cash held up the fence for her as she scrambled through. As soon as she was standing, he grabbed her and hugged her to him.

"Are you all right? Oh God, I was so worried. How I kept away, I don't know. Don't ever ask me to do anything like that again, okay? Are you sure you're all right?"

It wasn't just him expecting an answer; they all were.

"I'm good, really good. What about you? How'd you get on?"

"It's been a long night," Theo replied, "but it's also been a resounding success. I have to say Kelly's a dab hand with the tea and sustenance. Wherever we were, be it the Barkers, the Griffiths, and several other houses besides, she kept joining us, all through the night; kept us going. I'm not sure what I'd have done without her, wasted away probably." Corinna raised an eyebrow at this, but Theo steadfastly ignored her. Instead she turned to look at the building and sighed. "You know, it's a beautiful building really, the brickwork is quite superb, and that ballroom inside – they don't make 'em like that anymore, do they?"

"No they don't." It was Ness who answered her. "Thank God." Afterwards she addressed Ruby. "Is our work here done?"

Still with her arms around Cash, Ruby nodded. She noticed the relief in Eclipse's eyes, the sheer joy of a promise kept. "It's done. Brookbridge is what it is now, what it's supposed to be – just another housing estate, nothing more than that."

Chapter Twenty-Nine

THOUSAND Island Park had proved such a hit at The Lamb in Lewes that they were asked to play in several other pubs too, including The Waterside Inn in Shoreham.

"And for the Psychic Surveys team it's free drinks all night," the landlord declared. "You know this is like a different pub since you cleansed the cellars, I've been able to retain some really good staff, instead of them heading out the door after a month or two. This gig business is their idea. They said the punters would love it."

Ruby winced at how convinced he was that they'd done their job, but Corinna, Theo and even Ness had no such qualms. Even so, whilst the band was in full swing – Corinna staring starstruck as Presley's voice filled the room – Ruby herself a little awed at the sight of Cash on drums, she had a word in the landlord's ear and asked if she could go and have a quick look in the cellar, just to see how different it was.

Although bemused, he agreed. "Go ahead, love. It's as clear as a whistle down there."

Except it wasn't, she knew that as soon as she set foot in the dark, damp surrounds.

She addressed Joel and his cohorts in a whisper. "Are you okay, all of you? Are you sure you want to stay here? Honestly, there are much better places."

Where's that redhead? One of them murmured, Joel probably.

She expected a clout to accompany that remark, but there was only a muffled squeal and some giggling – Joel's paramour was clearly not jealous anymore; more confident in her own allure. Which was progress, Ruby supposed. Good progress.

"If you want to stay," she continued, "that's up to you. Maybe you'll drift off to the light one day, individually or together, who knows? But one thing I wanted to say was thank you, for keeping your end of the bargain."

A promise is a promise. It ought to be kept.

"That's right, a gentleman's promise, I remember. And you are, you're gentlemen all of you, apart from the ladies, of course; you're strong women, the best."

Clearly they approved of the compliment, as there were cheers all round.

"Sshh!" she said, bringing her hand to her mouth. "You know what happened the last time you got over-excited, you nearly got yourself moved on."

Ha! You'd like to think!

That'd take a bit of doing.

Get off with ya.

Still smiling, Ruby left them to it and returned upstairs. Theo and Ness turned to look at her as she re-entered the bar, but made no comment. Corinna was still enraptured. Then Eclipse walked in. Ruby hadn't invited him, Cash had. They'd got quite pally that night on the Brookbridge Estate, Cash, like Molly, feeling more secure in himself too. Going up to Ruby, Eclipse gave her a hug and offered her a drink, which she declined as she already had one on the go. She insisted on buying him a drink though, and a few minutes later, they stood together, watching the band.

The hospital building had been demolished according to schedule, but the light that had filled Ruby in the darkest part of it, was still in her; a feeling of calm, of peace, of happiness even. This prevailed despite the loss of Gran, despite what Ness had told her about Hames. He had indeed gone completely wild that night, just as Ruby had witnessed, but had since fallen into a catatonic state, even without drugs. But he wasn't staying at Ash Hill. He was being sent to a high-security unit in the far north; he had already gone, in fact, he'd been removed that day. Despite having felt she was meant to meet him, Ruby decided she wouldn't visit him, ever; but what she would do was send him light on occasions. She'd also remember the despair that was at the core of him, which may have prompted him to choose the path he had followed. Whatever the reason, she was on a different path and she wouldn't seek to merge the two again.

The band had finished their set, but enthusiastic cheers meant they weren't going anywhere unless they played an encore, Theo and Corinna were perhaps cheering the loudest of all, whilst Ness rolled her eyes at what she probably considered an uncouth display. Smiling again, knowing that Ness was enjoying herself really, Ruby felt a vibration in her pocket – it was her phone, someone was calling.

She ignored it. It was Friday evening, she deserved a bit of time off. If it was urgent, they'd call back, which of course they did, less than a minute later.

"Bloody hell!" Ruby moaned, ignoring it again. To be honest, she was having trouble taking her eyes off Cash. He really was quite mesmerising, never missing a beat.

When it rang a third time, she caved.

Turning to Eclipse, she held up her phone whilst mouthing that she was nipping outside to answer it. He pulled a sympathetic face and nodded.

As she left, she noticed Corinna jumping up and down, practically squealing, she was so happy. Tonight, in private, when she and Cash were alone, she resolved to show him how appreciative she was of his talents – a thought which warmed her as she stood outside on a night that was actually much colder than she expected. The phone had stopped ringing again, but only for a moment. As soon as it started up, she answered.

"Hello, Psychic Surveys. How can I help?"

"Oh, there you are," said a female voice. "I've been trying for ages."

"Sorry, I was at a gig, I couldn't pick up straightway."

"Oh right, I see, of course. Look, I'm sorry to disturb you, but, well, there's a problem, with our house. A big problem, I think. It's not quite right, the atmosphere I mean. Actually, it's far from right. And yesterday I had the most terrifying experience. Whilst I was in the kitchen I thought I saw someone in the garden staring at me – a man. A really strange man. He was in the far corner, and his eyes... they were just... I blinked and had to look away. When I looked back he was gone."

"Could it have been a trespasser?" Ruby checked.

"We live down a country lane and the nearest house is a short drive away. No one would normally be in the grounds other than me and my husband. Besides," she paused, "he wasn't dressed in modern clothes. He had some kind of robe on. I just knew he wasn't... you know what I mean, not flesh and blood. That's why I'm calling you and not the police."

"A robe?" queried Ruby.

"A black robe," the woman confirmed.

"How did you find out about Psychic Surveys?"

"You've got a website, that's how."

"Okay, great. I'm going to need some details. What's your name and how long have you lived at the house?"

"My name is Rosemary, or Rosie for short, and my husband is Dan. It's just us who live here, we're renting. It's a big house, and my husband's a painter and decorator. There's a lot of room for him to keep his gear. It's perfect in every way. The rent is really cheap considering how the size of it, but now I'm beginning to wonder why. Two months we've been here, that's all. I want to leave but Dan doesn't. In fact, Dan's downright resistant. That's why I'm ringing you now, because he isn't here, he's just popped out. It's best to visit whilst he's out too, I reckon, I can let you know when that'll be. It'd be handy to see what you think, whether it is the house or whether it's me and I'm going mad or something."

"Mad?" Ruby queried. "I shouldn't think so."

"Feels like it sometimes though, I can tell you. I work from home, I make jewellery and supply local shops, but lately I haven't been able to focus. I've started to miss deadlines. It *is* because of this house, I'm sure of it. Please help me."

"Rosie, of course I'll help you. That's what I do. I'm not sure where Dan will be but I'm free Monday morning—"

"Monday? Crap, that's ages away!"

"Do you feel you're in danger now, this very minute?"

'Danger… erm… no, I suppose not, not really."

"And Dan's due back soon?"

"Yeah. He's getting us a takeaway because the cooker's gone on the blink; brand new it is as well. Look... Monday's fine, it's good actually. Looking at his diary, he's leaving early to go to London to price a job. Sorry, I think I panicked a bit there."

"It's fine, it's okay. What time should I come on Monday?"

"Say ten? It's only two days, after all. I'll manage two days."

Ruby started frowning. "If you do need me before—"

"No, no. It's fine."

"Okay, I'll be at yours bang on ten."

"Thank you. Thank you so much."

Fishing around in her bag for a pen and a small notepad, Ruby asked Rosie for the address. The house was just past Ringmer apparently.

"Oh, and rather than a number, the house has a name," Rosie said. "It's a strange name actually. On the one hand it sounds grand, on the other... a bit odd."

"Oh? What is it? I'll jot that down too."

"Blakemort." Her voice was barely a whisper as she said it. "The house is called Blakemort."

THE END

A note from the author

As much as I love writing, building a relationship with readers is even more exciting! I occasionally send newsletters with details on new releases, special offers and other bits of news relating to the Psychic Surveys series as well as all my other books. If you'd like to subscribe, sign up here!

www.shanistruthers.com